A Different Kind of Angel

A Novel

Paulette Mahurin

Copyright © 2018 by Paulette Mahurin

ISBN: 978-0-9993116-9-1
Published by Early Girl Enterprises, LLC
Printed in the United States of America

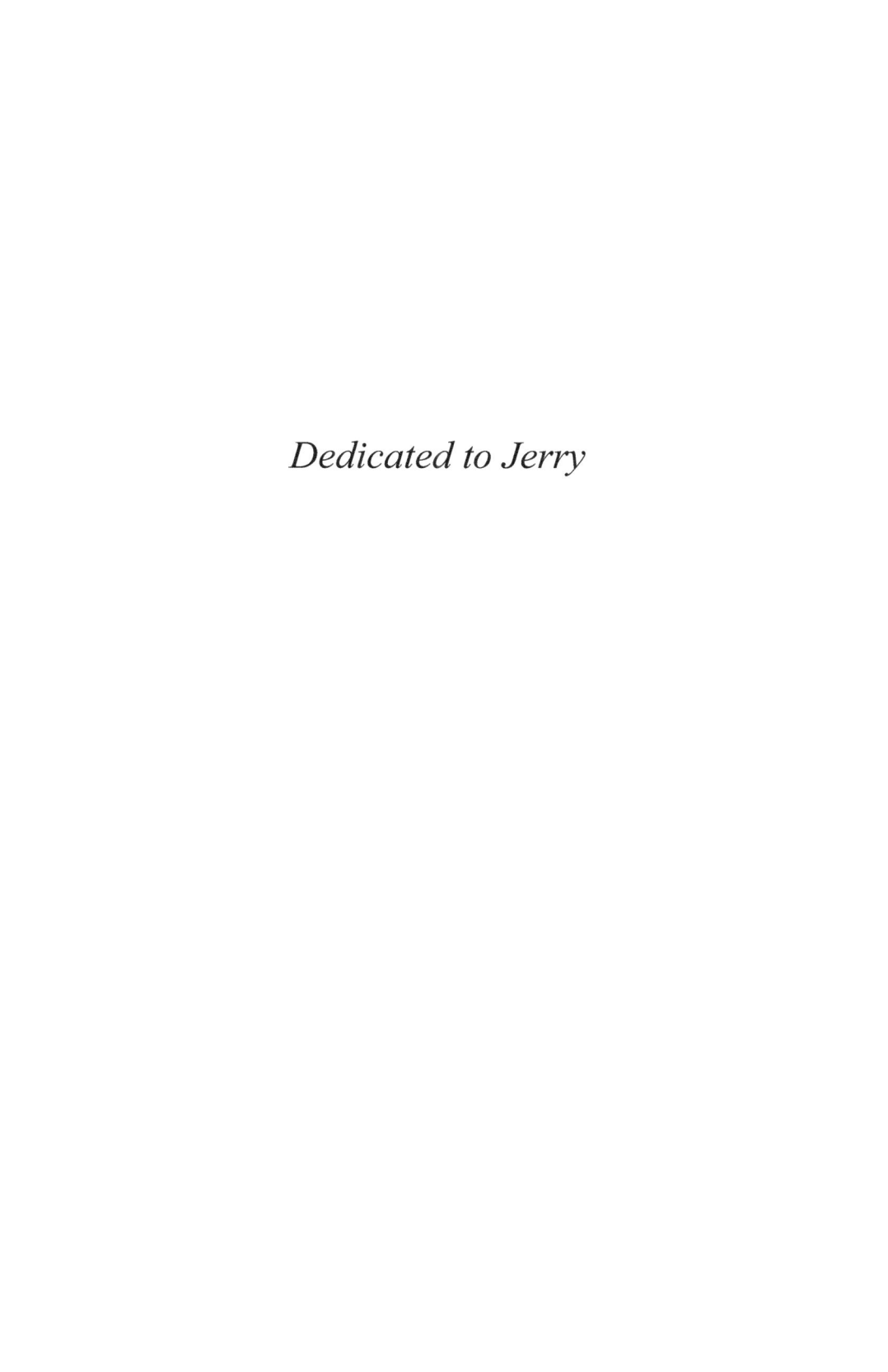

Dedicated to Jerry

Other Books by Paulette Mahurin

THE PERSECUTION OF MILDRED DUNLAP

HIS NAME WAS BEN

TO LIVE OUT LOUD

THE SEVEN YEAR DRESS

THE DAY I SAW THE HUMMINGBIRD

Acknowledgements

We sometimes think of an author as a lonely writer banging away on the keyboard, creating characters for readers to love and hate, forming the core of the story. Yet what brings these tales alive on the page is never a singular task.

To my talented critical readers, Jeannie and Terry, a heartfelt thank you.

To my incredibly detail-oriented, brilliant editor, Dr. L. Lee, this book would not be possible without you. And to the publishing house of Early Girl Enterprises, thank you for believing in Klara's story and helping her voice reach the world.

To Peter and Caroline at DesignerBespokeBookCovers.com, I'm grateful for the perfection you bring to the great cover design.

To the love of my life, words truly fail me when I say I couldn't have done this without you, my hubby and my best friend. You were there with your support, kindness, back and foot rubs, prepared meals and millions of read-throughs. You are positively the best.

"Love and compassion are necessities, not luxuries. Without them, humanity cannot survive."

His Holiness The 14th Dalai Lama

Preface

Although much of this story is based on factual historical occurrences, namely the Kiev pogrom of 1881, fictional license has been taken. While the 1881 Kiev pogrom was the most destructive attack to property, later pogroms were more violently devastating to life and limb. In describing scenes, the author has incorporated some of the later brutalities. Documented history fails to accurately portray much of what happened due to the suppression of data. Additionally, with regards to the Women's Lunatic Asylum on Blackwell's Island, fictitious characters have been added and names changed with the exception of a few of the publicly known historical figures like Elizabeth Cochran, aka Nellie Bly (the journalist who worked at the New York World and went undercover to write an exposé on the asylum). As the population of the women's asylum was over 1,500, not each patient's story was incorporated individually but rather combined into fictitious composites in the protagonist, Klara Gelfman, as well as other characters: Catherine Bigsby and the other four women housed in their dormitory. It was with great attention to detail that the scenes involving brutal cruelty were kept as close to what actually happened as possible. Some liberties were taken with a scene involving a patient's death and an account of sexual abuse.

A Different Kind of Angel

Before Elizabeth Cochran embarked on her exposé as Nellie Bly, a colleague warned her against entering the insane asylum for the sole purpose of making sensational revelations, to which she replied, "That such an institution could be mismanaged, and that cruelties could exist 'neath its roof, I did not deem possible. I always had a desire to know asylum life more thoroughly…a desire to be convinced that the most helpless of God's creatures, the insane, were cared for kindly and properly. The many stories I had read of abuses in such institutions I had regarded as wildly exaggerated or else romances, yet there was a latent desire to know positively."

When Nellie Bly left the institution she wrote, "The insane asylum on Blackwell's Island is a rat-trap. It is easy to get in, but once there it is impossible to get out." The following story shines a light on the living hell of a "rat-trap" Nellie Bly inhabited for ten days and thousands of unfortunate souls endured for years.

Prologue

The Blackwell's Island Asylum was the first civic mental hospital in the city of New York. Starting in the early 1830s, it was established to take care of the large number of indigent insane. Within the first decade of its opening, conditions were described by some of the staff to the commissioners in charge as "a miserable refuge." Despite constructing a new building in an attempt to improve conditions, the patients' living environment remained substandard as evidenced by inadequate nutrition, numerous outbreaks of disease, and the use of convicts from Blackwell's Island Prison as attendants to curtail costs. The asylum's large census was a result of its use as cheap custodial care to house insane immigrants. It also became a warehouse for disposable citizens who were not insane. A powerful or wealthy married man who wanted to dispose of an inconvenient mistress could easily arrange for her to be deemed a lunatic by the necessary doctors and sent to the asylum. Women who were regarded as troublesome or spoke a foreign language, etc. and stuck in the craw of the police were also treated like refuse to be dumped on Blackwell's Island. For these victims, transport across the East River was a one-way ticket.

When Charles Dickens visited the Women's Lunatic Asylum on Blackwell's Island in the 1840s he wrote, "...everything had a lounging, listless, madhouse air, which was very painful. The moping idiot, cowering down with long disheveled hair; the gibbering maniac, with her hideous laugh and pointed finger; the vacant eye, the fierce wild face, the gloomy picking of the hands and lips, and munching of the nails: there they were all, without disguise, in naked ugliness and horror."

By 1866, the asylum had grown to several buildings. Patients were housed in a building with a wing for men and a wing for women. These two wings were separated by spaces used for physicians' apartments, offices, and parlors. Women patients outnumbered male patients by two to one with conditions continuing to deteriorate.

It was due to these attendant circumstances that the Women's Lunatic Asylum on Blackwell's Island became famous when in 1887 a young female undercover reporter entered the hospital pretending to be insane. Her assumed name was Nellie Bly aka Nellie Brown. It was there she verified earlier descriptions of the horrible conditions when she described her torment with rotten food, cruel attendants, and diseased conditions. "What, excepting torture, would produce insanity quicker than this treatment?" she wrote.

It was in the Women's Lunatic Asylum, under unthinkable conditions, that Nellie Bly met twenty-year-old Klara Gelfman, a very unfortunate Jewish Russian immigrant who had escaped from the 1881 Kiev pogrom. (It was considered the worst of the pogroms that swept through south-western Imperial Russia in 1881.) This is Klara's story.

Chapter One

Klara

1882, New York City

On a late September afternoon, I lost the only thing I had left—my freedom.

I was on my way back to the boardinghouse where I rented a room when I spotted an unkempt man at the edge of an alleyway. Something about him made the back of my neck tingle. His smile was more of an upturned smirk and he had squinty, shifty eyes. Not heeding the nagging feeling in my belly that advised me to cross the street, I kept walking in his direction.

Just as I passed him, he grabbed hold of the back of my dress. Startled by the sudden attack, I lost my balance and started to fall forward. My arms flew as I tried to regain my footing and my purse, which contained all my worldly possessions, landed in the alley. That leech let go of my dress and grabbed my purse. Without thinking, I lunged at him to take it back.

He smacked me on the head with such force that I fell backwards even further into the alleyway. I heard the sound of my head hitting the pavement. A blinding flash of pain left me breathless. Then everything went black.

When I awoke the sun was edging over the horizon, and the air was filled with the strong smell of urine and booze. My head hurt. My whole body was trembling. I lifted my shaky arms to feel my scalp to make sure it hadn't been ripped off my head, which was how it felt. Rubbing my eyes, I tried to focus on the blurred figures of two men approaching. Scrunching my eyes to get a better view, I saw their loose-fitting, navy-blue uniforms with bulky objects hanging from their belts. I instantly felt safe. The police had discovered me, and I assumed they would rescue me. But when the taller one tilted his square-topped hat off his forehead and intentionally puffed out his chest to flash his badge, the look in his eyes—a deliberate glare—gave me a bad feeling.

I had only been in America for a couple of weeks, and I didn't know enough English to make sentences longer than two or three words. But I could understand a little of what others were saying. Getting by on hand gestures and facial expressions had worked well enough with the few kind and patient people I met in the boardinghouse, but these uniformed men looked neither kind nor patient. At the time, I didn't understand much of what was said by them or anyone they would subsequently bring me to. So, to tell this story, I must rely on my good memory in recalling the few words I understood, their rough treatment of me, and the looks of disgust I received from the people who were supposed to protect or help me to piece together what I imagine they were saying to me.

I tried to smile, but my lips trembled. I must have looked a pitiful sight.

The taller man nodded to his partner and shifted his jacket to display the baton and sidearm at his waist. He wrinkled his nose. "Smell the sauce?" he asked the shorter, pudgy officer.

The little man replied, "A lawbreaker. Looks like the whore is in violation of the Drinking Excess Law." He made a motion with his open hand as if he was holding a glass and tossing back a drink before he laughed. Then he bent to grab my arm.

Although I didn't fully understand what he was saying, the intent was clear by the harsh grip he had on my left forearm. I mumbled the few intelligible English words I knew, streaming together a thought that I knew didn't make sense. Too many missing words spewed from my mouth in a foreign tongue. "No English. Not speak. Please. You come. Come to me. To help." I mumbled still dazed and confused.

The little man's grip tightened around my arm.

"Noooo! Please." I was so confused and panicked that I barely understood what I was trying to say.

"Damn whore can't even speak, she's so drunk," came from the taller man. He then kicked my ribcage and shouted, "Get up, you whore!"

When I turned my head and looked at him, a cold chill ran up my spine. His dark, bloodshot eyes held no warmth. He acted like he was kicking an animal. "Please," I begged him to let me get up on my own. I tried to find the words to explain that I had not been drinking. That the state I was in came from being attacked. And robbed.

Here I was in New York City, where I was promised I would be safe from the oppression I had left behind, free from the tyrannical persecution of Jews in Kiev. So why was this happening? Why was I was accosted and beat up by a stranger and now being rough-handled by the very men I was told would protect me? Their yelling was deafening. All I wanted was simple human kindness from them.

I needed a way to ask for an interpreter; that would surely clear up this mistake. "No—"

The taller man kicked me again before I could get out the second word to form the sentence, no English. I did not speak the language that he understood, and why that seemed to infuriate him scared me even more than the repeated blows to my body.

The shorter one looked like a rabid dog with slobber coming off the sides of his angry pinched lips. "Help me get this pig up." With not a wink of compassion, without waiting for his partner to synchronize their actions, he yanked me up at an uneven angle causing me to fall back to the ground. My head hit the pavement. Again, the pain. The blackness.

When I regained consciousness, I was on an examination table in a room with the two policemen, a clean-shaven man in a well-tailored brown suit, and a nurse in a white uniform. I had never seen such a stark outfit. Flowing from a small band around her neck, pinched at the waist, the fabric went all the way to the floor. Barely visible out the bottom were the tips of white, pointed shoes.

The man in the suit then bent over my body, looking at me through his monocle. "Hmm," his gravelly voice vibrated in my temples.

The taller officer smacked his lips so loudly it sounded like horse hooves on hard ground to my pulsing ears. He looked at me and then at the man with the monocle. Both were shaking their heads. "She's one for the lunatic bin, ain't she," the officer probably said as he laughed. It didn't sound like a question.

Once again, not understanding all of what he said at the time was to my disadvantage. But what was clear was how much he liked demeaning me. The disdain that dripped from his tone of voice and his smug smile told me he enjoyed my distress.

My eyes widened like a scared rabbit sensing its predator. Surrounded by what felt like beasts of prey, I broke out in a cold sweat. Afraid to utter another word for fear of a repeat of what happened earlier, I bit down on the inside of my mouth—a nervous habit. That used to annoy my mother. My beloved mother would send me a look of disapproval but attempt to gain my attention with a gentle touch so as not to embarrass me. Eventually, Mama's mild reproach that it wasn't ladylike broke me of the habit. Now overcome with nervousness, it returned. Remembering the last time I saw my mother alive sent me into a dark place. The harder I bit down the deeper the ache in my broken heart. These men reminded me of those days of horror in Kiev. My once-loved Kiev was now a nightmare memory to be stored in the deepest hidden recesses of my mind. I came here to escape persecution! Why is this happening to me in America?

My thoughts were interrupted by the man in the brown suit with neatly trimmed gray hair. He put a wooden tube to my chest. I felt a hot flush move to my face. My cheeks were aflame with shame that he dared to touch me so close to my breasts. He held the other end of the tube to his ear, mumbled something then nodded. He stepped away quickly and washed his hands. "Healthy enough for a filthy harlot," he said as he crossed his arms against his chest, raised his chin, and scanned the length of my body with his narrowed eyes. He then turned to the officers. "You found her smelling of alcohol in the alley? Slurring her words? Incoherent and unable to respond to questions?"

It was then I assumed that this man in the nice suit was a doctor. I later learned he was a psychiatrist.

The short, fat officer raised his shoulders and puffed out his chest. He looked like a frozen figurine, reminding me of the ones I used to make in the snow back when I was younger. "You bet we did!" His smile looked daft.

"She's a mess, she is," came from the taller officer. He pointed to my head and grimaced. "That brown frizzy hair of hers flying about, those suspicious-looking brown eyes, and big lips that can't utter a sensible word. She's a batty tramp if ever I saw one," he smirked while shaking his head.

To this day I can't be sure if what I recalled is how it all happened, but once I learned to put a few more English words together, my memory replayed the scenes in that room; and this is how it seemed. They treated me as if I was some wild, loony strumpet. I might not remember all the words accurately, but I certainly recall how they made me cringe. Even the recollection makes me want to shake my body to rid it of that awful sense of helplessness.

When the man in the suit turned back to face me, I thought I saw a softer manner. I didn't know if it was the light that came in through the window playing tricks or if the expression in his eyes had actually changed. I wanted to believe he would help me. I wanted to savor a morsel of trust. I needed to regain my ability to see people as kind, especially men. But any hope I had was sadly dashed when he shook his head and mouthed, "Pathetic, how they roam our streets." Then there was something in the expression on his face that made my heart beat irregularly. Disgust? Hatred? Something much too intense for someone who didn't know me…and never would. He stared at me and said, "What do you go by? Your name?"

My shoulders sank, and I lowered my eyebrows expressing non-comprehension.

"Your name!" he demanded.

I jolted back.

On his last nerve, he slapped my face. "Christ, lady, do you not understand anything!"

My eyes pleaded with him to calm down. His escalating tone and rude manner were heading to a dangerous place. This was not a nice man.

Perhaps there was something in my body's response that gave the nurse pause. She had remained quiet up until that point. She looked to the doctor saying, "Let me have a try." Then she faced me and pointed to her chest, "My name is Miss Rudman."

The word miss was familiar, it rattled something in my brain and registered a connection. "Name?" I pointed to myself. "Klara?"

The woman nodded confirmation that I had answered correctly.

"Klara Gelfman." I attempted a smile for the first time since the officers found me on the street.

As soon as the words left my mouth, Miss Rudman raised her eyes to the ceiling and shook her head. Her denigrating expression deflated the slight sense of success I had momentarily felt. She motioned a hand gesture to the doctor that she was finished with me.

The doctor turned to the officers. "Has she been before a judge yet?"

The shorter officer's demeanor changed. Losing his erect posture, he pushed his hat back and rubbed his forehead. He hesitated then stuttered, "No…um, no, sir." He kneaded the skin on his left thumb, leaving a red mark. That repetitive motion was familiar and mirrored my own nervous inclination. My fingers itched to rub my neck, to relieve the building tension.

The doctor looked at the officer as if he wanted to say something. Then his wrinkled brow tightened as he pointed a stiff finger at me. "Why do you think you're here?" He jabbed my shoulder.

Trying to understand, I slanted my head.

"Talk to me!" His yell stiffened my posture. "For your life woman, speak!"

I wish I had understood that this would be the only attempt at compassion I was to receive for many years. Again, hoping that if I tried to communicate, maybe I'd break through this ordeal, I attempted to utter no speak English, but all I got out was, "No—"

The shorter officer, with his big belly protruding more than before, interrupted and (I suppose) thought he was claiming his redemption, "That's all she did when we tried to get her to talk. Sassed us with that foul mouth."

The doctor shook his head as he jotted something down on a piece of paper. Little did I know that in addition to signing his own name to my diagnosis and admission into the insane asylum, he had also forged another doctor's signature. He did it to make up for the officers' omission in not having me brought before a judge. It was much later that I learned that all that was needed to bypass the police courts was the signature of two competent doctors. Failing to make eye contact with me or the officers, the doctor made his way to the door and left with Miss Rudman.

Gone no longer than a few minutes, Miss Rudman returned wearing a coat. She held the piece of paper the doctor had just signed. "Let's get her to the boat," she said to the officers in a brusque voice. She led the way with that piece of paper sealing my fate flapping against her hip.

Being overpowered and feeling overwhelmed, I followed along as these three frightening strangers shepherded me out, not realizing others dressed like the nurse were about to become my new tormentors.

A Different Kind of Angel

Chapter Two

My head was a whirling mess of confusion. What is happening to me? Where are they taking me? Desperately, I clung to the hope that I would be taken somewhere meant to help immigrants so that I could tell someone that I was robbed. I thought of the helpful people on the ship when I came across the Atlantic. My worries and heartache grew as the distance increased from Kiev on the way to New York, but the kindness and gentle compassion those sailors showed me is something I will never forget. When tragedy befell my heartbroken father and he took ill, the crew took pity on me. While my papa, Isak Gelfman, was in his last throes of life, they brought extra food to try to proof him up. When he failed to respond, the captain assisted him to a private cabin. "These are good people, Klara," my breathless father whispered to me. "They will see you clear to America. Your new home."

"Papa," I cried, "save your breath."

His sunken eyes held a sorrow as deep as the very ocean we floated upon. He knew he was dying. But in his last moments, he tried to ease the inevitability for me. "Klara, my darling, you hold yourself strong and proud. Enough with the crying! We've shed all our tears. Now we grow strong and survive."

"Yes, we do."

His weak, pale fingers reached up to my wet cheek. Wiping the wetness, he smiled. "Listen to me, my daughter." His hand dropped back to his side.

A hot pang hit my abdomen—the fire of fear—the same sensation I felt when I watched my mother and siblings being murdered. I wanted to shut it out, all the memories of loss. I sat quietly pushing down my thoughts.

A loud rattling gurgle came from my papa's throat. "I'm dying."

I inhaled sharply. Quickly. Jaggedly. As if my very lungs were quivering. Then I sobbed. "No, Papa, you're going to get better." I refused to accept what his pasty, pale skin and parched lips told me. "You rest now." Laying my hand atop his wrist, I felt his feeble pulse fluttering against my palm.

He stretched out his fingers as if to say, Stop. Listen to me. In days past it was an outstretched gesture followed by, "Enough, Klara!" Back then, he had vitality. Now I only saw a fading light. "You...you cannot hide from...from what is happening. You...will be all...all that is left...of...of us. Do not despair."

The heaviness in my chest intensified as his words dimmed. The reflection in his widely dilated pupils mirrored the image of my face. Sorrow wrapped itself around me.

He gently clasped my hand. "Stay...strong." Hesitating to slowly suck in air, he did his best to raise his tone. "Never forget, you...you are a... Gelfman. We come from...st...strong stock. And you...you can do any...anything you make up your mind...to...to do."

As he rapidly puffed through pursed lips, I felt like my world was crumbling. I wanted to scream, No! Not you, too, Papa! Where is your strength?

His rheumy, bloodshot eyes flickered adoration. "Come," he lifted a flaccid arm, "give…your papa a…a hug, my dar…darling."

I leaned down to nestle next to him and draped my arm over his chest. A wisp of warm air hit my forehead. Followed by another weaker one. My elbow rose and fell with his breathing. When my arm stopped moving, I thought my heart would also stop. Feeling the movement of waves pitching, my forehead grew cold. Nausea hit my belly. I knew it wasn't from seasickness but rather the loss of my beloved papa.

For days after that, the crew tended to my needs. The captain was a good man with compassionate features: a soft unwrinkled brow atop downturned eyelids and a seemingly perpetual soft smile. For days I mourned. Not just for my papa's passing but also for all my family: my mother Lucinda, my siblings Abram, Shakna, Josel, and Anna. I was the last of the seven Gelfmans.

* * *

Horse hooves clip-clopping distracted my attention off the memory of my long, sorrowful Atlantic crossing. I was back beside the woman in white and the two police officers. We were in a horse-pulled carriage, going God knows where. The bounce of the chamber jolted my already rattled nerves. Each bump made me queasy. I swallowed hard as images of Papa took shape in my mind only to dissolve into nothingness, like the sweep of a broom dispersing a spider's web.

The nurse watched me wiping my sweat-drenched face with the back of my hand. She pinched her sliver-thin lips into a disapproving scowl. "We're here," she nodded ahead to a pier where a boat was docked.

I started to panic. My neck muscles tensed into knots. I had only landed in America fifteen days ago, holding a sign that read: No speak English. Need housing. Russian. A man on the ocean crossing made it for me. He had taught me a few words in English. He also told me not to tell anyone I was Jewish. He understood what had happened to us in Russia. He warned me, "Prejudice and persecution exist everywhere. Why advertise something that could bring harm to you?" When he saw puddles of tears in my eyes and my lower lip tremble, he realized how frightened I was and took his time to help me understand by explaining, "Better to be careful than to regret. Once you say something, there's no taking it back. Feel your way around before you share things about yourself."

I didn't get a chance to use any of his kind advice. Now, here I was back at the water, fearful that they were about to send me back to Russia. Back to the slaughterhouse. Hold yourself strong, my father's words echoed in my mind. I didn't feel strong. God help my weary soul, I felt helpless as I gazed upon two masts holding large sails. A man dressed in navy-blue wool pants and a turtleneck sweater threw ropes to another man on the dock. As they moored the vessel, we descended from the carriage.

The nurse greeted the boatman, to which he responded, "We're all set for you, Miss Rudman."

Each officer took hold of one of my elbows and guided me up the short, wedged gangway onto the deck of the small vessel. We were the only passengers. Once I knew it was unlikely this was anything but a quick voyage across the narrow water passage to a visible island, butterflies replaced my fear of being sent back to Russia.

I was brought down another plank to a dirty cabin with a foul, musty odor. Feeling nauseous from the stifling air, I put my hand to my nose to try to block out the stink. It smelled like someone had been ill and no one bothered to clean it up. I was walked to a narrow bench. The shorter officer pushed down on my shoulders to make me sit. Then Miss Rudman turned to the taller officer and commented (in a manner not demonstrating good manners or refinement) about what I assumed was women who were ill. Turns out they were talking about patients in the asylum, laughing at their antics and their suffering.

It took me a while to become adept at memorizing English words that I didn't understand. I played memory games and made stories inside my head when I felt it was something I wanted to understand. It was later when I received more help expanding my English vocabulary that I gained the understanding sorely lacking in my first few months at the institution. Words like lunatic, whore and asylum stayed with me. At first, my response to such words was neutral since I didn't understand their meaning or their negative implication. Once I learned what these things meant, I felt differently. I felt anger. Fist-clenching anger that made me chew the inside of my mouth.

Once we made it to shore, I saw an ambulance. It was waiting for me.

But I'm not sick!

With a guard's fingers sunk into the flesh of my left arm, I was put in the back and hastily driven to the Women's Lunatic Asylum on Blackwell's Island.

A Different Kind of Angel

Chapter Three

Blackwell's Island, a two-mile-long stretch of land in the middle of the East River, was the home of the New York City Lunatic Asylum, which included separate men and women patients' wings. It was the place where not just the mentally disturbed were kept but also, especially as was the case with women, those who were considered a "nuisance." Among the sane women committed to asylum were women who could be an embarrassment to their married lovers, those who caused undue trouble to powerful people, the homeless who were a blight on the streets of New York, and women (like me) who spoke a foreign language. Mixed in with the sane were seriously troubled, deranged patients. Through no fault of my own, I arrived at the place where, in all probability, I would spend the rest of my life. Unless a miracle happened. Given the events in Russia and America that brought me here, I thought to myself, I seriously doubt there will be any miracles for me.

* * *

As we moved along the drive to a stone building, we passed one low-lying structure that had a stench that made me gag. I made haste to hold my breath to stop the acid rising to my throat. I assumed it was a waste collection area. I discovered later that my assumption was wrong. It was a kitchen! Finally, the ambulance came to a stop. The nurse screeched something that sounded like, "Get out!"

The harshness in her tone gave me a start. I grabbed hold of a swatch of material on the skirt of my dress to calm my nerves. I wanted to respond, to tell her, "I just came to America. I don't speak English. Someone robbed me and beat me up. Please help me return to my boardinghouse. I won't be a bother to anyone anymore." I had no hope of communicating any of this to the severe woman in white without a translator; I didn't even know how to ask for a translator. But then, I knew better than to speak up to authority. I knew where that got me with the police. Fearing that if I did anything but obey it would make things worse, I just sat there not fully grasping what she wanted me to do.

The taller officer roughly pulled me to my feet. He clamped onto my arm as the other man prodded my back with his club like I was a cow to be herded. The indignity of it all, the humiliation of being treated like an animal, replaced the nervousness in my gut with anger for the second time that day. I tightened my clenched hands and moved along, obeying the physical jabs as we exited the ambulance.

Outside, the tall building loomed over me. It hurt my neck to look up to past the fourth-floor windows to a tower. We moved to the inside and made our way up a flight of narrow stone steps. Timidly, I continued to follow the nurse as the officers tailed behind poking that wooden baton into my lower back every few steps. I was delivered to a room to see the admitting doctor. Dr. Lucas Koch was the name on the plaque on his desk.

Miss Rudman sneered at me. Shrinking into myself, I felt small and insignificant under her judgmental countenance. She spoke to the officer holding my arm. "Sit her here." She pointed to the chair in front of the doctor's desk.

The officer obeyed her command, nodding in compliance. "We're all set then?" He scratched his chin. "Shall we move on now?" Shifting from leg to leg, he seemed anxious to leave.

The doctor knocked on the door behind his desk, and in came another nurse dressed in the same uniform as Miss Rudman. Well-built with broad hips, bleach-blond, straight hair with dark roots, green eyes and toothpick-thin eyebrows, she was pleasant to look at. The fact that she made eye contact with me lent some relaxation to my tensed neck muscles. When she smiled at Miss Rudman and said, "I'll take it from here," my erect-shouldered posture eased.

Doctor Koch nodded his head in concurrence to Rudman. She and the two officers left.

"Sally," he said to the nurse with him. "I'll have a look at this," indicating the piece of paper Miss Rudman handed to him, "then take her to the ward."

Nurse Sally smiled and stood silent.

As he lifted his hand to wipe a few wisps of graying hairs off his right temple, his eyes moved back and forth over the written lines. I quickly scanned the room. The large, brown wood desk created an unfriendly barrier between us. There was another straight-backed wooden chair beside mine. Behind the desk was a cabinet, on which stood a glass oil lamp that lit the room.

A crinkling of the paper in the doctor's hand redirected my attention back to him. The way he held the sheet cast a semi-circle shadow on the desk. It looked like a smile. It reminded me of my mama: her large chocolate-colored eyes and sweet, comforting, upturned lips when I needed support. The vision of my beloved mother and the violence that had happened to her made me feel sick inside. But before the tragic events in Kiev, there was so much that was good. I had to remember the good in my life. Little did I know then that it would be my memories that would keep me strong. It turned out to be an irony that in this mental institution, instead of losing my mind—going crazy—I became more sensible, levelheaded, and wise. My papa's voice sang to me, over and over, You can do anything you make up your mind to do.

My mind. My best defense weapon.

Another crackle of the paper. The doctor stopped reading. "Found on the street, drunk and disorderly," he glanced at me over the top of the monocle on his nose. "Tsk, tsk. Pitiful but all too common." He rolled his eyes then shook his head. Were it not for the calloused lines around his mouth, the harshness and the disgust his clinched lips held, he might have been attractive, distinguished even. But to me, he was an ugly man with a gruff, arrogant voice. He said a few more unintelligible words to the nurse before he stared at me with narrowed eyes. Predator eyes.

His look made the skin on my back feel as if armies of small bugs were marching over it. I pulled my shoulder blades together in an attempt to rid myself of that horrible feeling.

Doctor Koch took in a slow, deep breath through his nose, and just when he looked like he was about to say something to me, he nodded to the nurse. "Take this Gelfman woman to the ward."

The way he spoke my surname made me shrink inside down to an inconsequential nobody. I was no longer Klara Gelfman, daughter of Isak and Lucinda and loving sister to my four siblings; no, I had been reduced to a thing, referred to with such ill will that it made my skin prickle. As I watched this man, this professional—a doctor—through lowered lids and bowed head, I wanted to disappear. To be anywhere but in this room that felt like death, this

24

tomb that robbed me of my last trace of identity. My name is Klara, I wanted to scream. Klara Gelfman! I'm a person, just like you!

I felt Nurse Sally's attention shift to me. Again, for some inexplicable reason, it helped me relax a little. Perhaps she would be friendly. When her hand slammed down on my back, I was disabused of that idea. Consigned to this lunatic asylum without a chance of making myself understood, I was ushered out of the room and into the nightmare that would become my life.

A Different Kind of Angel

Chapter Four

It was late afternoon when I was shuffled past a large room filled with women patients sitting on wooden benches. I was taken down a long hallway to a cold, wet bathroom. Exhausted, I hadn't had a thing to eat or drink all day. I had been in the same disheveled, smelly dress for over twenty-four hours and looked a mess. This went against my nature, being that I was raised with attention to tidiness. My mother instilled the importance of conscientiousness in us. Although we were not a well-to-do family, my mama kept a neat, clean home. Papa's trade as a carpenter enabled us to have enough: a roof over our heads, beds to sleep in even if we had to share, food on the table, and clean clothes—two outfits for winter and two for summer. I prided myself in wearing things Mama sewed for me. Although the fabric was not fancy or expensive, our garments fit well and were flattering. We were a proud and respectable bunch, we Gelfmans.

The nurse motioned at my outfit. "Undress!" she commanded.

I understood the word dress but not what she was ordering me to do. I looked down at the filth I was clothed in. Confused about what she wanted from me, I tilted my head.

"You ignorant simpleton. Take that piece of garbage off!"

The harshness in her tone frightened me. I shook my head trying to indicate I did not understand what she wanted. She grabbed the front of my dress and then pointed to the floor as if she wanted me to take off my clothes. That scared me more. I was modest. I didn't want to undress in front of a stranger. The room was wide open, and anyone could walk in. Holding my hands over my chest and in the softest way I could muster, I begged, "Please…" The rest that came out of me in Russian asked her to please help me. I don't know where I am or why I'm here and I'm scared. Again, I tried to explain that I didn't speak English.

Suddenly all hell broke loose. She took a whistle out of her pocket and blew on it.

Two male guards came running in. Her hand gesture to them, her pursed lips, her lowered eyebrows and hardened eyes all indicated that she was disgusted with me. She screeched something to them.

They moved toward me.

I backed up until I was flush against a damp wall.

"Roy" she hollered to the medium-built guard with brown hair receding at the forehead and with long, frizzy sideburns. "Get her out of that rag."

My legs were shaking, and my forehead itched with hot needle pricks. I wanted to scratch my skin raw. Remember the words, I thought to myself. I needed them to try to piece together what was happening to me. I had to find a way to understand what they were saying. To find a way to come to terms with what they were doing to me.

Roy's voice faltered with saliva spewing from an opening between his front teeth when he responded to Nurse Sally, "She, uh, she won't cooperate?"

Sally took a rapid, snorting breath through her expanded nostrils. "Does it look like she's cooperating? Handle it!"

What did "handle it" mean? I didn't like the rough sound in her voice or the mean and foreboding look on her now-reddened face. I chewed on the inside of my cheek.

Roy made a hand motion to the other man he referred to as Albert (sometimes Al, depending on his mood). Pointing at my chest, his look gave me gooseflesh.

Albert was huge at six-feet-three-inches tall. His red, flushed cheeks and bulbous nose began to sweat as he approached me. He shook his head to clear the overly grown hair covering his eyes. That man was badly in need of a haircut.

Roy slurred something unintelligible.

I closed my eyes.

They both descended on me.

I pressed myself firmer against the wall. Images flashed inside my mind's eye. Russian soldiers. Whips cracking. Bayonets piercing. Bullets ripping. Blood splattering. Bodies falling. The decapitated head of a young girl. Then nothing.

When I opened my eyes and regained my bearing, the two men were holding me next to a tub of water. Undressed down to my camisole and petticoat, I prayed they wouldn't remove more clothing. I slid down to the ground to resist them when they tried to further undress me. Albert secured my arms while Roy grabbed at my remaining clothes. My screams and kicks were met with a fast, sharp smack to my right cheek. I desperately tried to break loose, to gain the nurse's attention, hoping that a woman would have some mercy. Surely, I thought, she understands a woman's modesty. But when my attention went to her, my shock doubled. She was in the corner laughing. My humiliating suffering was, to her, nothing more than amusement.

A Different Kind of Angel

Another hard smack to my head and my body went limp. They had beaten the fight out of me. Item by item they pulled off the rest of my clothes. I shivered before them in my nakedness, head hung low. Helpless.

I looked up when I saw one of the men step closer to me. When Roy gave me a lewd, wide-eyed look and moved a hand to my breasts, Nurse Sally finally came to my defense. "Hands off her, Roy." I learned later that protecting me wasn't what prompted her objection but that Roy was her boyfriend. What I assumed was an act of proper guardianship was merely a jealous rebuke.

Refusing to be further manhandled, I rose by myself and got into the bath. The minute my body entered the ice-cold water, I yelled. I didn't mean to (knowing it would give them more of a show); it was simply a reflex. My outburst drew a crowd of patients to the door. Again, I began to protest not just the freezing abuse but also the indignity I felt from all the onlookers. "No, please," was all I could utter before more Russian words came forth. My frustration over my inability to communicate and to be understood worsened after this intolerable, terrifying situation. Giving up on being understood, I stood up to get out.

Roy pushed me back down.

I looked to the door and shook my head in an attempt to plead for the observers—all women, all disheveled—to help me. It was of no use. Sally made it worse by pointing to one of the onlookers and motioning for her to come over.

A crazy-appearing woman with wild hair and eyelids that seemed to rise to her scalp came forth. She grabbed a dirty rag from a bucket on the floor and bent to scrub me. Taking some soft soap from a small tin pan, she rubbed my body, my face, and my long hair. She stroked, scrubbed, and abraded my skin while I sat there

30

with chattering teeth and limbs turning blue with cold. That torture continued with bucket after bucket of bone-chilling water poured over my face, into my eyes, into my ears, my nose, and my mouth. I imagined that was how a drowning person felt as I inhaled and coughed up gulps of water. Just when I thought the agony would never end, I was pulled—gasping and trembling—from the tub.

My hair was dripping, and I had pains throughout my body as if I had rheumatism. The nurse flung clothing, consisting of one underskirt made of coarse dark cotton and a cheap white calico dress with stains on it, on the wet, dirty floor. She said, "Put it on," while motioning to the garments then back to me.

I tied the strings of the underskirt around my waist and put on the dress. It had a straight tight waist sewn on to a straight skirt. While buttoning the skirt, I noticed that the underskirt was several inches longer than the outside dress. This was the outfit all the patients wore. Our feet went bare.

Still not fully understanding where I was or what they were going to do with me, I was moved out of the bathroom. With a lowered, defeated face, I was walked through the sitting area with wooden benches. Seated women, dressed like me, rose and lined up to follow behind another nurse and male guard. Some of them looked so lost and forlorn with slumped shoulders, trudging single-file like herded livestock. One was chattering what seemed like nonsense to an invisible person; others were laughing or crying indiscriminately. But one woman caught my attention and smiled. The gesture felt warm and appropriate, intended to offer comfort. My attention gravitated to her. Like a ship adrift finally headed for land, I hoped I had discovered some ground for a friendship with her.

The marching continued with stops only when the nurses had to put the patients back in alignment, one behind the other. I was placed between two women toward the end of one of the lines that had been formed. We were marched into a long, narrow dining room. The women rushed toward the long table. I watched the backless benches on each side fill up with women grabbing for a place to sit. Bowls lined close together were already arranged on the table.

I found a place to sit between two larger-sized women. The one to my right grabbed hold of several bowls and poured the soup into hers. Beside the bowls were thick, cut pieces of stale buttered bread. Accompanying the bread was a small saucer with five prunes.

I took a spoonful of the watered-down broth that tasted like dirty water and almost spat it out. In it were a few particles of gristly tough meat, with shriveled peas and carrots. I ate the bread and prunes to give my aching, empty stomach some nourishment. The commotion and noise were maddening. Above the din, the nurses blew their whistles and screamed for the women to shut up and eat.

Another whistle blew and anyone still eating stopped. We were marched back out in rows to return to the hallway lined with benches—a place I came to call the "sitting room." Two long wooden benches were up against the walls with barred windows. I looked for the woman who smiled at me earlier and was glad when our eyes made contact. A nod of her head and I went to sit beside her. She whispered something I didn't understand before the whistle blew.

Silence descended upon the sitting room.

We sat there for a couple of hours. No one talked. When one woman grabbed her knees to her chest and started to rock back and forth, a nurse (who, earlier, I heard referred to as Edith Preston) went to her to make her sit up straight. Small-framed Edith had what I assumed was a sympathetic look in her hazel eyes. Her slightly parted and thin-as-a-horsehair lips let out a sigh before she attempted to help the slumped patient sit up straight. With each effort, beads of perspiration formed between her wide-set eyes. When Roy saw the nurse having trouble with the woman, he pulled out his club and made haste over to them. He smacked the patient's knees until she cried out, yanked her legs off the bench so her feet touched the ground, then pulled up on her shoulders to straighten out her back. That's how we were to remain, day in and day out, sitting on those benches with a straight posture. In silence.

We were offered no mercy or pardon (to attend to aches, pains or urgent needs to relieve ourselves). Thus, time dragged on. My only respite from the uncaring environment, the uncertainty and the fear was the warmth of the body of the friendly woman sitting next to me. Our connected thighs brought an odd comfort. I needed touch to be reminded I was still a human being. So much that defined me as a person had already been violently ripped from me: my entire family, my life in Kiev, my religion, and the clothes on my back. All that was left of me—the last vestige of hope—was my attitude (what I would make of this unbearable situation). And my memories. They couldn't take those from me. Be strong, Papa's voice rang in my heart. An image of his face, etched with lines of wisdom on his brow, his soft, comforting, light-brown eyes, the edges of hair by his temples turning gray, gave me something real that belonged only to me to hang onto.

An index finger moved next to my hand. A gentle pat, seemingly indicating everything will be okay. At least that's what I wanted to believe. That repetitive motion from the woman beside me brought me home. As my body sat erect on that hard bench, the last remains of sun drifted over the horizon. Women stirred in the darkening room as my thoughts meandered to Kiev.

Before 1881 and the pogrom that devastated the Kiev Jewish population, my family had a good life. Simple but good. Days were filled with the aroma of bread baking in the oven while Abram and Shakna were discussing what they had learned. And Papa coming home with a surprise treat for us. "A candy bar," smiling, he held out his hand. We all ran to him, the little ones, Josel and Anna, jumping up and down in the excitement. On the palm of Papa's hand was the wrapped gift. He handed it to me, the eldest—nineteen at the time—and said, "Divide it equally my darling, Klara."

A cough in the room and the dropping temperature directed my attention back to the asylum. Holding back oceans of tears, my mouth watered at the memory of that candy bar. I felt the woman next to me flex her thighs as if anticipating to rise from her sitting position.

A whistle blew.

Before darkness completely enveloped us, the women stood. I joined them.

The kind woman stood behind me and whispered in my ear, "Stay with me."

There was something about the way she spoke that gave clarity to her message. And so, when we moved down the narrow hallway and came to a door that she turned to, I followed. In that room were six beds, and (to my luck) one was empty. Seeing the indentation of a body still remaining on the thin mattress, I wondered what had happened to its occupant. Since no one had assigned a bed to me, I assumed I could claim that one. Claiming a bed. Responding like the others to the whistle. I don't think I realized it then, but I had already become a patient in that asylum. My fight to hold onto myself had begun.

When Nurse Edith saw we had all taken our beds, she shut the door leaving us alone. I was relieved I hadn't been pulled from that room. My friend came to me. She seemed different than the remaining four women: more aware and normal is the only way I can put it. Although unable to really observe the others, they felt distant—not fully present.

"What's your name," she asked.

Before saying anything, I wanted her to know. "No English."

"Oh, I see. That's too bad. There are others here just like you. And a few like me. My name is Catherine Bigsby. Do you have a name?"

Finally, I was not met with punishment for trying to open my mouth attempting to clarify my situation. My neck and shoulder muscles relaxed when I said, "Klara. Klara Gelfman. Russian."

Without another word, that warm hand of hers found mine and gave it a squeeze. In a natural, spontaneous gesture, I hugged this kind woman. And I cried as quietly as I could.

I don't know how long I felt her breathing into my gasps of sobs, or how much time had actually passed, but she stayed with me repeating over and over, "It's okay. You're okay."

It would be this woman, Catherine, who became my sanctuary in this hellhole prison. With her help, I would learn to be more open and trustful. With one exception. Perhaps someday I would shed my fear to mention that I am a Jew. But until I felt safe from persecution, until I no longer had apprehension that I could be killed because of the religion into which I was born, it would be my secret.

Not only would Catherine be my shelter and savior, but in five years another woman would walk through the doors of this insane asylum prison who would change my life. In those years, I often wondered, What crime did I commit to be put in such a prison? Was it because I was Jewish? Could people somehow tell I was a Jew? Would the fate that befell us in Kiev happen again here, in the land of the free? At the end of those long five years, I would have my answer. In the meantime, I had to find a way to survive, physically and mentally.

Chapter Five

Klara

1881

My mother had no sooner put the younger children to sleep when a wind picked up outside. Dust and particles swirled into the air. Horse hooves in wild motion intensified the clouds of dirt. As the turbulent mass of haze increased, the noise grew louder. But before the chaos and the screaming rout began, there was an eerie silence that sent a chill up my spine.

We were dreading and expecting trouble ever since the news of the assassination of Tsar Alexander II and the proclamation that the Russian Jews were responsible for his death. Riots had broken out against Jewish communities around Russia. It was just a matter of time before they landed at Kiev. That time was upon us.

Earlier, we had seen the Southern-Russian Worker's Union leaflet which read: "Brother workers. You are beating the Jews, but indiscriminately. One should not beat the Jew because he is a Jew and prays to God in his own way – indeed, God is one and the same to all – rather, one should beat him because he is robbing the people, he is sucking the blood of the working man."

Although this aggression was fueled by economic conditions (such as debts owed to Jewish moneylenders) and was mostly falsely perpetrated by the Russian press, there was a kernel of truth in the proclamation in that a close associate to one of the assassins was born to a Jewish home. The fact that the other assassins were atheists and the broader Jewish community had nothing to do with the assassination bore little impact on the spread of anti-Semitism. Thus began retaliatory attacks on Jewish communities. We knew an attack was coming in Kiev. What we didn't know, however, was how wanton the cruelty would be.

My papa believed in keeping us informed. "Preparation can save lives," he told our family that was gathered together after that leaflet arrived. And he continued to keep us informed as the Jewish populations of villages and city upon city fell. Thousands of Jewish homes and businesses were destroyed. Jewish families that survived the attacks were reduced to poverty. Significant numbers of men, women, and children were killed. We heard the news and waited, hoping that it would end before reaching our doorstep. That was a futile wish.

Yes, my papa advocated readiness. But no family meeting, no means of advanced preparation could have prepared us for the rioting and slaughter that was about to take place.

Papa stood up and looked around our minimally furnished living room. He quickly moved the brown couch closer to the wall and surrounded the ends with tables. While hurrying about to rearrange our furniture he motioned a frantically waving hand to Mama. "Gather the children!"

Papa's demanding, no-nonsense tone in his otherwise calm, self-assured voice scared me. Seeing Papa react with such intensity before running for his rifle gave me no reassurance that we would be safe.

Before we were all gathered into our living room and had a chance to blow out candles or close the curtains, a window shattered. Glass burst into the room. A shard hit my brother Abram on his right cheek. As his hand flew to the wound to remove the fragment, Mama ran to him. Without thinking about it, she ripped a piece of her apron from her bodice and had Abram hold it over the cut. "Oh, dear God! Please keep us safe," she prayed.

We hadn't made it to our hiding place behind the couch when two Russian soldiers entered. "Get that!" shouted the taller one who motioned an index finger in Papa's direction. He pointed his gun at my family while the other shorter one rushed to confiscate Papa's rifle.

"You think you'll use this, you Jew pig?" The shorter soldier rammed the butt of the rifle into Papa's belly.

Doubled over, Papa yelled to us, "Run! Find a place to hide!" He grabbed and pulled the soldier's pant leg to throw him off balance.

The taller soldier's attention was now off Mama and the rest of us. He rushed to where Papa was. "Not so smart, Jew!" He spat while holding his gun to Papa's head.

Papa's distraction worked. Some of us made haste to get to outside. We were safe.

Momentarily.

Out of breath, I made it to a dark corner with overgrown brush. I flattened myself on the ground. Panting, I peered out between the dense branches. I saw Mama race out. Her left hand was latched with Josel's. She carried Anna clutched in her other arm, her little body bouncing on Mama's side as she ran. They made it no further than ten feet. The shorter soldier shot them down.

The sound of those three gunshots reverberated in my body. My heart felt like it was going to explode. I wanted to run to them. Trembling, I stayed put. I knew what my fate would be if the soldiers saw me. I hoped they wouldn't remember how many of us there were. I prayed they wouldn't hunt us down until we were all dead.

Waves of nauseating, disabling and painful shock lurched through me as I watched Josel and Anna die instantly from shots to their little backs. Mama, covered in their blood, fell to the ground and cried roars of agony. The murderer just walked off and left her there in her misery to continue to suffer the torment of seeing her lifeless babies beside her, Anna yet in her arm. God, why? Why... My bleeding soul mourned.

I don't remember how many more shots rang out. How many more innocents were dead or dying?

And then silence.

That same eerie quiet that I experienced before the outburst began filled my ears. Like slithering snakes on the ground moving to their target before the rattling, that horrible stillness led to a terribly misguided sense of safety. To generate an iota of hope before destruction. Could there be a more vicious way to attack your own people?

I started to tremble so badly that the branches surrounding me shook. I continued to wait. I was frozen with fear, afraid to move. After I don't know how long, the quiet was disrupted. The soldiers—now disorganized and wild-eyed—got on their horses and rode off. The last plume of dirt from the graveyard that Kiev had become settled back to the ground, covering the still, cold bodies of my people.

When the sound of horse hooves thundering was long gone, I crawled on my belly over to Mama. Through my wet, blurry vision,

I saw the light from the moon reflect in her fading, glossy eyes. "Mama, stay with me." I kissed her cheek and continued to whisper in her ear, "Don't die."

She tried to talk. Her barely-parted lips only emitted a shallow breath.

I moved my hand over her body to try to find where she was wounded to attempt to stop the bleeding. But it was no use. She had already lost too much blood from a bullet hole in her thigh.

She raised her limp, heavy hand to my wet cheek. Gently caressing it, she stroked a finger to wipe my tears. That was the last living thing my mama did.

Grabbing hold of her, I screamed inside my head, Noooo! I put a hand to Josel then Anna's face with my bloodied fingers and caressed them. My warm tears splashed on their cold little bodies.

A noise in the bush startled me. Leaves moved. I froze like prey avoiding a predator.

When the motion stopped and the foliage calmed, the knotted tension through my neck and back remained. I pretended to be dead next to Mama and my siblings until I heard nothing for a long time.

Where was Papa? And Abram? And Shakna?

I had to find them. But I was afraid to stand. Afraid I'd be seen and shot.

Ever so slowly (and under cover of darkness), I crawled to our door. I saw Papa with a lifeless Abram and a moaning, bleeding Shakna. Shakna's chest wound was bad, and I knew with each gurgling breath she took, she wasn't long for this world.

As I began to edge my way to Papa, his bloodshot, tear-filled eyes made contact with mine. And like those hideous soldiers had done with my mama—leaving her to bleed to death watching her children die—they left Papa at the side of his beloved children to witness a parent's worst nightmare.

"No, Klara, not here. Go hide. Save yourself."

His words were like a bayonet piercing my heart. Leave him? No! I couldn't. I continued to move toward him. None of what had happened had really sunk in. It was all too unreal. I didn't want to be in a world without my family. I continued to edge toward my papa. I yearned for his touch. I needed the comfort of his love. I needed him to tell me we would be safe now. I needed to wake up from this nightmare and find my family alive.

When he reached an arm out to me, I saw blood on his shirt. Dark reddish-brown blood.

"Papa! You're bleeding!"

"Shh, my darling, shh. It's just a flesh wound. See?" He looked at the stain that had changed from bright red to a dull coffee color. "It's not fresh."

Thankfully, the bullet wound on Papa's torso was superficial. Having passed through an outer pouch of fat, it sealed itself closed.

"Klara, you listen to me. Go! Find a safe place and stay put until the commotion calms. That is an order, young lady! We need to separate to ensure one of us stays safe should they return."

"Papa," I moaned. I knew he was right, but I didn't want to leave him, afraid it would be the last I'd see of my papa.

"Go, my darling." His outreached arm motioned me to move. "I'll find you."

I grabbed his arm. "Promise me," I begged.

"Yes, now go."

Heartbroken, I went back to the corner I hid in earlier. Lying there, it felt like the pain in my chest—the mountain of loss—would smother me. As I breathed in dust, I waited. The noise of the turbulence, bloodshed, pillaging, and victims' outcries screamed in my head. Again, I began to shake uncontrollably. Nausea filled my belly. I cried into my tightly closed eyelids.

After what felt like hours, no soldiers returned. I crawled back to the house. To my papa. He hadn't moved from Shakna's side. From her labored-breathing and the blood bubbling from her mouth. When Shakna's wheezing stopped and her body went limp, Papa grabbed her in his arms. With mournful, sunken eyes, he shook his head at the unbearably grief-stricken situation. He stayed quiet for a long time, then he put Shakna's body down and asked, "Where's Mama? The others?"

My eruption of tearful sobbing was answer enough.

"Oh, dear God!" He quickly looked at the door, the broken window, and to me. "We need to keep you safe." His look changed. Like a bear protecting its cub, he went into action. He scrambled to the kitchen on his knees. There he cleaned and bandaged his wound. He also grabbed some bread and filled a jug with water then crawled back to me and said, "Stay crouched down. Follow me."

We made our way to a field behind our house and into the scrub and tall growth. We stayed there for days. Papa was right to have us stay put because the soldiers returned with a vengeance that burns in my brain to this day. On the last of their three-day rampage, four soldiers rode up to our house. One went in and looked around. He came out laughing. Laughing! How dare he laugh at death, at what was inflicted on my family? What calloused heart does such a thing?

When I thought I'd seen the worst, when my overwhelmed mind swam in disbelief, when I could envision nothing more devastating, it happened. A frightened little girl with brown, curly hair and small, short legs ran past where Mama, Josel, and Anna's bodies lay. I glanced through the scrub that hid us to see her look at them. She screamed.

I pounded a fist on the ground, attempting to make a noise to get her attention. To stop her from drawing attention and danger to herself.

Papa, wanting to keep us safe, grabbed hold of me, put his hand over my mouth and whispered, "Shh."

My clouded vision went to the little girl, turning in circles, wailing, "Mama!"

Please move little one, I silently pleaded. God, please help her! But that late afternoon, no God was helping us Jews.

What happened next made me vomit in Papa's hand.

A fat soldier rode up to her on his horse. Laughing while spewing vulgarities, he took his sword out of its sheath and made a slicing motion through the little girl's neck.

Papa sniffed a shocked breath. He held me so tightly that I had trouble inhaling. When the sadistic, ugly curse of a human being rode off, my last meal was all over Papa's hand and arm.

Before that day, I'd never seen my papa cry. He was a stoic, strong man. A loving, compassionate man. A good provider and decent human being. But he kept his emotions hidden. Not on that day. He held me, and we both cried like babies.

By nightfall, when all of the unfamiliar sounds of violence, destruction and death had dissipated, and the city fell still, Papa had had enough. "We're leaving."

I was too afraid to speak. Too frightened to move. And too shocked to think straight. I had witnessed more evil and suffered more grief than anyone should ever have to in ten lifetimes. I sat there unresponsive.

Papa shook my shoulders to snap me out of it. "We need to leave! Now!" Papa had made up his mind. And there would be no changing it.

When he shook me again, I moaned. "What about Mama? Josel? Anna?" I choked out the names of my other two siblings. The smothering lump in my throat felt like the size of a boulder preventing more words.

Papa looked to Mama's body, and the two small ones beside her and lowered his head. "Yes. We'll take care of them, then we must leave."

A Different Kind of Angel

Chapter Six

I moved through the rest of the day as if in a frightening dream. But this nightmare wouldn't be one I'd awake from. No, this one was real. Painfully real.

In 72 unbearable hours, the Kiev pogrom reached its conclusion. The soldiers moved on to their next target for annihilation. The first thing we did was dig graves to bury Mama, Abram, Shakna, Josel, and Anna.

Our tears turned dirt to mud as we shoveled holes in the ground. The ghosts of a lighthearted Gelfman family waltzed in my head as the yard we so often sang and danced in became a graveyard. We dug where we used to sit outside in warm weather sharing meals. We hollowed places in the earth where Abram stood tall and proud practicing for his bar mitzvah. We bore through seedlings planted by Mama to grow a vegetable garden. And when their bodies were covered with dirt, we sat down by their graves.

Papa cleared his throat. In a solemn, gravelly voice, he recited a Kaddish. When I heard the words "blessed, peace, and consolation" from that prayer, I wanted to pound my fists to the ground. Where is the God who allows this to happen? To innocents! My father's faith was stronger than my waning belief that somewhere a God was watching over us, and somehow there was meaning to all this suffering. My papa used to bring me to his lap when I was little and got hurt. He would say to me, "God has His reasons. We can't see through His eyes. But never lose the faith. We are here, we exist, by His miracle." At that moment—sitting by the graves of my mama and siblings—I didn't care if I existed at all. I just wanted the painful, tortuous mental images to stop. I wanted to dull my mind and purge my soul of all I had witnessed. Of all I had been robbed of.

As we continued on, each moment seemed to last an eternity shadowed with heartache, I thought I would explode with grief. Finally, when it was time to leave, Papa grabbed hold of my arm to help me up. Once standing, he took me in his arms and, as if carried on a gentle, healing breeze, he softly whispered, "I love you, Klara. We will get through this." His touch, his words, his aliveness made a difference. My papa had given me many precious gifts, but the most important two were strength and hope. At that moment, I felt a glimmer of hope. He had that ability. He infused me with love. It helped me endure.

I followed his lead the rest of the day, in awe that he was able to think logically about our future survival so soon after our unthinkable loss. While I had trouble concentrating, he had clarity about what we needed to do. "We need money—valuables—for travel. To live on. To get to a place where we will be free from persecution." When he went to his bedroom and began to look through a small chest of drawers, he told me, "Search through the rest of the house for valuables that we can carry with us. Nothing heavy. Coins. Jewelry. Gold. Silver."

When I nodded and turned to leave, the sound of something clanging caught my attention. In Papa's hand was a gold mezuzah. He kissed it and placed it back in the drawer.

"You're not taking that?" I asked. "It's gold,"

"No, nothing marking us as Jews. Nothing to put a pox on us. From now on until the day we will be safe to practice what we believe, we will carry our religion only in our hearts."

I knew how much he loved our religion. Although we weren't Orthodox, he held a firm belief in the Old Testament, the Jewish Bible, and had centuries of Jewish blood pumping through his veins. It was such an essential part of his life. Leaving the mezuzah, that trinket that held a small piece of a parchment scroll with sacred texts from the Torah (the body of wisdom and law contained in Jewish Scripture), was like him leaving part of his soul behind. And so, my papa placed the symbol of what gave his existence meaning back with the clothing and other mundane items and shuffled through the remainder of the drawer looking for assets to barter.

When finished rummaging through our home, we packed two small bags of clothing and food. Before we left, I took a long look at the living room. Never again would I see Anna toddling after Josel, or Abram sharing things he learned, or Shakna helping Mama with meals. Never again would I smell their baking and share the joy of family time over warm food cooked with love. Never again would I see our possessions, the small items that meant nothing to a stranger but represented our lives: candles, books, a doll, a doily Mama made, and the mezuzah Papa said we had to leave behind.

"It's too dangerous to be a Jew," he whimpered. That was the last time I heard that tone come from Papa. His bereavement would come second to his fatherly instinct to protect me. To be strong. From then on, our survival was his priority. And he was determined to fortify me so that I would rise through this horrifying time. God bless my papa, for it was this lesson—and this alone—that helped save my life more than once.

We then went to other homes that were not burned down and were empty. We grabbed what jewelry, coins, and valuables we could find and carry. Papa spotted a hay wagon and a horse. While attaching the horse to the wagon, he told me, "Get under the hay and cover yourself." He then went to find more food and water to bring with us. Riding off, we left the only home I had ever known.

As the horizon filled with flames and screams from gathering mobs, we drove. And drove. Over bumps well into the night. I don't know how many days we traveled or exactly where we were, but Papa talked to people en route and formulated a plan as we headed west through Galicia and Hungary to Croatia-Slavonia. Papa continued to meet people who helped us with directions and offered us places to stay. Due to weather and political conditions, some of the stopovers lasted for weeks. Papa's carpentry skills came in handy around farms and homes in exchange for room and board, while I assisted with cooking and chores inside. Looking back on that lengthy travel time, much of it is yet a blur. What I vividly recall was the help of good people we met along the way and the kind deeds of those with compassionate hearts. By the Grace of God, we eventually met a kind, generous man, Boris Chernoff, who worked out of Rijeka, a port in Croatia-Slavonia. He transported cargo to America. For a reasonable price, he was willing to take Papa and me to this fabled land of freedom and endless opportunity.

In early 1882 we set out from Rijeka. The voyage took us through the Adriatic Sea to the Mediterranean Sea, through the Strait of Gibraltar to the Atlantic Ocean. For days we pitched and rolled. Just when my cheerless, cloudy mind started to relax, it looked like the skies were ready to burst with rain.

Then it happened. My papa became ill. My heart turned as cold as a Kiev snowstorm. The thunderclaps of unshed buckets of rain clashed in my head as I prayed Papa's illness was nothing serious. When I glanced at my ashen papa, I could see something going on behind those dull, brown eyes of his that made me feel uneasy. "Papa," trying to deliver a spoonful of soup into his mouth, I said, "eat this."

I knew he was in trouble by the way the skin around his mouth tightened when he tried to take air in. Attempting to spread open his lips, he coughed up a big glob of brown mucus. He reached a hand to the horizontal lines between my brows, now crinkled with worry. "I'll be okay," he mumbled through a weak smile as if trying to alleviate my apprehension.

"Yes, you will, Papa." When I caressed his hand, it felt warm. Feverishly warm. A panicky hot flame rushed into my belly.

He fell asleep. His breathing slowed and became less labored, and I was able to relax along with him. I watched the peaceful expression on his face, the unimpeded rise and fall of his chest, and felt the heat emanating from his flesh dissipate. Hope, as tangible as the sweater on my back, surged through me. It allowed me to doze.

My respite from worry was short lived. The next morning when I awoke, I could tell that Papa knew he was dying. He stopped telling me he would be fine. Instead, he tried to prepare me. Right until the end, he focused on preparation. "I'm dying." He was panting his last breaths when he told me to stay strong. You are a Gelfman. You can do anything you make your mind up to do.

But making up my mind that he would become well didn't bring back his health. All I could do was cry.

As his lifeless body turned rubbery and cool, my throat strangled with fear. Waves hit the bulkhead and rolled the ship. A candle in the room flickered. I tried to rouse him. "Papa," I begged his body to move, to show some sign of activity. "Please, Papa! You said you would be okay." I gently shook his torso. Then as my uneasiness turned to dread, my throat cramped from unshed tears. "No! Not you, too!"

I don't know how long I sat beside him, unmoving, blinking away seas of sorrow before I lumbered up to the deck, into the gray day that matched my mood, to inform Captain Chernoff. The rest of what occurred after that is a very foggy memory.

I do remember when the captain explained to me that a dead body could not be taken ashore in America—something to do with concern over disease—and that we'd have to toss my papa's body overboard. That was the painful last straw before I shut down emotionally.

Fatigued and emotionally crushed, were it not for Captain Chernoff, I probably would've sunk into a black abyss and remained there. My faith was as thin as a spider's web and as tenuous as a fly caught in it. God was fast becoming no more real to me than a childhood fable. If not for the captain's benevolence and attention to my welfare, my fragile belief in life's goodness would have shattered. Because of him and simple acts of kindness by his crew, the candle of my soul yet flickered. Barely. Just enough to cast a very dim light onto the dark, shadowy days.

Day after day, I was tended to with offerings of warm meals and an occasional walk on the deck. The crew was short-staffed, so I was grateful these busy men took time to let me just be among them. I didn't feel so alone, and that helped to lift me from a depressed, inert state. Slowly, very gradually, I felt less grim. Around three weeks after Papa's death, I felt enough determination to help in the galley. I needed to occupy my time, to distract my mind, and, most importantly, return the goodwill.

To my benefit, I worked alongside a bilingual Russian sailor who knew I was now alone and beginning a new life in a foreign land. He took it upon himself to teach me some English. Word by word, all his effort started to pay off. By the time I arrived in New York City, my limited vocabulary would help me find my way to a boardinghouse. I was still solemn at my core, but I could mask my doldrums—even submerge them at times—so I could face my next steps. Whatever they were. Little did I know that before long, I would encounter a whole other level of hell.

A Different Kind of Angel

Chapter Seven

Nellie

1887

In telling my story, it's important I that I describe how Nellie Brown arrived at Blackwell's Island Women's Lunatic Asylum five years after me. She's a significant part of my story, so her story must be told, too. I hope I'm doing justice to Nellie's motives for coming to be a patient at the asylum because she told me so many years ago.

Nellie Brown (her real name was Elizabeth Jane Cochran, and her pen name was Nellie Bly) didn't arrive at the asylum the same way I did. No, she knew exactly where she was going and why. By the time she arrived in 1887, I was already speaking English. Catherine spent hours at night helping me form words and gain an understanding of my new second language. That became my second secret—that I knew English. It allowed me the slight advantage of being an inconspicuous but effective observer to the loose-lipped, gossiping staff. Plus, I didn't want to get Catherine in trouble for helping me. Patients interacting with each other was strictly forbidden and savagely punished by many of our "caretakers."

When blue-eyed Nellie Brown arrived, with her brown, wavy hair and short-cropped bangs, I was taken with her beauty. She was wearing the same dingy "uniform" as the rest of us and looked a bit frazzled, but her loveliness was hard to hide. Into the sitting area, the five-foot-three-inch, small-waisted, thin woman arrived, her hair still dripping wet from her bath. She sat next to Catherine and me. Close enough to be overheard in conversations with the nurses and guards. To our collective fortune, she was roomed in the same dorm as us.

From the minute she arrived, she professed to be "normal." And by all appearances in speech and mannerism, I would say she was surely mentally sound. Like me. And Catherine. And we weren't the only ones of sound mind who inhabited that place. There were others. God only knew how many.

Many women routinely announced their sanity, but their actions cast immediate doubts about their claims. Not Nellie. When Nellie Brown proclaimed, "I am not insane," her assertion had an authentic ring to it.

I wondered about her. Why would someone with seeming sophistication of physical and verbal expression find herself in this horrible place? I wanted to ask her. Curiosity overwhelmed me. But it would be ten days before I learned her complete story. This is what she finally told me (to the best of my recollection). After all, she was a journalist with a keen observational sense and affinity for detail.

* * *

Elizabeth Jane Cochran was born in 1864 to Michael Cochran and Mary Jane Kennedy Cochran. After her father died, Elizabeth had to drop out of boarding school. The family, living in Pittsburg, fell on hard times, but that didn't deter Elizabeth's interest in advancing her skills in writing. When she encountered an article, What Girls Are Good For, in the Pittsburg Dispatch that suggested that women were only good for giving birth, raising children, and keeping house, she told me that she was irate. Under a pseudonym, Lonely Orphan Girl, she responded. George Madden, the editor of the newspaper, was so impressed with her response that he wrote an advertisement for the author to step forward. When Elizabeth went to introduce herself to Madden, he offered her the fortuitous break to write a piece for the newspaper under the same pseudonym. Once again impressed with what she wrote, Madden offered her a full-time job. Nellie said that it was customary at that time for women writers to use pen names. The name chosen for Elizabeth Cochran was Nellie Bly, after a character in a Stephen Foster song.

Nellie initially wrote articles focusing on working women, primarily investigating factory work. Then she was reassigned to cover women's topics like fashion, gardening, and the societal elite. Uninspired by the new subject matter chosen for her, she became discontented. "I hated it, Klara!" She shook her head when she told me. "They think women's brains can't comprehend anything but gossip, garments, and gardens!" She ventured to Mexico to write about government corruption involving the press. When she was threatened with arrest, she returned to Pittsburg and was reassigned to write about arts and theater (again, considered women's topics). Disillusioned, she left the Pittsburg Dispatch in 1887 and headed to New York City.

She spent several months without a writing job and was broke. Finally, she talked her way into the office of Joseph Pulitzer, the owner of the New York World. It was there she agreed to take on an undercover assignment: faking insanity to investigate and expose rumors of disregard and brutality at the Blackwell's Island Women's Lunatic Asylum. Nellie later told me that her response was, "This is what I was meant to do." Finally, there was a melding of women's issues with institutional corruption that she could dig her teeth into. Having faith in her ability to pull it off, she agreed to the assignment and set about immediately practicing physical gestures and verbal characteristics of the insane in front of a mirror.

The ten-day assignment to uncover what white-capped nurses and bolts and bars kept hidden in the locked-up wards began by wiping the perpetual smile off her face. In keeping with the initials on her clothing, NB, she assumed the name, Nellie Brown. Remembering what she had read about insane people, how they have wide, staring eyes, she practiced opening her eyes as wide as possible without blinking. She told me that she read ghost stories to create her dispirited mood.

When she felt she was ready, she put on old clothing and set out to secure a room to rent in a female boardinghouse. It was there that she pretended to be looking for work. After a few days, her real work began: to behave like an insane person.

* * *

Nellie told me that her career as an insane woman began with her walking down an avenue with a far-away expression. She had seen pictures in books of the insane with that distant, elsewhere look in their eyes. She had dressed simply. To give the appearance of not caring what she looked like, she had shifted the waist of her stained dress off to the side. Shuffling along to a boardinghouse, she passed a young girl selling flowers. Without looking at her, she sniffed the aroma of fresh cut roses. The smell made her nose run. Snuffling in the nasal discharge gave her an idea that she would later put to use. Nellie was such a smart woman. I always admired that about her.

She continued down the street until she arrived at the front door to a boardinghouse and pulled on the loud clanging doorbell. Fidgeting, she waited some minutes until a young girl answered.

After giving Nellie a head-to-toe looking at, the girl said, "Yes?" She couldn't have been scowling more disdainfully.

Nellie swiped a hand over loose strands of brown hair jutting out from under a hairpin. Avoiding eye contact, she cast her blue eyes to her dirty shoes. "Um…I need a room."

Nellie said the girl was speechless. She just motioned for Nellie to follow her to a drawing room where she was introduced to the matron, Mrs. Stansfield. Taking in Nellie's appearance and demeanor, Mrs. Stansfield coldly asked, "What do you want?"

Nellie, aware that she might be overplaying her part, and not wanting to lose her chance at a room, straightened her posture and looked at the woman. "I am Nellie Brown, and I would appreciate the opportunity to stay here for a few days if you have an available room."

Hesitant but satisfied, the woman nodded. "You may call me Mrs. Stansfield. There are no single rooms, but I can put you in a room with another woman. That much I can offer. How much money do you have?"

"Oh, ma'am, that would suit me just fine." Nellie smiled a purposefully crooked smile. "I have no more than eighty cents until I can find work." She never intended to look for work; instead, she would dawdle until her funds were gone, and she was put out.

The matron replied, "We charge thirty cents a night."

Nellie paid for the first night and settled into her room with a pudgy, red-cheeked, narrow-nosed, full-lipped woman as her roommate. As she was describing this woman, Nellie smiled. I think Nellie liked her.

"Martha. Martha Wellington," she held out a chubby hand to greet Nellie.

Nellie looked at her own hand and made no attempt to connect with the woman. Moments later, a loud bell clanged. Martha smiled. "That's dinner. Come down with me." She wasted no time in heading to the door.

Nine women were seated at the table, all engaged in lively conversations. Most were wearing modest working outfits and dresses. Nellie told me she assumed these women were factory workers. She found an empty chair near the end, at Mrs. Stansfield's right side. Martha took the seat next to Nellie. The din faded as the women noticed the newcomer.

A woman at the opposite end spoke up. "I see we have a new occupant." She smiled. Directing her attention to Nellie, she continued, "And what would your name be, dear?"

When Nellie did not reply, Mrs. Stansfield answered for her, "Nellie. Nellie Brown." The matron continued glancing over to her right side. "Go on, now. Don't be shy." She motioned to the steaming bowls and platters of food.

When Nellie reached for a bowl of potatoes without saying a word, the room went silent. Several of the women gave each other looks that varied: surprised, puzzled, amused. Martha had dismay spread across her scrunched pudgy cheeks as if her new roommate's bad manners reflected poorly on her. Martha gave the room a nervous smile, shrugged and grabbed a hunk of bread.

Before long the chattering resumed while serving spoons clanked against dishes. Nellie lowered her head and avoided conversation. Boiled mutton, potatoes, and bread made it to her plate. She chewed loudly with an open mouth and slurped the coffee that was served with the meal. More unkind looks passed between the women.

After supper, she returned to the cramped, cold room. She said nothing as Martha sat by a light and read. Nellie started sighing, sniffling and conjured up tears. Hearing her roommate in apparent distress, Martha looked up and inquired, "What's wrong?"

"Nothing," Nellie put on a grand, but fake, smile. To add to the drama, she covered her face with a handkerchief.

Martha did not offer further queries. Nellie told me she hid her genuine smile behind the hankie. Nervously banging a foot on the wooden floorboard, once again Nellie distracted Martha. Nellie was sure that if she kept acting in this unpredictable, bizarre, annoying way, Martha would soon wonder if she was rooming with a crazy woman.

Sure enough, by the next day, Martha went to the matron and stated abruptly she refused to room with "that batty woman." Nellie was moved to another room with a new occupant, a Mrs. Crane.

During the second night, Nellie sat on the edge of the bed and stared blankly into space. That sent Mrs. Crane into a tizzy, coming around to look at her every so often. (I would have worried, too!) Finally, when she couldn't take it any longer, she asked Nellie questions. Where was she from? Did she have any family? What kind of work did she do? Anything to get her talking.

Nellie never looked at Mrs. Crane but answered each question with a long pause followed by, "I don't remember." Then she gave her new roommate a little more information. "I think… Yes… It was the headaches." Still staring vacantly at where the ceiling met the wall, Nellie said she noticed Mrs. Crane move closer to her. "When the headaches started, everything else vanished. Poof! Memories all gone."

"Headaches," Mrs. Crane perked up like she was about to have a breakthrough with this poor lost soul. "Do please tell me about this affliction."

Nellie refused to indulge in any further talk; instead, she stared silently into a void.

That night Mrs. Crane woke up in a cold sweat, the result of a nightmare. She told Nellie that she had dreamed that Nellie rushed at her with a knife. Just before she was slain, she woke up. Nellie said she thought it odd that Mrs. Crane had shared the gruesome dream with her. "Perhaps she sought reassurance. But when none was received from me, Mrs. Crane spent the rest of the night somewhat agitated."

When Mrs. Crane started to nod off, Nellie eased her posture and kept her mind as stimulated as she could, so she wouldn't fall asleep. "I was afraid that if I slept, Klara, I might just babble the truth about my situation and who I really was." Nellie told me that she passed the time connecting lines on the floor into geometric configurations, watching a spider spin a web, and (for an hour or two) she sat face to face with herself in a way she'd never done before. She felt her heartbeat. Her lungs take in air. She put her hands together and felt the texture of her skin. She watched thoughts come and go: disturbing, funny, entertaining, uncertain all jumbled together in a stream of never-ending waves. Then the thinking slowed. Spaces appeared between ideas until she sat there unthinking. The quiet illuminated her. "It was then I knew I would be able to continue to carry out my assignment with confidence, Klara," she told me.

When Mrs. Crane awoke, she was surprised to see Nellie sitting at the edge of the bed yet awake and as active as a humming bumblebee. She tried to console her clearly agitated, unstable new roommate by asking Nellie if she had any friends who could help her.

Nellie barked, "I don't have friends. I don't have family." Then she frantically pounded a fist on her bed. She moved her head into seizure-like motions. "I have flowers," said Nellie in a softer voice. "And they talk to me." She turned around and glared at Mrs. Crane. "Do you have flower friends?"

Mrs. Crane was speechless. Averting her eyes from Nellie's fierce stare, she made haste to leave the room. It was then Nellie was sure that Mrs. Crane deemed her undeniably insane.

When word got out that Nellie was not of sound mind, the other tenants in the boardinghouse taunted her with questions. Nellie feigned instability by rolling her head back and forth and mumbling incoherently. She kept up her role until the matron, Mrs. Stansfield, went to her to try to calm her down. When that had no effect, the matron commented, "I think it's time for you to find another place to stay. There's simply too much disruption to the other—"

"No!" Nellie yelled, refusing to move.

Another tenant—a middle-aged, prudish, puckered-lipped, plainly dressed woman in black from head to toe—complained, "Someone needs to go for the police."

"Tsk-tsk," chided Mrs. Stansfield as she put on her bonnet and left the premises.

Whispers, taunts, and laughs erupted in the hallway outside of Nellie's room. It was all she could do to stay in character. She would have liked to have scolded these unkind women for being cruel and merciless. "All people, especially those who are suffering any form of illness, deserve to be treated with decency and kindness," she told me. I nodded in agreement. "Klara, I struggled to stay put inside that room, to say nothing to these heartless women, and let the charade play out. I took the assignment, and I had to let it play out."

Before long, Mrs. Stansfield appeared with two ruggedly-built, large policemen named Samuel and Thomas. "This here is Nellie Brown," she said to them.

Nellie refused to look at them or make a comment.

"If you don't come along willingly, I will drag you through the street," said Thomas.

Nellie told me that she believed Mrs. Stansfield was a merciful woman. The matron lowered her voice and lied to Nellie by saying, "These two men will help you find a job. Now, go on with them, dear." But Mrs. Stansfield did it to get Nellie some much-needed help.

Nellie yielded by standing.

"That's good now, you go with them. I'll follow along to assist."

Nellie left with the two officers. They all quietly walked to the station house. Upon arriving, the officer in charge questioned Nellie. "Are you Nellie Brown?"

"I suppose I am," replied Nellie.

"Where do you come from?"

"I don't know."

Mrs. Stansfield, who came along, interjected saying that Nellie had acted strangely in her home. "She has not slept a wink. And it is of my humble opinion that this demented woman must have been driven to madness by inhumane treatment previously." She went on to relay the events that took place at her boardinghouse since Nellie's arrival, including input from Martha Wellington, Mrs. Crane, and others. Even though Nellie thought the matron was showing her kindness, I have to wonder if Mrs. Stansfield was really concerned about Nellie or just trying to get rid of her.

The officer took notes while there was further discussion and questioning with Mrs. Stansfield. When completed, he commanded the other two officers, "Take her to the court."

Mrs. Stansfield left.

Before reaching for her elbow to take her out, Officer Samuel eyed Nellie closely, shook his head, and winked at his partner Thomas, a gesture that came across like he thought Nellie's mind was permanently gone.

They entered the Essex Market Police Courtroom where legally the question of whether or not Nellie was insane would be determined. Judge Duffy sat behind the elevated dark-brown wooden desk. His pale face was aged with worry wrinkles carved into his forehead. He had stern squint lines radiating out from the corners of his eyes. The judge's manner was gruff when he said, "Step forward." His demeanor gave Nellie the impression it would not be difficult to convince him she was ready for an asylum.

Nellie ignored his command.

I was shocked that she was so brave and told her so. Nellie said with a shrug and a wink, "I had to be convincing. Plus, that old judge needed to get his blood circulating."

Demanding a response, he raised his voice, "Did you not hear me?" Nellie played right into it, acting oblivious to his attempts to rile her. She began humming loudly enough for the judge to hear her.

"I said step forward," came a sharp gravelly tone from the judge. "And stop that noise you're making this instant!"

Nellie moved closer to the bench and looked down at the floor. Smelling cologne emanating from the judge, she was reminded of the girl selling flowers earlier and the idea she had. Now was the opportunity to put it to use. She stopped humming and began loudly sniffing in the aroma.

"What's your name?" The judge asked.

"Nellie Brown," she mumbled and again made a production of inhaling through her nose.

"Speak up, Miss Brown!" He demanded. "And face me."

When Nellie remained still, Officer Thomas put a hand under her chin, lifting her head to face the judge. Nellie closed her eyes. She took in several rapid, loud breaths through her nose and continued to sniff like a dog.

"Open your eyes." The frustrated judge slammed a fist on his desk. "And stop that racket with your nose!"

Remaining in the same stance, Nellie emitted a low, guttural groan to keep from laughing.

"I said open your eyes!"

Nellie opened her eyes and tried to turn away against pressure still exerted under her chin. Officer Thomas moved closer and used both his hands to hold her head toward the judge. Nellie looked in the direction of the judge, to the bulging veins on this neck that looked ready to burst.

"When did you come to New York?"

"I didn't come to New York."

The judge's face turned red. "But you are in New York."

"No," Nellie replied, trying to look suspicious (like she thought a crazy person would look). She curled a strand of hair around her index finger and lobbed her head back and forth.

The judge looked to Officer Thomas and then to Officer Samuel. He made a stern declaration, which (according to Nellie) sounded like his final decision. "This person is obviously of unsound mind. She does not know where she is from. She does not respond with attentive disposition."

Nellie made her body shake as if she were on the verge of a breakdown. She opened her eyes wide and, like in the boardinghouse room, stared into space. For a sane woman, Nellie knew a lot about acting crazy.

"I have seen and heard enough. Get her out of my courtroom," the judge said quickly while shuffling papers in front of him. "Make out papers to send her to Bellevue for examination." He slammed his gavel down so hard, the court reporter flinched.

A Different Kind of Angel

Chapter Eight

Before being carted off to Bellevue for evaluation, Nellie told me that she overheard the judge tell one of the officers that he thought she had, "Hopelessly gone mad. Her lucidity is simply irretrievable." But this time when he spoke, Nellie heard a changed tone. His harshness had softened. It didn't sound like that gruff, patronizing attitude he had displayed moments before.

Avoiding looking back at the judge, Nellie wondered if his abrupt treatment of her had caused him to feel guilt pangs. She worried he might change his mind. She said to me, "I never heard of a judge that suddenly came down with a case of remorse, but wouldn't that have just been my luck?" She was concerned he would call her back and withdraw the insanity judgment. "My undercover assignment would've been hopelessly ruined because of a judge with a conscience! Mr. Pulitzer would've thought I had gone insane if I told him that," Nellie smiled at me, shaking her head. But her worries were for naught. The judge made no further comments, and the officers guided her out the door. "I realized I had been holding my breath the whole time, so I let out a big sigh and inhaled deeply. Klara, I nearly laughed out loud when one of the officers said to the other, 'Good grief! All that sniffing from that lunatic. Another one who thinks she's a dog!' I bit my lip to contain a smile."

The last thing to happen before leaving the courthouse was an exam with a doctor for the final okay to transport her to Bellevue.

She entered a room in which two chairs sat facing each other. A small wooden table was set off to the side. On it was an oil-lit lamp. Nellie told me that the newspaper building she worked in had been renovated to include the new electric light bulb. This room still had the old glass lamps lit from burning fuel. They gave off irritating-smelling fumes that made her sneeze.

The doctor sat in one of the chairs, while the officers brought Nellie to the other. He looked sharp with his finely pressed wool suit, brightly polished shoes and neatly crimped hair. "I took one look at him, Klara, and thought he would see right through my act." She sat in a chair before the doctor.

"Put out your tongue," he said.

"No, I don't want to."

The doctor sternly straightened up in his chair. "You must," he protested. "I am the doctor, and you are sick."

"I am not sick. I never was and never will be," replied Nellie. "I won't do it!" She then stuck out her tongue.

The doctor jerked his head back making her want to laugh. "Hold still," he said, trying to have a look in her mouth.

Nellie wagged her tongue, and spit flew in his eye.

Wiping his eye with a handkerchief, the doctor stamped a foot to the floor and harshly said, "If you refuse to cooperate, I will have you restrained."

Nellie then opened her mouth but refused to stick out her tongue. He gave it a quick look. "Ah, yes, okay."

He continued his superficial examination of her face and head. He said "Ah" and "Hmm" and sighed a lot but wrote nothing down. Nellie told me that she had overestimated this doctor from his professional appearance. She relaxed in the chair.

He then felt a pulse and listened to her heartbeat while Nellie held her breath in an attempt to make it irregular. When she gasped to regain her breath, he shined a light in her eyes to see the reaction of her pupils. She wondered what an insane person's pupil reaction would look like. To test him further, she gave him a wide-eyed stare. She held her unblinking glare upon his hand, leaving it there for moments after he finished what he was doing. When he shook his head and puckered his lips, like he'd had enough of this mad woman, Nellie felt more confidence in her ability to succeed in her mission.

After the exam, the doctor told the officers, "It is pointless to ask any further questions of this...she is incapable of answering."

Relieved, Nellie said she was then moved to the ambulance waiting to transport her. Feigning resistance when the officers forced her in, she accidentally banged and cut her knee on the metal door. With blood oozing through her ripped dress—the smelly one she had been wearing the last several days—they drove out of the gate.

Holding a hand to her knee to stop the bleeding, Nellie noticed a crowd of people gawking at the crazy girl. It prompted one of the officers to lower the curtain. Thus far, Nellie had successfully presented herself as hopelessly insane. When Nellie arrived at Bellevue, a gruff-sounding man opened the ambulance door, and asked, "Only one today?"

"Yup."

The burly guard with a thick, scratchy-looking beard came at Nellie quickly. In an instant, he was looming over her. Without query or any effort to gain Nellie's cooperation, he took hold of her in an attempt to drag her out. Mustering up the strength of a bear, once again Nellie resisted. He lifted her out like a sack of potatoes—a screaming, kicking sack.

"Were you frightened?" I asked, having a hard time believing that her journey to the asylum was worse than mine.

"Perhaps a bit, but I was more incensed to be treated in such an uncivilized way." Nellie paused. "I must admit, Klara, I was also intrigued. This barbaric domain is one I had never suffered."

I simply nodded, not knowing how to respond. Nellie was like no other person I knew then and now. I finally said, "Then what happened?" She gladly continued.

Nellie was brought to a small, dark office where several men worked. The one behind a desk, whom she assumed was a clerk, opened a book and began to ask her questions. When she refused to answer, another man in the room, a doctor, said, "That won't be necessary."

"But sir, the pa—" protested the prim man behind the desk as he rubbed a finger inside his high-starched collar.

Interrupting him, the doctor said, "All the papers are made out. She is too insane to coherently answer." Satisfied that he'd completed his task, the doctor ordered, "Take her to the insane pavilion."

When the same big brute that manhandled Nellie out of the ambulance came forward to remove her, she squirmed. He grabbed hold of her arms so tightly that a razor-sharp pain ran through her. As he lugged her, her feet dragged all the way to the insane ward.

A white-capped nurse met Nellie upon her arrival. "The persnickety woman tugged on her uniform to straighten a wrinkle and flicked off a particle of lint. She didn't speak to me or even look at me. That nurse gave lint more attention than she gave me." Nellie rolled her eyes when she told me.

I knew that demeaning attitude. I often felt less valuable than lint in the asylum. "What did she do?"

"She stood firm with her finely polished shoes anchoring her to the grimy floor. She gave me a quick look up and down and said in a dull, monotone, 'You. Wait here for the boat.' I think it was painful for her to acknowledge me even that much."

Nellie wanted to ask, how long? But she knew better. Instead, she stood at the door and looked down the long, uncarpeted hallway with dull walls that were distinctive to public institutions. An anxious flush ran through her as she noticed the doors at the far end of the hall. They were fastened by a large iron padlock. A few wooden chairs were lined under windows by doors on the side that she assumed opened to bedrooms.

Nellie was surprised that she was only the fourth patient present. The other three were sitting on the chairs lining the hallway. Nellie avoided contact with them. As the cold air began to seep in through the open windows, she wrapped her arms around her chest to stay warm. The other women also appeared to be catching the chilled draft. One of the women put her shaking knees together; another rubbed her arms. Nellie assumed that the third woman, who stood to stomp her feet while she walked in circles, was also uncomfortable with the dropping temperature, as were the nurses who buttoned their heavy garments. When it became almost unbearable, Nellie raised her voice and said, "Cold!"

A nurse curtly responded. "Don't expect much else from this place! Be grateful for the charity we're giving you. This is not—"

The nurse's arrogant reprimand was interrupted when the ward's hallway door opened, and an officer came to get Nellie. Before departing, Nellie was given another exam by a different doctor, which went pretty much as the first. "She is positively demented. A hopeless case." A few more choice words came from him before the final paperwork was signed, and Nellie was made ready for departure. "There was no point to all those routine procedures, other than to keep an evidence trail in the inconceivable case that anyone bothered to inquire if a woman no one cared about was being treated fairly," Nellie later told me.

Finally, she was hauled out and taken to the wharf to be boarded on the boat that would bring her to her final destination: Blackwell's Island Women's Lunatic Asylum.

Chapter Nine

Klara

1882

When I was attacked by the drunken man who stole my purse with all my valuables and identification in it, I realized that I didn't escape brutish criminals when I left Kiev. Wherever human beings with hardened hearts lurked, the suffering of innocent people would persist. But I had never imagined that policemen, doctors and, sadly, even nurses were capable of such intentional cruelty toward their fellow human beings. To recapture my heart, I needed to encounter people with selfless, earnest motives; that would be the only antidote to the suffering I had thus far endured. How else would I regain trust and a sense of security?

I was raised to believe what's important in life are decent people's actions. Altruism is the only benediction a good heart seeks, my papa frequently intoned. If I were to believe this principle that Papa instilled into our family—to counter all the hostility I had endured with compassion and goodwill—then infusing my soul with grace would have to become my prayer.

Before the 1881 Kiev pogrom, I felt secure, confident, and self-sufficient. But after the devastation, that changed. I changed. I became dependent on the charity of others—not just for my physical well-being but also to hold together what was left of my broken heart.

Initially, I found the goodness I needed in the people who helped Papa and me on our journey to Rijeka, and later from the captain and crew during the ocean crossing. They helped me connect with Russian-speaking people who set me up in a boardinghouse. Not long involved with them before I landed in the asylum, it was Catherine Bigsby who became a keystone figure in my life, the rock upon which trust would be rebuilt.

* * *

My first night on Blackwell's Island was met with moans that filled the very air I was breathing. Whatever sleep I managed to get was light and fitful. The bright illumination from a nearly full moon shone through the unadorned, barred windows. It lit the room, creating an appearance of daylight on a cloudy day, which disoriented me and made falling asleep even more challenging.

The other five women, including Catherine, were in their decrepit beds. As I tossed sleeplessly on my sagging, lumpy mattress, mental images of the day flashed before me. Attempting to avoid agonizing recollections, I brought my thoughts to Catherine and the way her beautiful amber eyes made me feel safe. I envisioned her dull, straight, black hair that clumped to her scalp from lack of washing. With so many of the women in this facility looking unkempt, I wondered about the hygiene they received. And yet even with the lack of grooming, I saw that Catherine was lovely. She had a thin nose and slightly upturned lips that were shaped like a dove's wings, lending to a soft smiling appearance. I needed to focus on her, the only good thing that happened that day. The simple stroking of my hand with her finger when we sat on the hard bench, the invitation to follow her to share this dormitory, and the attentive way she stayed with me before taking her leave to her bed helped me see that her beauty transcended her physical features.

Exhausted but awake, I kept my eyes on the movement of her chest rising and falling. I willed myself not to go back in time, to all the painful memories. My restlessness was interrupted when another patient suddenly sprang out of her bed and started to scream. "They're here! Hurry!"

I found it odd that her eyes were closed. Later, Catherine explained to me that she was in sleepwalking hysteria. Once again, not understanding what her words had meant, Catherine mimed it for me. As I pieced together instances like that with Catherine, and more to come, I began to understand where I was. But not why I was there. Nor Catherine, who by all means acted normal.

That poor sleepwalking woman woke up Catherine. She went over to the pacing, bowlegged sleepwalker who looked unsteady on her feet as if she suffered from a mineral deficiency. I had seen that before back in Kiev with the street urchins begging for food. Their wobbly bones were hardly able to hold them as their deformed arms held out a shaking hand. It made me feel so sad. Mama said they weren't properly fed and their bodies hadn't grown as they should. I wanted to feed them, but Papa forbade it. That was the only time in my life I thought him unreasonable. "You can't feed the world, Klara. We are in need ourselves."

"But Papa," I whimpered.

"You've got a kind heart, my beauty, but you feed one and the others crowd and follow you. You must learn boundaries."

He was right about my sensitivity to others, the compassion that was my joy and curse. He was also right about boundaries, which my mama reinforced and took a step further. "You don't allow someone to touch you," she would say, trying to communicate what she never seemed to find adequate words for. It would take me being in the lunatic asylum to fully come to learn what Mama meant to say.

These images and words came to me as I watched Catherine with the sleepwalking patient. And like she had done with me, Catherine gently took the woman into her arms. "Shh, Tillie," she whispered as she glanced toward the door.

Another patient, whom I had earlier heard referred to as Annette, jumped out of bed and acted as if she were in the bathroom. She began to wash her body. She had no water, no soap, no washcloth, but there she was scrubbing her skin through her nightgown. By the light of the moon, I got a closer look at her bare arms revealing eruptions: pustules, blisters, red patches, and scabs. It gave me a sick feeling that I may be doing bathroom ablutions near her. "Cleanse the evil," she intoned. She looked to the ceiling and in a raised voice said, "God, I haven't heard from you lately." Casting an ear upward, she waited for what appeared to be a response. When minutes passed, she banged a foot. "There's much evil to purge. Evil man. Evil!"

I felt a chill. The night was cold, and the room had no heating. Our blankets were flimsy. I curled into a tight ball on my side to try to keep warm. It was then the door flung open and a night nurse, carrying a lantern, came in yelling, "What's all this commotion!"

She looked at Catherine who was still with Tillie. And then at Annette. I peered at them through squinted eyes, afraid the attention might shift to me, the new patient in the room. But I wasn't the intended target. While she went to Annette, Catherine edged Tillie back to her bed.

Once close to Annette, the nurse put down her light. Rather than trying to calm her, she gave Annette a beating and a black eye. Crying out, Annette soiled herself. The nurse then dragged her out of the room by her hair, slamming the door so hard it shook the beds.

My body vibrated. It was the aftershock of all I had been through. All it took to rile me was the mere loud bang of a door. What is this place? Why am I here? Afraid to cry aloud, I sniveled and silently wept. My right hand clutched the threadbare blanket. Just when I thought I could no longer contain myself, Catherine came to my bed.

"You're trembling." She gently touched my arm.

I shook my head. With lowered, questioning eyebrows, I did my best to try to express I didn't understand what was happening.

Catherine nodded. Whether she actually comprehended what was going on with me or not, she calmed me down when she faintly spoke in my ear. "This is not a nice place. Not what I consider a decent hospital…It's more like a warehouse for some women…women who men want to get out of their lives. Like me."

I turned my head from the pillow to look at her. Catherine's beautiful soul spoke to me through her glimmering, tear-filled eyes. Words didn't matter. Her compassion went right to my heart, into the shattered parts that were torn asunder. Her facial expression was the comforting emotional glue that held together the pieces of my life that had been ripped apart. We stayed together in silence sharing a rare moment of solace.

The door to the dorm burst open. Annette stumbled inside, and the door slammed shut behind her. Was anything handled gently in this place?

Annette returned soaking wet—nightgown, hair, every part of her. Catherine, in what I had just begun to learn was her true nature, went to Annette. Catherine helped the despondent woman remove her wet clothes and wrapped her in her blanket. I later found out that we were forbidden from sleeping in our day clothes; if found in bed in them, we were punished with a severity not fitting the "crime."

My eyes grew heavy, and I finally drifted off, escaping to a sweet time when the mouth-watering aroma of sushki permeated our home. I loved to help Mama in the kitchen. Being I was the oldest girl in the family, I was the first daughter she taught to cook. And oh, I loved combining flour, eggs, water, and salt together. Kneading my fingers through the soft, rubbery texture until it became firm dough was magical. Then cutting and rolling it into thin strips, forming it into rings, and briefly dropping my creation into boiling water before baking in the oven made me feel so proud.

The smell of baking made its way to the living room and bedrooms. It took no time before the whole family landed in the kitchen. Because of what I had helped to create!

"The rolls are hot," said Mama as she bent to remove them from the oven with a dish towel. "Watch that you don't burn your tongues."

Salivating, Abram playfully nudged Shakna's shoulder. "God forbid, my sister should burn her tongue and not be able to use it. She'll surely lose our debates."

Laughter broke out as we pushed each other aside to get at the hot rolls. "Me!" laughed Shakna. "I'm first."

"I was here first," joked Abram.

"No, actually Klara was here baking with Mama." Shakna joshed back to Abram.

"Oh, so we agree, that I'm first," I quipped.

"Children," smiled Mama, "there's plenty for all."

This was our game. It was our joyful way of being a family and a community at the same time. For in the playful competition was love. We never tried to outdo the other or wanted to succeed at the expense of another's failure. We shared and wanted to. We all equaled our individual parts, and together, in this equality, we were whole. That was Papa's doing: weaving fairness into our moral fiber. And it was Mama who set us free to enjoy and delight in life. But it was both my parents who taught us about personal boundaries and respect. I hoped I would never have to put it to use with a man violating my body. And as quickly as that thought came to me, I was swept away from my fond memories and plagued with a sense of dread.

I don't know how long I was asleep before I heard a strange noise. Snoring? Disoriented, I opened my eyes to get my bearings. And there I was back in the asylum. In a room with five strangers.

A nervous flush moved through my body. I rubbed my forehead and felt the scar that mirrored my hairline. The thick, elevated, inch-long section of healed flesh was a reminder of escaping Kiev. I had banged my head getting into the hay wagon. Other than the dried-grass feed, there was no bandage. There was nothing to cover that wound, so I made do with what I had.

Be strong. Why my papa's words had returned to me in that terrifying moment was yet unclear. But before long, I would find out that, like in the hay wagon, I would learn to soothe my wounds and make do with what I had.

A Different Kind of Angel

Chapter Ten

That first night in the asylum seemed as if it would never end. After the nurse returned with a soaking wet Annette, I was afraid to fall asleep for fear someone would enter and harm me. Since Kiev, I had been excessively alert. Overly reactive. With every strange movement or sound, I felt like a crushing weight was pressing in on me, making it hard to breathe. I couldn't get my mind to settle down. The mental pictures of the slaughter I witnessed kept returning. I had to try to distract my attention off the agonizing flood of images that yet seemed unreal. I still couldn't believe my entire family was dead. Oh, how that loss constricted my throat. Even if I could speak English, it was doubtful I would tell anyone. My grief had sunken too deeply within me.

How am I going to get through this? This life of mine? My next idea was interrupted by a cough. And a shadow. A cloud had just moved past the moon, leaving a scene on the wall opposite my bed. I watched it change as the motions of the dark night sky shifted. It looked like rabbits dancing on water. The illusion of rabbits made me feel slightly better, a little lighter. I loved animals. And nature. It surprised me how drawing on that affection changed my feelings. Subtle, but nonetheless a change. Right then, it felt easier to make things up than relive what I had already experienced. Was this the answer I sought for how I would continue to exist and carry on? Was this the beginning of my salvation in this hellhole? Creating fantasy?

And if so, would I ever come out of the make-believe and return to reality? Or would I stay out of touch, unable to relate to or understand others? Is this what happens when someone goes crazy?

With my curious nature somewhat ignited, I looked to the wall for other scenes. I searched to make some sense—something recognizable—out of nature's seeming randomness. As a child, I stared up at the clouds until I found something recognizable. So now, where a shadow existed, I created wall-drawings. Mirage and reality merged, and from my brain sprang sunflowers' flaring yellow petals and orange centers with their distinctive brown seeds. Then came the hollyhock and crocus. Beautiful purple crocuses. I relished that miniature member of the iris family, its tubed flowers and slender linear leaves. Blooms from plants turned into lush foliage, and I recalled the green territories and waterways right in the middle of Kiev. My beautiful Kiev, you will always remain pure and unsullied in my heart. I refused to have the last vestige of goodness robbed from me: my fond memories of a life well-lived with a family full of love. No, I will not lose you Kiev, or Papa, or Mama, or you Abram, Shakna, Josel, and Anna. I will find a way to bring you back. I will find a way to release the love that my heart carries and bring it back to life if it's the last thing I do.

Another cough and the artwork I had created on the walls dissolved into the cold, dank room. The cough sounded the same, but I had changed. The tightness around my throat had eased a little. I must have dozed off because the next thing I remembered was being abruptly woken by an object poking into my side.

"Up," commanded Sally, the day nurse. Not allowing me to stretch, she poked me again. "Now!"

I sprung to my feet and immediately felt lightheaded. Whether from hunger, lack of sleep, getting up too quickly or something else,

I couldn't keep my balance. I grabbed hold of the bed to stop myself from falling.

"Clumsy idiot," Sally's voice was unpleasantly thick. Her frown and the way she slapped her poking rod on my bed told me I had best hurry.

Gaining my bearing, I glanced at Catherine and saw her getting dressed. With my eyes now cast downward, I took my dress from the side of the bed and did the same. Once ready, the six of us were marched out to the line forming in the hallway. The procession then advanced to the dining room.

Again, I sat next to Catherine. The woman across from me grabbed hold of her porridge. When she lifted her bowl to her mouth, I saw that she had no teeth. As I picked up my spoon and scooped up a portion of the mostly liquid gruel, I heard her toothless gums smack food around. The suction noise and droplets of food landing on her chin and up her nose turned my stomach. When she swiped the back of her dirty hand to clear the mess she had made over her face, nausea rose from my belly. I bit down on the inside of my cheek to calm the sensation. My abdomen heaved a wave of sickness making me gag. A few deep breaths stopped the retching.

My papa would have stopped eating and given that sloppy woman with poor manners a look to scorch her soul. Swallowing what was on my spoon did not help reduce the feeling I was going to vomit. It tasted awful. But I had to get some sustenance into my body. As squeamish as I felt, I forced myself to eat that dreadful slop. More slow, deep breathing through my nose between swallows, and I kept it down.

I knew there was more to my reaction than just feeling repulsed from one woman making a noisy mess. Perhaps it was moments like this when I allowed myself to feel, allowed my emotions to surface.

I was smart enough to know what keeping everything inside could do. Mama used to encourage me to let it out when it concerned how I felt. When I stubbed a toe and jumped around in childhood agony, she'd say, "Go on and cry." She soothed me and made me feel safe. No doubt as a result of her tender attention, I felt better. Now, I had to find a way to be delicate with my own wounds. I had to find a way not to sink into a personal hell. But I also had to honor my mama and my papa. I had to be strong. Painfully strong.

Out of the corner of her eye, Catherine noticed what must have been a change to my skin color. I knew what I looked like when I felt sick to my stomach and could well imagine how I appeared to her. Some shade of pale yellow. To distract me, she tapped a finger to her spoon and said, "Spoon."

My father used to tell me, you can become anything you make up your mind to be. He validated what others have said was my keen intellect. And so, when Catherine pointed to her utensil and said, "Spoon," I had the correct notion she was beginning to teach me English. At that moment, she saved me by refocusing my awareness.

I wanted to say spoon out loud, but instead, I sat quietly, glad to have my attention off the toothless woman across from me. From the odd way she gyrated her head and rolled her eyes upward, I couldn't blame her for her lack of etiquette. She didn't seem to have enough mental awareness to comprehend her own habits.

As I finished the last of my meal, a dry piece of bread, I glanced around the hall noticing others with equally odd behaviors: one woman fitfully flapped her hands, another had her eyelids open so wide that it seemed her eyeballs might bulge out, a different woman tipped her bowl around as if creating waves for her pretend boat at sea, while yet someone else broke her bread into tiny pieces and lined them up on the table before her.

The last woman caught the attention of Sally, who was still in a rotten mood. Sally strutted over to the woman who was lining up her bread. The nurse's hand grabbed a wooden object hooked onto her belt. Approaching the intended patient, she whipped out that stick and smashed it onto the patient's right hand. Out came a scream that unsettled several of the other women.

Sally smirked and probably said something like, "Keep playing with your food, and you'll get worse." I heard her say it many times after I learned enough English to understand.

The startled, disoriented patient squeezed her hand around the piece of bread she was still holding.

"Open your fist," ordered Sally.

Whether it was being yelled at or having been struck so brutally, the woman became even more unhinged. She began to whisper, "No. No. No. No."

Sally's face turned bright red, and her nostrils flared like a cow in labor. And like a heifer giving birth to her first calf, Sally began to strain so hard that strings of tendons showed on the sides of her neck.

The patient, completely oblivious to the danger she faced, spun out of control screaming, "No! No! No!" over and over while Sally beat her black-and-blue.

As if that wasn't enough, Sally yelled, "Roy! Come over here!" out through the open door, where Roy must have been on guard.

Roy lumbered in, boots pounding on the wooden floor. His frizzed sideburns stood out like he had been sitting by a steaming liquid.

Catherine moved her hand from her waist to my thigh where she rested it heavily. I took her motion to mean remain still, do nothing.

A Different Kind of Angel

Sally was speaking so loudly that I could easily hear her over the increasing commotion in the dining hall. "This one," Sally pointed to the object of her revenge, "is not obeying." She pushed the poor woman's head so that her forehead hit the table. Nurse Sally's smile was absolutely evil.

Without hesitation, Roy descended upon the woman and grabbed hold of a clump of hair on the back of her head. He ripped her off the bench and dragged her, legs trailing behind, out of the dining hall.

The sight sent a shiver up my spine. Nervously rubbing the scar on my forehead, I shoved down the distress I felt from witnessing that rough handling. I stuffed my fears and anxieties down into a mental box that I kept locked. If my genuine reactions were to surface and be expressed, what would happen? Would I get worse treatment than that unfortunate patient Roy dragged out? Would I even survive more torture? I thought of some of the other patients I'd witnessed who were apparently unable to control their conduct. Did they arrive that way or were they driven to their madness? Contrasting myself with the patient who lined up her bread, I was aware that I was able to discern and control my emotions. I believed Catherine was able to do the same which only added to my continued confusion as to why we were in that awful place.

Breakfast was over, and we were marched out to sit in the long hallway (the sitting room). For hours. Until the next meal. The maddening routine—the inescapable tedium—was almost as bad as the physical torture and emotional abuse. Day in and day out, we sat motionless for hours. Determined not to succumb to the irritating repetition, I continued to find things to occupy my mind. I created artwork from shadows and cracks on the wall. Particles of dirt on the floor, stains on clothing, a glimpse of a cloud through the window and I was painting stories. I'd hear an innocuous sound like a sneeze and imagine music. Someone clearing her throat would become a bird's song.

The real respite came at night in the dorm. It was there Catherine expanded on what she started earlier with the word spoon. She'd tap an object and say its name. I was a quick learner, to our mutual delight.

She pointed to me and said, "Klara."

Smiling, I nodded at Tillie. "Tillie," I said. Then motioned to the next bed. "Annette." I remembered hearing their names earlier.

"Very good, Klara." Catherine gestured toward the other two women in the room. Her finger wagged to the one closest to us, to the woman with red hair and wild, blue, shifting eyes. "Rosie, like the flower," she said.

I tilted my head, not understanding the sentence.

"Oh, sorry. Rosie," Catherine nodded at Rosie. "Rosie."

"Rosie," I repeated.

"Yes," she smiled. "Yes," she reiterated with a pat to my hand—a reinforcement of touch—like I had done with a pet in the past.

I had a dog when I was around nine-years-old. A large, attentive, black, furry dog that would rather be petted than given treats. Catherine's mannerism reminded me of my interaction with Artemis. I loved the name derived from my favorite Greek goddess, Artemis—mistress of animals and protector of young girls. I felt very protected and safe with Artemis. And just like with Artemis, I was beginning to feel a sense of security with Catherine.

Breathing in, I felt air move deep into my hollow lungs.

Again, Catherine motioned to the last, yet unnamed, woman who had suspiciously-narrowed eyes and scrunched, lowered eyebrows, "Amelia."

"Amelia," I glanced at the skittish-looking, tall, thin patient with skin hanging from her chin, arms, and legs. She had wrinkles in places that once must have held fat to round out her figure. Her skin now hung on her like rumpled curtains. Malnourishment was an enemy to all of us in that horrible place where near-empty stomachs gurgled night and day.

Wherever I looked, whatever I heard, I was constantly reminded of inhumane treatment. Too little nourishment. Cold rooms and cold, filthy bathwater. Lumpy, stained, withered mattresses and paper-thin, dirty blankets, hours of sitting on hard benches in silence. Physical and emotional wounds inflicted at the whim of the nurses and guards. The exception was Catherine. I hoped that there might be someone on the staff who possessed the decency to find and help us innocents.

Catherine cleared her throat to regain my attention. In what I will never forget as a very sweet gesture, she placed her hand upon mine and said, "Hand."

I felt her fingers which were cool to the touch. Her heart pulsed from her near transparent flesh and beat upon my index finger. "Hand," I said feeling her aliveness and smiled. I had learned another new word. There would be many more to come. These lessons were good for both of us, distractions from the insanity of life in the crazy house. I looked forward to the nights and my time with Catherine and hoped nothing would ruin our special friendship.

Chapter Eleven

The sun was just breaking over the horizon, and soon Sally would arrive to shock us awake. Amelia woke up screaming. I was already awake and saw why Amelia was upset. A rat scurried from her bed and ran through a crack in the wall. Amelia's shrieking woke the other four women and brought Nurse Sally bounding into the room with a bat in hand.

Amelia's head contorted in wild circles, whiplashing her dirty, oily long brown hair. Her screams intensified. Her eyes narrowed, and her eyebrows lowered into an apprehensive gaze. She continued to scream, "He'll kill us," as she pointed to the hole in the wall that the rat escaped through.

"Shut up!" hollered Sally, landing a blow on Amelia's left thigh.

That set off a ruckus of shrieking and howling like a dog hearing a high-pitched whistle. The blows continued until Amelia was silent. Unmoving. She was unconscious. Blood seeped from her legs, arms, and smashed-up face.

I didn't want to watch. And I certainly didn't want to remember the brutality that the scene with Sally and Amelia reminded me of. My forehead began to tingle. I swiped the palm of my hand across the itching scar on my forehead. The uneven skin sat next to my filthy, disheveled hair. As my fingers rubbed the healed tissue, a fingernail snagged into a knot of hair.

I wanted to cry. For Amelia. For myself. Instead I shut down. Push the brutal attack down. Way down. Don't feel the pain. Think. Think of something else. Tears threatened to overflow. Don't cry. Hold it in. They'll see it as weakness and punish me, like poor Amelia. Weakness should be helped, instead it was reprimanded. Sick! Sick! Sick! I swallowed down the bitterness rising in my throat. My hand, still on my forehead, moved across my grimy face. I wiped it on my dirty sheet. Filth. So much filth. I hate the filth. I want to cleanse myself of the filth. My mind drifted to the despicable conditions in the facility. My thoughts took me back further to times when hygiene and cleanliness were a way of life.

Nightly before going to bed, Mama came to me. "Time to wash. Then bed." Bless her sweet heart, every night my mama arranged two buckets of water: one heated and another to rinse our washcloths in. Mama insisted we were clean before putting on our pajamas. When I was ten, I was old enough to assist Mama with the weekly washing of sheets and helped her to hang them on the clothesline to dry. The smell of fresh bed linens after having a bath was something I always cherished. Yearning for a wash and a good combing to untangle my hair, tears trickled down my cheek.

While I quickly wiped away my tears, Sally stormed out and returned moments later with Roy. He looked down at Amelia's mangled body. "You did this," he smiled at Sally.

Sally moved closer to him and stroked his upper arm. The risqué way he looked at Sally, first at her breasts then down to her private area, made me feel very uncomfortable. When the tone in her voice softened and she swayed her hip next to his thigh, I lowered my gaze. My mama had warned me about those behaviors and where they led. I had been parented to avoid them.

"She asked for it, honey," Sally responded to Roy in a voice I hadn't heard from her when she spoke to any of us.

Honey? The way she said it was so intimate. I wondered about their relationship. Again, I felt ill at ease with the sensual air between them. What exactly would he do for Nurse Sally? There was something about the two of them that smelled dangerous to me.

Roy cleared his throat. It sounded like a growl, a low guttural lion's snarl that meant danger for the prey. The next sound I heard was a loud slap. "Wake up you bitch!" When silence with barely the sound of breathing was the only response he got, Roy repeated, "Get up!"

I tucked further under my rotting blanket. Eyes squeezed shut. Quaking from the cold and fear.

A loud thud on the floor was followed by what sounded like feet thumping on the ground and something scraping the floor. A body being dragged out? Then Sally's voice, "Out of bed the rest of you!"

Keeping my head bowed, I sniffed back more tears, took in a deep, slow breath to control myself and rose to change into my dress. We were funneled out to breakfast, which was all but over due to our being detained by Sally's flare-up. Remaining quietly next to Catherine, I ate rapidly. My attention was focused on Amelia.

The rest of the day was more of the same as the day before with one exception. It was a bath day for some of the women. Once a week, we were scheduled for a bath or shower; at least it was supposed to be once a week. Showers were rare but would have been welcome since the same bathwater was used for multiple women. The fact that the more desirable cleansing option was rarely used was more evidence of the intentional cruelty by the staff.

I soon discovered that bathroom privileges fluctuated with the on-duty nurse's whimsy. Everything was subject to change, depending on the mood of the dictators with all the power. One of the nurses, whose name I didn't know, must have decided she'd had enough of my foul body odor and took pity on me. "You," nodding to a group of women in line, "line up with that group," she ordered. Next, she pointed to Catherine.

The bathroom was kept locked, so patients couldn't bathe at will or use it to obtain drinking water. Baths were the only time we saw soap.

There were around thirty women in the room at one time with two old, frayed towels. I saw a woman who was scratching her arms raw. The eruptions on her skin looked infected. When she wiped herself with one of the towels, I cringed that I may have to use the same one. I determined that I would rather use my dress as a towel than that contaminated rubbish.

On bathing day, one tub was filled with cold water in which the patients were bathed—one after the other—without changing the water. This was done until the water became so grimy and concentrated that it was like rubbery mud. Then it was refilled without the tub being washed. Fresh dresses were handed out once a month, which again depended on the dictates of the tyrannical, lazy nurses.

Before I had completed my bath, I put my head under the water and soaped my hair. As I was toweling myself dry, Nurse Edith, who was also on duty that day, came in with combs. To my dismay and utter embarrassment, Roy and Albert entered carrying a bench. Most of the women, including myself, were in various stages of undress. Feeling a hot flush run through my body, my heart pounded on my ribcage as blood pulsed in my ears. I grabbed my dress to cover myself.

They placed the bench down. Before leaving the room, I noticed Roy give Catherine a look, similar to the one he gave Sally earlier that day. It burned into my eyes and made my insides feel scorched.

Sitting on the bench having my hair combed was painful. But not as painful as the vulgar, lustful look in Roy's eyes and what I feared he would do to Catherine. That was the first time I feared for her.

A Different Kind of Angel

Chapter Twelve

Three days passed before Amelia returned to the dorm. She had various shades of black, blue, and yellow bruises patchworking her arms. A red, puffy left cheek and eye gave her a morbid winking appearance. My heart ached for her as she stumbled around moaning like a wounded animal. As the moon drifted behind clouds, and Rosie unmade and remade her bed several times, Catherine went to Amelia to gently assist her back to her bed.

After watching Catherine calm Amelia, my attention shifted to the others in the room: Rosie's frantic, repetitive motions, Annette's babbling an odd prayer in which she spoke to God and answered for Him, and Tillie's thrashing about trying to find a comfortable position. An overwhelming sadness of our collective situation sat in my bones. Tears eked out of my eyes. I thought I was too dehydrated to cry, but down they came. My sunken-in chest made it hard to breathe. The last three days of sleeping next to Amelia's empty bed kept returning me to my empty soul, deserted of all whom I loved. Dreading my inability to get my attention off of my family and the bullets that ripped through the flesh of my blood, I focused my gaze on Amelia and Catherine.

In the time since Amelia was brutally beaten and dragged away, my heavy feet trudged from room to room. Pick up your feet. Walk like a lady, Mama would scold with Papa's concurrence that, no one likes to see you sulk. Then he'd hug me, and Mama would smile.

They didn't need to make their words sting with harsh action. It was enough to receive a scolding. I moved a hand over my chest, holding onto the place where they now resided. I felt like I could cry enough to bathe my body.

All day long, I was forced to sit on a hard surface listening to the repetitive sounds of breathing, coughing, moaning, shifting positions, bones or joints cracking, fingers and mouths clicking. I breathed in the same stale air comingled with body odor. Foul smells made me feel nauseous and scant food lacking in nutrition didn't help. Hard as I tried to find something akin to pleasurable (like the time I had my hair washed) to distract the pit I was sinking into, all I could conjure up was the sound of my wet head dripping on the floor. Drip. Drip. Drip. The morbid monotony was deadening my spirit. I even lost interest in the one activity that was my private retreat: creating magical scenes from the moonlit shadows on the cracks in the walls.

Not until Catherine went to Amelia, and I heard her soothing voice, saw her soft, stroking hand on Amelia's back, did I remember that love still existed. Our humanity was smothered and suffocated by the evildoers, but it was there like a seed; and, like a seed, it needed a chance to grow. Just a simple chance. The opportunity for kindness was there. And when it shone its beautiful face, my heart recaptured its possibility anew. I would look for love. I would look for kindness. I would see that in the darkness there are cracks, and it's the cracks that let the light in. I would find the light. My light.

I surprised myself when I got up and went to Amelia and Catherine. Sitting at the edge of Amelia's bed, silently wishing her well, I began to feel a little lighter. I started to see that wanting to help another and doing something about it ended up helping me feel a bit better.

Catherine extended a hand to me, the one that wasn't on Amelia's back. As we touched, the coldness of our hands melted into warmth, and our blood pulsed together. My breaths slowed. As if by some small miracle, it was then that Amelia's moaning shifted to snoring. A sweet, peaceful, relaxed posture overtook her. I felt the same sense of safety I had when Mama would hover over me when I was ill, not leaving my sickbed until I could sleep. This time, my sense of security came from my comfort with my friend Catherine. It felt good to be reminded of Mama without aching. Without feeling like my heart would explode. It felt good to feel the love. Then and now.

Back in my bed and still feeling a need for consolation, I tightly cocooned my sparse blanket around my waist and legs. Praying that peaceful sleep would come, I drifted off.

When morning arrived and the frigid night moved into the promise of a sunny day, I felt better than the day before. The painful routine had been broken, and once again I partook in wall artwork: shifting cracks into forms and imagining shadows into scenes. Several days continued like this. And an unexpected event occurred while in the dining room. I overheard Sally talking to Roy about her upcoming vacation. Finally, a reprieve from her day-in-day-out bad moods, hostile attitude, verbal and physical abuse, and flaunting her body around Roy, which I feared was stirring him up. Sadly, I would soon learn I had good cause to be concerned about Roy becoming sexually stimulated.

It happened on another bath day. Several of the women were lined up as usual. When Roy came with Nurse Edith and pointed his finger at Catherine, I wondered why she was chosen again so soon. Sitting next to Catherine on the bench in the hallway, I felt her thigh muscle tense against my side. She took in a breath and held it.

When Roy moved closer, I smelled something sharp, a rotting sweetness. It was the same sickly, repulsive odor I detected on the drunken men on the streets in New York. "Get up." He spat on me as he motioned to Catherine, his eyes focused on her breasts. The stink was more noticeable when he opened his mouth. Much later, Catherine would wrinkle her nose in disgust and tip her hand to her mouth to indicate Roy took to the liquor.

Roy grabbed my friend by the arm and forced her to the front of the line. Why are you taking Catherine? What are you going to do to her? Up until that time he had only gawked.

* * *

In the many months that had passed since being admitted to the asylum, I had learned enough English words to start to piece sentences together. Outside of Catherine, I never let on that I understood English. It was better to keep quiet and have staff think I was stupid than to reveal my newfound language skills and lose my advantage of being an invisible, competent witness to the daily horrors patients endured at the hands of nurses and guards. My words became consequential. And those consequences would not be good. It was then I had two things to hide: I was a Jew and clearly intelligent. Intelligent enough to learn English and to use it for my own survival. Other than Catherine, I could trust no one. Especially Roy, whose words I now better understood. They heightened my understanding of his intentions.

With Sally away, Roy strayed like a big cat on the hunt. And similar to a hunter cat at dusk when he was out prowling, his eyes glowed a hungry, devilish look. It was an unusually quiet night in the dormitory as the other women drifted off to sleep, and I began to doze.

That's when the door creaked open.

In stumbled Roy.

Not daring to move, I squinted open an eye to see him enter holding a dimly burning lamp.

Lumbering clumsily, he almost tripped as he approached Rosie's bed. He held the light over her face and spewed, "Where's she?" Groping a hand in the air as if milking a cow's teat, he drooled, "Where's Catherine?"

Rosie, fast asleep, remained undisturbed.

"Where's that woman's flesh. Oh, Catherine…Catherine," he hummed. "I want to feel your body."

It was then that it dawned on me why earlier that day he chose Catherine for a bath. It was most likely that he wanted to watch her undress. First Nurse Sally, now Catherine. I couldn't help but wonder how many other women he had relations with (consenting or not). That man couldn't be trusted around women. And, where was he? Working in an insane asylum for women run by nurses!

I watched Roy move onto the next bed repeating his drunken maneuver and waking Tillie.

She sat straight up and laughed.

"Crazy bitch," responded Roy as he pushed her back down with such a force she half fell out of her bed. She continued to laugh until Roy smacked her on the mouth, cracking her lower lip. Splattered blood on his hand and the lamp sent him into a tantrum. "Shut up!"

Tillie scrambled onto her feet. The last of Roy's screaming sent her into a fit of laughing and squealing hysterics as she ran in circles around her bed. When Roy went to whack her with his lamp, the oil spilled on his shirt and caught fire. Quickly ripping his shirt off, he threw it on the floor and stamped out the fire.

At that point, the entire dorm was awake. Annette was curled in a tight ball on her bed mumbling a prayer while Rosie was on the floor hiding under her bed. Amelia was on her side shaking. Catherine sat up. Tillie continued to run in circles while I remained quiet in my bed. The noise level between Tillie and Roy must have been what brought in the night nurse, who I hadn't seen before.

Holding her light to a shirtless Roy and visibly disturbed patients, she motioned to Roy. "You sir, out!"

Roy stared at the nurse in her stiff, starched uniform, making no attempt to leave. His demeanor and appearance were more bizarre than the rest of us in the room. He moved toward the nurse, who was close to me. He belched. Out came a glob of spittle that smelled of stale booze and something else repulsive. "Now, Harriet, come on. Don't be like that. I just come in to help and got me involved in a little fire."

Standing erect, the nurse's eyes were sharp like nails when she pointed an index finger at him, and demanded, "Out!"

"Okay, okay," he staggered toward the door. Before exiting, he turned around and shot the nurse a look.

"Out!" She motioned to the door.

"No one's gonna mess with me," he threatened before slamming the door shut.

Nurse Harriet then marched over to Tillie and moved her back to bed. "Go on now, get in there, Tillie." The tough firmness expressed to Roy moments earlier had left her voice. She waited until Tillie was covered. "That's good now. You go back to sleep."

As Nurse Harriet made her way around the room, I loosened the tight grip I had on my sheet. My knuckles relaxed, but I doubted I'd get any sleep that night. I was worried for Catherine. Making lewd motions with his hand earlier, Roy had called out for her. From his actions and what he said, it took no wit to figure out what he was after. That time, Catherine was lucky, but how long would her luck last?

A Different Kind of Angel

Chapter Thirteen

As if by some godly design, Roy was absent for several days. With Nurse Sally still on vacation and Roy gone, we had a new day nurse along with Albert. Right away, I noticed that the mood felt different and wondered if it was the new person's influence on Albert, who seemed less callous than when he was around Roy. Sally and Roy, a gang of two, incited others toward cruelty, disrespect, and harm. Those two appeared as if they enjoyed inflicting pain on us and making us fearful all the time. Worse, they were bad influences on their peers.

At first glance, the new nurse, Barbara Lincoln, looked frightful, but thankfully (in her case), looks did not represent the person she was. Of stocky build and with broad, masculine shoulders, she turned out to be a decent woman, a good person. Albert lowered his shoulders and politely nodded to her when she gave him an order. I thought it odd and fascinating that a woman appeared to be in a senior position to a man. In every family, group, or experience I had been involved in up until then, it was the male who ruled. But it was clear from the very beginning that Barbara Lincoln's no-nonsense attitude was kindly and not intended to be confrontational or competitive. It brought out a less aggressive side of Albert. In that otherwise suffocating institution, she was a breath of fresh air.

A Different Kind of Angel

I had lost so much—had so much taken from me—yet here in this hell, I found angels who lifted my spirits. Like Catherine. And on that particular day, Barbara Lincoln would be added to my very short list of those in my life (after leaving Kiev) who showed me compassion. They gave me a reason to believe that goodness still existed in this world and that good prevails over evil. I had abandoned all hope, but these sweet angels restored my will to survive. Even in that den of Hades where torment was commonplace, and souls were ripped to shreds, the embers of kindness created a tolerable balance.

Barbara Lincoln scratched the back of her neck where her brown hair curled up at the bottom of her cap. Looking at the patients in various stages of disorientation and semi-alertness, she made her way one at a time to several of the other nurses on duty. When she returned to where I was sitting, she swiped a pointed finger to a line of women and indicated that we should follow her. The other nurses were doing the same. Once in line formations, we began to move through the hallway.

When we came upon a group of patients linked together by a long cable rope that was fastened to their wide leather belts—chained like prisoners—my heart sank. One of the women was flailing her hands in wild gestures. When a nurse and guard tried to contain her, she broke loose and slammed her fist on the bench beside her. She hit it so hard that the wood cracked. I could tell from the appearance of her instantly deformed hand, so had her bones. At that moment her eyes looked at me, but I doubt she saw me. Her attention was lost in some remote thought or place.

We moved on. My body filled with pity as I caught sight of an old, gray-haired woman talking aimlessly to space. Next to her was a woman in a straightjacket being dragged along by the others. There were more scenes like this: crippled, blind, old, young, wrinkled, pretty, unkempt, homely, tall, short, a sampling of human beings with tragic circumstances.

Worried that my fate would be the same—constrained with my freedoms reduced even more than they already had been—my forehead itched. I started to sweat. Feeling like a raw, exposed nerve, similar to when I had toothaches in the past, I sucked in a deep nose-full of air to settle my trembling limbs. Thankfully, we passed them and made our way to an exit door. But still feeling shaky and confused, it took me a minute to grasp we were outside in the garden.

Looking at the lush, green garden, all the madness I had just passed by trickled away. I yearned to walk on the grass, but the moment I ventured a step in that direction, I was halted. "No walking on the grass," scolded one of the nurses I didn't know.

Jerking back, I avoided the no-venture zone.

Barbara Lincoln was a little way from where I was standing but within earshot. She turned to see what the commotion was. When our eyes met, she gave her head a gentle shake and sighed as if to communicate to me she wished this weren't how we were treated. Barbara walked over to me, smiled, and calmly took hold of my hand. She walked me around a corner out of sight of the nurse who demanded I stay off the grass. There, by a tree with flowers, she said, "They have a nice aroma."

Not understanding, I squinted my eyes. I was afraid to speak, to use any words for fear that what I had been learning would expose me to trouble.

"You don't understand? Well, no need to use words." She reached for one of the flowers and rubbed it between her thumb and index finger then held it to her nose.

When I hesitated to lean into the plant, to repeat what she'd done, she motioned with a side nod for me to go ahead. Lifting my hand to a white flower, I filled my fingers with fragrance. As the perfume lingered in my nostrils, I looked around at the view outside our confined walls. The East River, a narrow waterway, was calm with a few ripples of white caps left from the wake of boats. Sparking ripples of sunlight reflected off the waves. I could easily see across the water to the buildings in New York. I saw small bodies scurrying about. Just the feeling of not being confined helped me get air into my lungs. My tight neck muscles loosened as I became aware that my heart was not pounding. The simple pleasure of being outside was heavenly.

Other patients gathered near where I was with Nurse Barbara. I watched them stand and gaze with yearning desire toward the city they would (in all likelihood) never set foot in again. That I may never set foot in again. That stretch of land across the river meant freedom and liberty. It seemed so close, so tangible. A woman next to me coughed. I looked at her and the dark circles under her eyes. I only saw her in the dining hall. She never spoke, at least I never saw her speak. Her lips seemed sealed like an envelope in perpetual silence. I pondered what was behind those sealed lips. Had she once been a dreamy-eyed, happy girl like me? Had she gone from that normal existence to an overly-alert, constantly guarded state like mine? Did she even know she was confined to an asylum? Did she converse with silent individuals inside her head like so many others I'd seen? I looked away from her to the vibrant green grass, out to the river, to the city beyond full of life and living, and wondered if I'd ever get out.

A chilly breeze kicked up; it was time to return inside. Although I was surrounded by loss and devastation, that was one of the better days on that hellhole island.

The next several days passed and Roy returned to work. We never found out what happened to him after that incident with Amelia. For his first week back, and before Sally's return, he was somewhat subdued, and his breath didn't smell of liquor. When Sally returned, the mean old Roy returned, too. Liquor-breath and all. As miserable as Sally was, she kept Roy relatively constrained. I suppose that's what's called a silver lining. Most likely, she sexually satisfied him, so he didn't need to drunkenly wander through the women's dorms at night. But in time that would change.

A Different Kind of Angel

Chapter Fourteen

Nellie

1887

By the time 1887 rolled around, I had become convinced that I would spend the rest of my life on Blackwell's Island living among the mentally unsound. Life had become a chain with links made of misery. There was some relief, though, in the comfort of close relationships. Thank goodness for the friendships. But I am getting way ahead of my story. In hindsight, I see how my mind learned to cope. I'd seek more comfortable things to contemplate by moving back and forth in time to escape the sorrow or pain that was too difficult to bear at that moment. Like now as I'm retelling my story. I feel emotional pressure constricting my heart, and I want to digress and shift my thoughts away from the ache. It's too much for a body to embrace in one sitting. A respite from my story is necessary. Thinking of Nellie, that remarkable woman, always helps. A memory of Nellie's arrival comes to mind. And my chest feels lighter envisioning how animated her facial expressions were as she shared her experience with me.

When Nellie arrived at the wharf, a mob surrounded the ambulance she was in with two other passengers. They remained quiet avoiding eye contact. The police accompanying them had to move the crowd away so that they could reach the boat. Nellie told me that she was hauled out last and nearly lost her balance as she stumbled down the plank to a boat. She was taken to a grimy cabin where the other two women were already seated on a narrow bench. The small windows were shut, and she said the smell of filth in the air was smothering. At the end of the compartment was a small bunk that, "probably smelled much worse than it looked. And it looked like it was rotting from mold." Nellie wanted to hold her nose but said she didn't want to break character. Breathing through her mouth, she sat on the bench next to the other patients. Two intimidating female attendants, one chewed and spat tobacco on the floor while the other lowered her brows and glared at the three patients aggressively, guarded the door. Nellie told me that the way they spoke about patients was not proper or civil.

When they arrived at the island and went ashore, Nellie was roughly grabbed by the woman who spat tobacco. Her hand left a red indentation on Nellie's upper arm. An ambulance was waiting for them with a man holding open the rear door.

"What is this place?" asked Nellie. Thus, she began her mission to prompt information for her exposé.

"Blackwell's Island, an insane place, where you'll never leave," he smirked. With that, she was shoved up into the passenger compartment. He jumped on behind her and shut the door.

As the ambulance drove past lush green lawns, Nellie felt satisfied she had gotten this far in her objective to infiltrate the asylum. Although she had an inner sense of satisfaction, she was concerned by the expressions on the other two women passengers' faces. She told me, "They appeared distressed. There was a tightness in their faces. Even to their comportment. The elderly woman with gray hair avoided eye contact. The other one had watery eyes. One got the sense that if either of them fell, they would shatter like glass." Nellie wondered if they were unjustly sentenced to this prison (in all likelihood) for life. She referred to the island as a prison—a tomb of living horrors—which was, from her perspective, a fate worse than being walked to the gallows. I couldn't disagree.

When the ambulance stopped, the guard told them, "Get out." Once they had obeyed, he mentioned to the driver of the vehicle, "Good thing they came quietly."

The driver looked them over before replying, "What a mangy-looking lot."

Nellie planned to drop the facade of insanity upon arrival at the asylum. Now it was time to be herself. She responded to the men, "I can hear you!"

Nellie's reaction got the attention of one of the patients transported with her. She swiped a strand of messy brown hair off her perspiring forehead and gave a discreet nod to Nellie.

"You want to talk back?" The guard at the door threw a fist across Nellie's face sending her tumbling backward. "Maybe that'll teach you to think before opening your mouth!"

The woman who had just made a connection with Nellie came to her defense. "Let me help you." She offered a hand.

The guard smacked the woman's outreached arm back from Nellie. In a loud voice, he said, "Keep your hands to yourself." Pointing to Nellie, he demanded she get up. When she didn't respond promptly, he kicked the bottom of her feet (the closest part of her to him). Nellie scrambled to stand. The guard grinned. "I don't want no more trouble, you hear that?" He directed his comment at Nellie who stared at him, rubbing her jaw.

"I heard."

The guard shook his head, turned to the others and yelled, "Now move!" He shoved the old woman in the direction of the asylum's entrance. He trailed behind them.

Nellie strode beside the brown-haired woman and whispered, "Do you know where we are?"

"Yes," she softly replied. "Blackwell's lunatic island."

"Are you crazy?" asked Nellie.

"No," she replied, "but I've been sent here to be out of an influential man's hair."

"Oh dear, I see."

"My husband," mumbled the woman. "He must have paid off the two doctors who admitted me and signed the paperwork." She wiped a tear from her watery eyes. "I'll have to be quiet about it until I can find some means to escape."

Despite Nellie's knowledge that she would be released in a few days, she felt sick. She later communicated to me, "That injustice was pathetic. The woman's husband disposed of her in such an ungodly manner. And others in charge of tending to the ill went along with him."

Nellie took note of that hateful crime. "I'm so sorry," she sighed in the woman's ear.

When they arrived at the building, two nurses were waiting for them. Nellie was taken in a different direction than the other two women. She wondered where they were going and why she was going somewhere different. Curious about where she was being taken, she entertained thoughts of eating and sleeping amongst senseless chattering? After experiencing first-hand the complete disrespect and outright hostility directed toward patients, imagining what was to come made Nellie feel uncomfortable. I recall her telling me that she attempted to remove the lump in her throat by swallowing hard, but it didn't help, and she felt like she was being strangled. She hadn't anticipated all the emotional reactions she would experience. "Nor had I imagined how despicably the patients were treated before they even entered the asylum," Nellie remarked.

It was later that day when I first met Nellie Brown. Catherine made room for her on the bench next to us. There was something about her bearing that felt comfortable, not at all dangerous or threatening. To me, she seemed normal, like Catherine. I wanted to trust my first impression of this new woman. Later, when I discovered I was correct about my intuition, it reinforced what would help guide me through the rest of my life with regards to my relationships. There were things I became aware of in that crazy place, things that helped me grow. Like trusting my instincts.

Right away, she looked at Catherine's alert smile and asked, "Who sent you here?"

Catherine looked around to be sure it was safe to talk. Then looking into space as if not indulging Nellie, she said, "The doctors. My boyfriend paid them off. My married boyfriend." She then leaned into Nellie. "You?"

Nellie reflected back on the fact that this was the second woman (of two she had asked) who had unjustly been put away by her male companion. Determined to protect her real identity as an investigative journalist (but stay true to her plan to be herself), she replied, "They say I'm insane. I am not."

Just then a nice-looking blond nurse named Greta Smidt walked by us. Her hair was in buns atop her ears. I wondered if she was German. I had seen drawings of German women who wore their hair like that. And, like Nellie, it was her first day with us. Had I not seen the hard lines around her mouth, I would have assumed she was a kind nurse. But the minute she opened her mouth to speak, I knew kindness was not in her character. "Quiet, you two idiots," she barked.

Nellie protested. "What harm is there in talking?"

"I said shut up," Greta repeated.

Just as things felt as if they were going to get ugly, I heard Greta's name being called. She turned away from us. Another nurse at the end of the hall apparently needed her. I sighed in relief.

The conversation between Nellie and Catherine continued. I was surprised when Catherine put a hand on my wrist and said, "This is Klara." With tightened lips forced into a flickering smile, I side-glanced over to Nellie and nodded ever so slightly.

The whole time Nellie was in the asylum, she never revealed that she was a reporter on assignment. She did, however, admit she was not insane and was sent to this place incorrectly. Five years after my arrival and what felt like centuries of witnessing torture and enduring unthinkable cruelty, my friendship with Nellie began. I would soon feel safe enough to share with Nellie that I spoke English.

When Nellie arrived in1887, things in the asylum had changed somewhat. Depending on who was on the staff for the day, patients were allowed to wander about more, talk to each other without blaring interruptions to be quiet, and had more frequent trips outside to the garden.

Other changes were not so welcome. The frequency and severity of brutality and torture waged on the patients by the nurses, guards and doctors increased (again depending on who was on duty). Some of the staff were new but with them came an escalation of abuse. With few exceptions, it was as if mean-spirited people were hired to work in the asylum. There, patients were invisible— easily forgotten by those in responsible administrative and political positions, the press and society at large. As a result, we were easy prey for our cold-blooded captors to abuse us in any way they wished without consequence.

Nellie may have heard shocking rumors, but she would soon find out how inhumane life at the asylum could get. Unfortunately for her, she never had a chance to meet the rare, kind nurses like Harriet Brownstone or Barbara Lincoln. They were never on duty during Nellie's ten-day stay. It was Nellie's bad luck that only malicious nurses and guards were on duty for the short time she was there. She would have more than enough material to validate all of those rumors. I often wonder if the cost of her journalistic work—no matter how significant—wasn't too high because, once in the asylum, your life was in the hands of people who took pleasure in your suffering.

A Different Kind of Angel

Chapter Fifteen

Klara

1883 - 1886

As the weeks moved into months and another bitter winter was upon us, our suffering took on a whole new meaning. A cold shower in the summertime was bad enough, but bathing in ice-cold water in a freezing room with no means of warming ourselves before bed was particularly hard on us. Still moist from my bath, I curled on one side with my arms and legs drawn up and head bowed to keep myself as warm as possible. My teeth chattered, and gooseflesh covered my skin as I tried to stop my body from shaking. Trying not to freeze to death was awful; what happened that frigid night to poor Annette was ghastly.

Nightly, when Annette wasn't involved in some ritual prayer activity, she fixated on cleaning herself with make-believe washings regardless of whether she had just come from a bath or not. And she went about it loudly. "God." She pounded a fist on her bed and paused, appearing to be listening to His response. "Dirty man! Filth!" On that night, her tone was different—harsh and rapid as if each word was a dagger aimed at some evil target. "The earth needs to be rid of him!" She rubbed her right hand up her left arm. Scrubbing harder, as the intensity of motion increased so did the volume in her voice. She yelled, "He! Needs! To! Die!" Her words were sharp and clipped. Red lines she had scratched into her arm oozed blood as her nails continued to dig into skin.

Catherine was usually able to get to Annette and return her to her bed before a night staff nurse noticed the commotion. But on this particular night, Catherine was not able to calm Annette's odd squawking sounds before the door flew open with such force that it banged a hole in the wall.

Candace Millhouse, a relatively new night nurse, scanned the wall damage she'd just made and, with an arrow of hatred shooting from her narrowed eyes, stormed toward Annette and Catherine. Nurse Candace was a pudgy woman who looked like a pig: over-stuffed sausages for arms and legs; a bloated, chubby face that made it hard to make out her features; an over-sized head that sat on a cumbersome body with no neck adjoining the two; and very straight, short brown hair in a man's cut. She was a nasty human being through and through. I never once recalled seeing anything on her face but a scowl with her lips drawn in as though she had just sipped vinegar. Just looking at her made my belly ache.

Candace walked up to Annette and pointed a pudgy finger at her. Then she motioned back to the damaged wall. "You made me do this, you crazy pinhead!"

Groaning something unintelligible, Annette continued to scratch her scabby, bloody arms.

Catherine sat frozen next to Annette.

Nurse Candace moved in on Annette. Open-handed slaps turned quickly to punches with her fat (but powerful) fists. When Annette was writhing on the floor, the big bully began kicking her. Annette's cries and moans were drowned out by the nurse's panting, grunting, and gasps for breath.

But Annette's muffled moans only grew louder.

"Shut up!"

The force of Candace's tone looked as if it hit Catherine's body like a lightning jolt, flinging her backward.

"Get her up." She directed her command to Catherine. "Now!"

Catherine made a gesture to try to quiet Annette, who had resumed a frantic bath-like activity of rubbing her bloody arms. The more Catherine tried to soothe her, the wilder Annette's motions became.

The situation exploded with Candace grabbing Annette's ear and a clump of her hair and lifting her to her feet. "You," she stuck her chin out at Catherine, "up. You're a useless idiot."

Annette stood there shaking, swaying back and forth, and moaning.

Catherine, forehead down, looked at the floor and stood up. Discreetly, out of the nurse's eyeshot, she put a hand on Annette's trembling back.

The furious nurse flung her lantern in a circle around the room. "All of you pieces of garbage," she spat her words. "Get up. Now!"

Amelia and Rosie instantly rose while a confused looking Tillie started crying, "Mama. Mama. Mama!"

The whole scene sent my head spinning. Annette's wildly erratic and scary sounding prayers about a man needing to die made me very nervous. I hated that a nurse, who was supposed to help, hurt a patient. But it was Tillie's yearning wails that unleashed the torturous grief I had tried to lock inside me. The heartache I worked so hard to suppress. Mama. I sunk to a dark place, where the madness and brutal behavior was as crushing to my spirit as the dropping temperature. Shivering, I went to Tillie to help her up before we became the next victims of Candace's unjust abuse.

Nurse Candace continued to shout, "Get a move on! You'll be next if you don't move now!"

I gently put my hand to Tillie's arm to help her up. When her unfocused pupils widened in my direction, I saw my reflection. A strange woman I barely recognized with stringy, yet moist, hair looked back at me. My cheeks were sunken, and lines of sorrowful memories were written all over my face. All the healthy color was gone from my skin.

When Tillie gazed up at me, she smiled. Reaching up to hug my shoulders, she whispered in my ear, "Mama, I knew you'd come for me."

Nurse Candace didn't stop yelling commands at us while impatiently stomping her foot on the floor.

As I took Tillie in my arms, I could no longer contain the river of tears that flowed out of me. I took a few quick breaths while holding onto Tillie, and I regained some of my composure.

Once in the hallway, Candace caught the attention of the night guard. He smiled at her and scanned the rest of us with a furrowed brow. "Help me get this one to the shower," said Candace. She still had a sniveling Annette by the hair and ear.

His response took me by surprise.

"In this freezing weather?"

"Are you questioning the night duty nurse? I believe I outrank you. Should we take this up with the supervisor?"

"Whoa! Hold your horses! No need to involve the Super. I just don't want to get wet." His smile faded, and a brooding took over, darkening his skin. "I don't care what happens to them, but it's damn cold."

Candace stood akimbo. With her eyes bulging and eyebrows elevated, her countenance was one of a ferocious ocean wave— nothing was going to stop her. She threatened, "I will tell—"

"Hey," the guard interrupted. His shoulders slumped, he looked around as if to see if anyone heard what Candace said. "Okay," he cowered, "okay. Settle down." And to placate her, he added, "You know I'll help you."

What happened next was agonizing to watch. When the daily boredom, fear, panic, and haunting thoughts in the space between my ears didn't make me feel like I would go insane, it was times like this when I seriously doubted my ability to remain rational.

Through her yellow, cracked, clenched teeth and with her fists held tight, Annette screamed bloody murder when she was flung into a cold tub of water. Then they hung her up spread-eagle by ropes attached to cleats on the wall. Her flimsy dripping nightgown was ripped from her body, and she was left to hang there in a temperature no more than thirty degrees. Her body shuddered. She howled in anguish so primal that I thought my chest would implode. It reminded me of an incident I'd once experienced with Papa. We came upon a wounded wolf in so much pain my papa had to shoot it to put it out of its misery. I realized then that killing was an act of kindness—the humane option—under the proper circumstance and with compassionate intentions.

There would be no kindness for Annette. Her body went into spasms and contortions that made the muscles in my neck cramp. She wailed one long, lucid-sounding, "No!" That was the last sound she made before her emaciated, bruised, bloodied, pocked body went limp. We were ordered back to our dorm while Annette remained strung up, unconscious. With my earlier nervous reaction from Annette's words about killing a man all but gone, I prayed she would live without awareness of her outrageous crucifixion.

Catherine wiped the tears from her red eyes and stayed quiet for the rest of the night. So did the others. I tossed and turned until the wee hours of the morning when, all of a sudden, Tillie sat up singing. She had a surprisingly lovely voice and sang as if nothing horrible had happened just hours earlier. Tillie was even smiling. To my amazement, she made me smile. Perhaps there was more to this thing called insanity than I had witnessed. And I pondered, is the fantasy world of illusions that lifts the spirit all that terrible? I know it seems absurd, but crazy Tillie helped me to see something that made me feel somewhat lighter. At that moment, something in the vast, intangible unknown became obvious. There was benediction in the simplest acts of goodwill, whether one is lucid or not. It was then I saw that, in the fabric of life, the beauty of goodness is magically woven, heartbeat by heartbeat. Not suppressed by cruelty or evil or even insanity, it arises and lends meaning to life. And quality to existence.

Several days later, Annette returned from the infirmary. She continued with her wild prayers of eliminating evil and her bathing rituals just as she had before that vile incident. Appearing unscathed made me wonder if perhaps, just like Tillie, Annette had her unique song inside her head. Just the possibility that, in her mysterious way, Annette was coping—and not suffering—made me breathe easier.

Chapter Sixteen

Annette recovered, and the nightly rituals in the dorm continued for months. That's how the cycles seemed to go, a period of relative calm followed disaster. Although monotonous, we had a long reprieve from the senseless cruelty after the night of Annette's shocking abuse. But I knew that this relative calm was temporary. Even in the quiet, a storm was brewing. The air, thick with unease, weighed heavy in that place of horrors. I never knew when more tragedy would strike any of us.

As the numbing winter melted into spring, I saw red, orange, and yellow flowering weeds erupting on the grass through the barred windows. Spring was my favorite time of the year back in Kiev, especially April and May when the whole city was covered in white and pink blooms. How I loved to see the fruit trees in full blossom—promising pears, apples, and cherries. The days were filled with a fragrant aroma and breathing (like my life) was easy. The city was at its greenest as birds migrated to the comfortable temperature and alighted upon welcoming tree limbs to greet the day with their songs. On walks through forested areas, I'd commune with nature. Among the pine, spruce, beech, and oak trees, I discovered my soul's desire: to stimulate my mind with as many books as I could read. I was lucky that my parents encouraged my desire to learn instead of stifling it like so many other girls in their teens I knew growing up. Your mind is your best friend if you use it well, my papa would say to me through my formative years. I had so many happy moments out in nature with a book. Sitting near a scurrying squirrel, listening to swifts and waders chirping, and noticing an occasional skittish fox wandering into proximity, I sifted through pages. When my eyes grew heavy, I'd nap on the cushy, moss-covered earth and drift peacefully into my fantasy world—the world where I would one day meet the perfect man and fall in love.

I used to have a life where I dreamed of a future filled with romance. The feeling of excitement and mystery associated with love would consume me. In the asylum, all I had were singular moments. Most of them were hard to endure; some were easier than others, like when Nurse Barbara was on duty.

On one sunny day when she came to wake us, there was something different in her tone. She sounded happy. Her voice was filled with excitement when she told us that some of us were going to be chosen for a ride around the island. "So up you go," she smiled at Catherine then looked at me. "You too, Klara." She continued around the room helping the rest to their feet. No harsh scolding, no slapping or hair pulling, no insulting words on that morning to start our day. Barbara showed us civility and kindness as we dressed and marched to breakfast.

After we ate, our little group was escorted out in the brisk morning air to pile into the back of a small wagon with large, open windows. We huddled next to each other. I could tell from the looks of worry etched on some of the women's faces that they were unsure if this was a trick. Seeing Barbara's relaxed, open posture and genuine smile, I felt confident that we were safe. I tried to assure the others by smiling, nodding, and patting the hands of those closest to me.

Barbara said, "I'm sorry it isn't warmer, but this is the only time I have use of the wagon."

Viewing the lush lawn surrounding the buildings that spread down to a fence separating land from water, I felt somewhat hopeful. Perhaps this was a promise of changes to come. Changes for the better. As it turned out, I was sadly disappointed when I later learned that it was Barbara Lincoln's way of making up for something awful she had witnessed on her last shift. Rumors spread, and Catherine overheard. She shared the story with me that night.

A pretty young girl was genuinely ill when she was brought in. She screamed and fought against the guards, not wanting to be brought to such a dirty, foul-smelling place when she was burning up with fever. She begged the nurses to send her to a hospital. A real hospital. Instead of being shown mercy or even calling in a doctor to see the girl, the night nurse beat her. She was held naked in a cold bath then thrown in bed while she was shaking, her body contorting in strange ways. The next morning, Barbara Lincoln was on duty. When she saw the girl, she ran to get a doctor. But it was too late. The young girl was dead. The doctor claimed she died from convulsions. A very distraught Barbara was overheard protesting to a charge nurse about the intentional harm inflicted on this patient. When Nurse Barbara's complaint was ignored, she told a sympathetic colleague, "Enough is enough! I took a pledge as a nurse to 'abstain from whatever is deleterious and mischievous.' If I'm going to continue to work here, I have to at least try to change things, even if it's one shift at a time." We were some of the lucky recipients of her goodwill. I often wondered if Barbara was one of the staff members who revealed the conditions in the facility to outside authorities. Perhaps she was one of the people who indirectly contributed to Nellie's undercover assignment and exposé.

As I shut my eyes and tried to settle my mind to allow sleep, the day played in my head. I thought of the flowers I'd seen interspersed on the island, especially the one with a spike of brilliant red petals. The walls in the asylum were so dull in contrast to the natural colors that filled my senses as we drove around for a couple of hours. The scent of the ocean opened my nostrils to a fishy, briny odor as I caught sight of seaweed rolling on white, soapy froth. I closed my eyelids and listened to the sound of water splashing ashore. It was a soothing sound. Taking in the earth's sights, smells, and sounds made me feel more alive. For this, I silently thanked Barbara Lincoln.

Going out for a ride was not the only change. Not long after that day, nurses started giving medications to the patients. At first, it was to help us sleep. And then they were given during the day. Not to all of us but to those who were "acting up," like Annette and Tillie. The two drug names I remembered were morphine and chloral hydrate. And they didn't always work as we were told they would. I recalled seeing a patient who went crazy after several doses. She became wild for water. And when the nurses' withheld drink from her, she tore off her clothes and ran naked down the hall, screaming and begging, "Water! Please! I need water! Water, water, water!"

The night after this episode, I cried when I heard that she ran to the locked bathroom and tried to scratch the door open. Blood dripping from her mangled hands, she was dragged away by two guards and chained onto her bed. A lucid patient in the same dorm retold the story the next day while Catherine and I were within earshot.

The intermittent relief from crushing fear continued when Barbara Lincoln was on duty during the day and when Harriet Brownstone was our night nurse. She had been assigned to our dormitory earlier when I first arrived, but I hadn't seen her for months. As the seasons changed, spring gave way to the stifling hot, muggy days of summer, which cooled to the shorter days of fall. That's when Harriet reappeared. She was firm but kind. I wondered if she had softened somewhat because of something that happened one night. She came in after lights were out holding her lantern and approached Catherine's bed. She then whispered something to my friend that I couldn't quite hear.

Catherine whispered her reply. "That would be really lovely."

A couple of minutes after Harriet left the room, I got out of bed and went to Catherine. Now speaking good enough English to communicate, I asked, "What she here for?"

Catherine looked up at me. Through the dim light of the moon, I saw her eyes light up when she said, "Books." She sat up and put her hands together mimicking a book in her palms. When she scanned her hands like she was reading, I understood that Harriet offered to bring books to Catherine.

"Books." I smiled.

"You read?"

I knew what she was asking. I thought of all my books sitting somewhere in the pile of my past in Kiev. The forest was my favorite reading place. Even though I feared I'd never see anything so beautiful as the naturally green, hilly and water-rich Kiev, I hoped to be able to read a book again. Someday. "Love to read," I nodded.

"I can use the book to help teach you better English."

"English. Yes. Better English," I repeated.

"Oh, Klara, yes! You will get much better at English." She sat up and wiped the tears running down her cheeks. "Harriet is a nice lady."

I understood the emotional reaction Catherine had experienced. In that fog of daily misery, it took so little to ignite a spark of life. And here I had a friend who was willing to share her good fortune with me. Catherine was a good influence on me. From her, I learned to better care for others. When one of our dorm mates was unsettled at night and Catherine was asleep, I went to her. Tillie (in particular) was comforted from my hand upon hers, a soft touch to her cheek and an occasional hug. I was moved by the reaction Tillie had to my touch as she continued to refer to me as Mama. As the days moved along, I felt less of a sting in my heart when she uttered that word. Although the ache in my chest never left, there were times it was replaced with contentment and kinship with Tillie. And the others I gave my time to slowly became like family to me. I like to think I have Catherine to thank for that.

As the rest of the year moved along, there were more good days when Barbara and Harriet had shifts. There were also horrific experiences, especially when 1884 arrived and we saw more of Roy and Sally. I had hoped that their absence from working directly with us meant they were no longer employed at the asylum. Unfortunately, that was not the case. I never found out the cause of their long absence. But what I did know was that where Roy went, Sally was posted. And the two of them meant nothing but trouble for us.

Chapter Seventeen

1884 brought change to the world. The first proclamation was made by the Federation of Trades and Labor Unions in the United States for an eight-hour workday. The United Kingdom suffered the Colchester earthquake, the most devastating one in recorded history. The cornerstone for the Statue of Liberty was laid on Bedloe's Island in New York Harbor. And the Democratic governor of New York, Grover Cleveland, defeated Republican James G. Blaine to win the presidential election. Years later while reflecting on that time, I saw that while the rest of world was moving forward in industry, technology and civil rights, we at the asylum seemed to be stuck in the unbelievable living conditions of prisoners in the Middle Ages. My small universe was taken up with Roy's growing fixation on Catherine. He scared me…and for good reason.

Surprisingly, his sick obsession was slow in manifesting. Roy had shown an interest in Catherine since I came to Blackwell's Island—perhaps even before I had arrived. In my time at the asylum so far, Roy had targeted Catherine twice, not including the leers and groping in the sitting hall and other public areas. The first assault attempt when he selected her for the bath was foiled later that night with that awful flare-up with Tillie. Then, like the incident I'm about to share, Nurse Sally was away. I overheard that Sally needed time off to tend to a death in her family. A relative of hers died, and she would be going to the funeral somewhere out west. So, like before when Sally was away, foul-mouthed, intoxicated Roy strayed.

Uncharacteristically warm fall weather kept the facility hot during the day. But at night, the sweltering humidity was nearly unbearable. I had just put on my nightgown and gotten into bed when Tillie started to whimper. When she continued moaning, I worried that her sleeping medication might not be working. I went to her. As I was rubbing Tillie's back, Catherine looked over at me. She smiled and blew a goodnight kiss.

Just as Tillie was relaxing into a snoring slumber, Roy staggered into the dormitory. He didn't bother to keep his voice down. "Catherine!" He stumbled near where I was with Tillie. Ignoring us, he absently looked around. "Oh, Catherine? You big-busted, sexy woman. Where are you?" He turned his head and belched. Smelly spittle landed on my cheek.

I cringed but didn't dare move. The feeling of that brute's slimy spit sliding down my face is something I will never forget.

As Roy's boot hit the floor near her, Annette jumped out of bed. Palms together in a praying stance, she asked loudly, "Now?" She inhaled deeply as if absorbing an answer only she could hear. Then she began, "I'm ready for—"

"Shut up!" Roy shoved her back down to her bed knocking the wind and the words out of her.

Annette shook her head and sputtered, "Evil! Evil! Bad! Bad man!"

Knots formed in my belly. Who is Annette referring to? And what is Roy going to do to her? I hope Annette stops talking!

"Shut that crazy mouth of yours." Roy took aim with his open hand and slapped Annette's face. Hard. She fell to her mattress and stayed there, mumbling "evil" over and over while holding her hand to the side of her face that met Roy's palm.

Roy straightened up his posture and adjusted his uniform. Then he turned away from Annette's bed and lumbered onward, intent on finding Catherine.

Catherine very quietly pulled her counterpane over her face to hide from him.

I watched him lurching around until he came to Catherine's bed. His hand groped her buttocks and moved up. Removing her blanket, he wobbled then sat down on top of her legs.

I could see her struggling to loosen herself from what must have been a very uncomfortable position. I was so frightened for her and sick to my stomach at what I imagined might happen. But I was too afraid to move. To help my dear friend.

He put the lantern down on the floor and pulled a flask out of his shirt pocket. After a few swigs, he belched again and broke out into song. "Honey. Baby. Mine," rang from his loud, hoarse, off-key voice. With each word, he upped the volume.

Why isn't another staff member stopping him? Why is he allowed to be so disruptive and shameful with one patient? I wondered who else was on duty and why no one had come to investigate the commotion. Perhaps they didn't care or were too tired to move or were purposefully overlooking Roy's behavior because they were beholding to him on some account. It didn't matter. Someone should have stopped him; what he was doing was criminal.

A few more gulps from his metal container and all that came from his lips were slurs and jumbled sounds. I was still at Tillie's bedside. If someone comes, my panicked brain told me, I'll be in trouble. While she snored, I slid down to the floor and belly-crawled back to my bed. My heart was beating so hard that I was sure he'd hear it pounding the wooden planks I was slithering across.

Just as I was about to crawl onto my mattress, I felt a circular object hit my face. A flush of hot terror ran through my body. When my fingers encircled the tiny metal article with two holes in the middle, I knew it was a button. A button? From where? Just then I heard a pop and another ping of metal hitting wood. Roy was undoing his pants! Right there on Catherine's bed.

Vomiting into my mouth, I swallowed as I heard his disgusting moans and groans. Then there was an odd, frantic, rapidly moving, swishing sound followed by a loud, "Oh, God." He seemed to be fumbling around Catherine's bed; it looked as if he was rearranging his pants. Then he picked up his light and left.

Fearing he'd return, I waited for a long time before softly speaking. "Catherine?"

"Yes, Klara." As if she read my mind, she said, "I'm okay," her voice quivered. "He...he did nothing to me." She sniffed, "Good night."

By the way her speech cracked, I could tell she'd been crying. She wasn't okay. Now moaning, I could also tell that Annette wasn't okay. One repetitive crying chant to heaven above was most unsettling: "He must die!" Wondering if she was referring to Roy or some other man (perhaps someone who contributed to driving her insane) played in my head. Are you here because of a man? Did a man hurt you? And then the world turned upside down. Did you harm a man? Is that why you're here? Are you dangerous? Topsy-turvy thoughts ran through my brain. I didn't know whether to fear Roy or Annette. Maybe both.

The next day was uneventful. In the dorm that night, I went to Catherine. "Good, no Roy today. Free."

"Yes," Catherine smiled, "free today."

A longing to be out of that place ignited in me. I wanted out of there. I wanted my freedom. On the few occasions when we'd been out in the garden or driven around the island, I contemplated escaping. But how? "Catherine," I hesitated, not entirely sure I had the right words and afraid even to mention what I was thinking.

"Um-hum."

I remained quiet thinking about how to express my desire to know if anyone ever tried to escape this godforsaken island. My thoughts once again went to why in God's name I landed there. Why Catherine had been imprisoned there. It boggled my mind that beautiful, kind-hearted Catherine was in an insane asylum. I had become convinced that she, like me, had been unjustly sent to this hellhole for some corrupt reason. But why? My only answer was that there was no answer. I had to accept that there are some things in life I will never fully understand. Like why the Jews were so hated in Russia. What did I ever do to deserve what happened to me? Or Papa? Or Mama? Or Abram, Shakna, Josel, and Anna? My sweet baby sister, Anna, was only two-years-old when she was murdered. Why? What hollowed the hearts of these assassins? What blackened their souls to make them so vicious, so filled with hatred? I may never know the answers to the questions, but I can't stop asking them.

From the vile human rights abuses in Russia to the icy shower a dying young girl received to the lecherous tormenting Roy subjected Catherine to, I was smothering in the filthy air of hostility. I wanted to scream and pound a fist on something hard. I wanted to break something. But to do anything other than silently comply with my "masters" would put me at risk for more abuse. My fingernails dug into my clenched hands. The scar on my forehead itched.

Before I had had a chance to rub my skin raw, Catherine interrupted my retreat into darkness. "It's okay. You're okay, Klara." Her soft whisper hit my cheek. "You're soaking wet."

I pulled my nightgown from my chest and fanned myself. I was so warm. Hot from rage. I was a wildfire inside a closed-off fireplace; if I didn't break free, I would be nothing but soot and ashes. Talking. Distracting my attention was all I could think to do…for now. Reflecting on an earlier question, I asked, "Catherine, how we get out here?"

"I wish I knew." She rubbed a hand on my sticky back. "I wish I had an answer."

There was no point in aggravating our situation by pursuing that line of questioning. I wasn't insane, yet I was committed to an insane asylum against my will. In a country that valued individual freedom so highly, there must be laws against such actions. So, if I escaped and told good people on the outside about how I had been treated, it would mean big trouble for those who unjustly committed me. They benefited by my remaining there and being beaten into silence. That was the logical conclusion I drew from the fact that no one was doing anything to try to help me. I hadn't even seen a doctor. This whole calamity was some unbelievable mistake and cover-up. Someone else gaining by my imprisonment in a crazy house was too depressing to contemplate.

Knowing I needed to shift the conversation, I asked, "How you get here?"

Catherine's upwardly slanted eyebrows and her frown, her wistful faraway look, made me feel sad I asked. I knew that look. I'd seen it in my papa's face on the ship coming to America when he spoke of Mama and the rest of the family. It broke my heart. Was there anyone in this awful place that didn't have a sorrowful story, a tragic past? I doubted it.

Looking downward, feeling deep regret and shame that I accidentally opened the door to Catherine's pain, I said, "You no like talk. Okay. I sorry." Attempting to relieve tension building in my neck, I chewed on the inside of my cheek.

Catherine snapped out of whatever it was that put that expression on her face. "Oh, honey, you did nothing to apologize for." Reaching a hand to my left cheek, she sighed deeply and slowly. "I don't mind telling you. You've already shared so much with me," she said.

Over the last couple of years, I had learned enough English to tell her about what happened in Kiev. I also revealed things to her about my past: growing up and learning to read, our family and how we loved to cook and sing, and the one time I had a crush on a boy in my neighborhood. Catherine enjoyed hearing about Isaac and how my papa admonished me. You are sixteen. Too young to be concerned with boys. Study and make something of your life, he'd say to me. I listened to him then but now wondered if I'd been wrong to do so. I may have robbed myself of my only chance to experience a relationship.

Catherine sighed again then began her story. She told me that she was born and raised in New York. Her father was an architect and her mother was a homemaker. She was an only child. Tears ran down her half-opened eyes when she mentioned that she had been away at a friend's house when a fire broke out in her parents' home. It took their lives. She went to live with her father's brother Stuart, his wife Mabel, and their son Jackson. That was when she was in her early teens. As she grew and developed, boys (and then men) were attracted to her. "Jackson was very smart. He attended law school." Clearing her throat, she blushed as she relayed how Jackson connected with some influential people while in school. He fixed her up with a lawyer he interned with. A married man. Originally the man kept it from her that he was married, but later on he went into politics and became high profile, so Catherine found out. She became a moral obstacle in his path to success. By then, Jackson worked for the man. Captivated with and swayed by his power, Jackson was drawn into an illegal corrupt world. Eventually, the politician had Jackson hire doctors to commit Catherine to the asylum. By then her aunt and uncle had died. Her own cousin did that to her! Disposing of Catherine was a convenient way for that immoral man to handle his problem. In the middle of the night, an ambulance came to her place and kidnapped her. The rest of her story was similar to mine. Although I didn't fully understand all the words, I comprehended enough to grasp the horrible nightmare of betrayal that her lover and her own cousin put her through. It was impossible for me to believe that anyone I was related to would ever do such a hateful, selfish thing to me.

"No one hear you?" I asked.

"Did anyone listen to my side of the story? No, I'm afraid not. He's rich. Powerful."

I put my hand on hers and gave it a gentle, understanding squeeze. "You no other family?"

"Not anymore," she sniffed. "My uncle and aunt are dead. And my cousin," she continued as her hand clenched mine, "is dead to me."

Feeling the warmth of her touch and heart beating so fast, I said "You. Me. We family now. You my sister."

I stayed next to her, crying along with her, as our hearts melted together. It was a comfort to be there with my friend. Were it not for her and our close bond, I may have shut down completely. She ignited a sense of belonging and family in my nearly empty soul. Conversation by conversation, touch by touch, I stayed alive spiritually by helping her and receiving help from her. We were kindred spirits.

"Yes, we are family," she replied.

Family. I already lost one family. What would I do if this precious, life-saving relationship with my new sister Catherine was ripped away from me?

A Different Kind of Angel

Chapter Eighteen

What Roy did that night on Catherine's bed unsettled me. I find it odd how some thoughts affix themselves in one's memory, repeating over and over, while others fade and are hard to recall. Of all the things I'd experienced, witnessed, and heard about, there was something about Roy's behavior that wouldn't leave me alone. Maybe my attention was drawn more to Roy because of Annette's nightly rantings to God about a man she was bent on destroying. I no longer feared Annette being a direct threat to me. She wanted some man dead, and there was a good chance he was already dead. But Roy was another matter. What he did to Catherine in front of the women in the dorm was one of the sickest behaviors I had witnessed in the asylum. Once I started taking notice of Roy, I saw that meanness and vulgarity were as much in his blood as was his liquor. I didn't see one patient he ever treated as a fellow human being.

On top of my fear of Roy, my monthly bleeding had slowly faded to a trickle then just ended. I didn't know for sure why but assumed it had something to do with my constant nervous alertness and with the perpetually gurgling sounds coming from my stomach. I can recall several times when I cried, but no tears came forth. My body needed water. My body needed better nutrition. Proper rest. And just as the times when my tears had dried, I also wondered if my womb had dried. My tears returned when I was able to get enough liquids in me. But the female bleeding stopped. Although relieved I didn't have to continue to find ways to attend to the bleeding, I feared that the whole incident in Kiev and everything that happened since could have sterilized my womb.

Perhaps it was also my deep fear of being damaged sexually and not being able to bear children that kept Roy's obnoxious behavior replaying in my head. And I couldn't help wondering if remembering was an instinctive warning, like a cat with raised hackles sensing danger. Just the mere presence of Roy unnerved me. His brutal attitude and forceful nature reminded me of the Russian soldiers who attacked my home. I tried to shove the stormy feelings down into the mental box where I stored those awful emotions that made me shake with both fear and agony. I admired Catherine's resilience and positivity; she seemed to handle life in the asylum—even Roy's behavior—with an inner grace I wished I had.

Luckily, months passed before we were subjected to more of Roy. The cold-hearted fiend had been pulled off to work in the men's facility for the rest of 1884 through the beginning of 1886. Also, Sally never returned. Rumor had it that, while out west at the funeral, she met someone. Not all of our luck was bad.

In the months that Roy was gone, we breathed a little easier at night in the dorm. Catherine and I continued increasing my vocabulary, and soon I was reading to her from the book that Nurse Harriet had brought.

One night when I looked at the title, Jane Eyre, I felt despair. I instantly thought of another book I had read when I was sixteen, three years before the Kiev pogrom. Anna Karenina by Tolstoy. It took me several minutes to make the connection as to why this earlier book was now coming to mind. The tragic story involved Anna, a married noblewoman and her affair with Count Vronsky.

Moving a hand over the cover of Jane Eyre, I thought of Tolstoy's book and what was happening in Russia at the time it was written. The action in the novel took place against the setting of liberal reforms implemented by Emperor Alexander II of Russia. I thought of all who benefited by the transformation of the military, the government, banks, industry, and the press. The rise of the new elite and the decline of the old aristocracy were vividly disputed in the story. While the book was stimulating to read, it was also sorrowful. In the story, as in life, so many were benefiting while devastation was in store for Jews on the horizon. I couldn't help feeling sympathy for Anna when she took her own life. I remembered thinking that nothing would drive me to that degree of despair. Looking toward a future of endless misery in this atrocious prison, I wasn't all that certain.

But I promised myself that I would survive. I would find a way to endure. So, Catherine and I continued reading and talking. I was curious about why Harriet gave her the book. On the one hand, I thought it was a nice gesture. But I also wondered if Harriet knew the circumstances behind Catherine's being kept in the asylum, her only "crime" having been a paramour to a high-profile man. But if Harriet knew, why not do something about it? Maybe she had tried to get Catherine released, but the corruption was too far-reaching for her to have an impact. It haunted me that someone would know of such wrongdoing but make no attempt to rectify it.

One night when we were to begin our reading, I asked Catherine. "Why you think Harriet give you book?"

"She's a good person. She knows that I don't need the sleep medication. Just like you don't. And she just wanted to offer me something to occupy my time in here."

"Do she know 'bout—"

"Me?" Catherine raised her eyebrows in thought. After a few minutes she spoke, "Perhaps, but even if she somehow found out, what can she do? We're talking about doctors, police, and a politician keeping the secret. Powerful men."

"All keep secret. Maybe Harriet, too?"

"Sad, but yes. If she does know anything. But I doubt anyone would have been so stupid to leave a note around or some evidence."

"Stupid? Evidence?"

Catherine, looking confused, scratched her head. "Hmm." Her eyes lit up when she opened the book and pointed to me then moved her finger over the page like she was reading. "You smart." She then pointed to a peacefully sleeping Tillie, motioned to the book then shook her head. That's how Catherine helped me learn words; she'd point to an object or pantomime them for me, like when she helped me learn the word dress by pointing to hers and mine then saying the word.

"No smart? Stupid is no smart?"

"Yes, Klara," she whispered. "Evidence?" She made a motion on the back of the book like she was writing something. Then looking at me said, "Doctor," and continued to pretend writing.

"Doctor no keep evidence he write?"

"Yes." She patted my leg.

"Men. Bad. And not stupid. Keep big secret."

With that, she handed the book to me, and we began for the night. Once we made it through several pages, she grinned. I enjoyed the experience more when Catherine appeared pleased with my progress. Not only was I improving but assisting me gave her satisfaction. "I know I'm making good use of my time by helping you...you and the others," she once explained to me after I asked her why she was helping me so much.

Looking pensive, as though Catherine wanted to say something else, a rustle and squeal from another bed grabbed our attention. It was Rosie. Catherine quickly shut and hid the book as I scurried to my bed. Rosie was now screaming loudly while holding her belly. "Cramps!" Her red hair was flying about. Her arms thrashed, and she had her knees bent, exposing her private area.

I thought she was having menstruation cramps. I was wrong.

Her next outburst was even louder and higher-pitched. It woke up Annette. "The baby's coming!" Rosie bounced out of her bed and ran to the door, still clutching her belly.

Annette, disoriented from the sleep medicine, tripped getting out of her bed. Landing face-first on the floor, she screamed. "I can't breathe! Help, I'm drowning. He threw me overboard. He's trying to kill me!"

As Annette continued to act out being tossed into the sea, Rosie pulled the door open and bolted down the hallway hollering, "Baby coming! Baby coming!"

I went to Annette to make sure that she was okay. Her large, unfocused pupils were glazed over like she was caught in some state between sleep and full awareness. When I saw there was no apparent damage, I helped settle her into bed. She quickly fell back asleep.

Moments later in came Nurse Harriet and a male guard, each holding one of Rosie's arms. They led her back to her bed. "Okay, Sam," Harriet said to the guard. "I'll take it from here."

When the door shut behind him, Harriet soothed Rosie by pretending along with her. "Not yet, Rosie. Not time yet. Now go on back to bed and get some rest."

"Okay, Nurse." A calmer Rosie straightened her sheet, puffed her pillow, and relaxed back to sleep as Harriet sat by her. When she got up to leave and noticed me watching her, she came to me. "She'll be okay, Klara. Happens sometimes with the sleep medication."

Tilting my head and scrunching my eyebrows, I looked up at her. I understood a little, but she didn't know that.

To help me comprehend what she said, she made a motion like she put a pill in her mouth. "Sometimes not enough." She tried to explain that inadequate medication sometimes worsens a patient's mental problems.

I shook my head, indicating I still hadn't understood.

Harriet held her palm out and drew a large imaginary circle on it and a smaller one inside. Pointing to the larger circle, "This right medication amount." She then pointed to the smaller one inside and said, "Too little. Will not help. Make patient worse."

I was rather taken by the way she took her time to come to me, noticed my confusion, and wanted to help me understand. Catherine was right when she said that Harriet was a good person. "Pills...need more?"

"Yes," Harriet smiled.

The next night when Harriet handed out the sleeping medications, she told Rosie, "A little stronger for you, so you don't wake up again in the middle of the night."

Rosie slept well that night. So did the rest of us. As time moved along Rosie had a few more episodes of going into hysterical labor, but nothing drastic became of it for her. Not yet.

Days passed. Months moved on. Soon another cold winter was upon us. A harsh chill came before the new year.

When 1886 arrived, so did Roy.

Chapter Nineteen

Unlike my life before the asylum (and unlike the lives of "normal" people), if someone had asked me, "What day of the week is this?" I couldn't give them an answer. I measured time by the blur of consecutive sunrises followed by moonlight. Time of the year? I guessed by the temperature, weather, amount of daylight and what little I could see through filthy windows of how plants and trees were fending. It's odd, I thought, how Mother Nature now defines time for me while I'm confined within a granite fortress.

All I knew was that it was cloudy and cold at the beginning of a new year. Another bleak day in what was now 1886. I had been in the asylum for nearly four years. Years of my life subjected to malnutrition and torture. I never understood how I could have been taken without my consent and without so much as the assistance of an interpreter. How hard could it have been to get someone to help the police or the doctor to understand what I was trying to say? Their carelessness—or indifference—was inexcusable. Criminal.

The endless days were interrupted by my few precious moments with Catherine. Reading. Talking. Sharing. Growing a friendship. And now that, too, was soon to be interrupted by Roy. I would have looked forward to it being a bath day were it not for him being on duty. And to make matters worse, he was acting strangely. He smelled of drink before he opened his mouth. A rectangular bulge in his left shirt pocket looked like the outline of a flask.

After breakfast, Catherine and I were walking in the hallway when Roy stopped us. He was alone. He stared at each of us in turn—a short glare at me and a lingering gawk at Catherine. His dark, chilling gaze reminded me of the wicked wolf in a fairy tale I was told as a child. The wolf's eyes, like Roy's, were wide and black and dangerous. After he had consumed Catherine with his beastly, intrusive eyes, he told her, "I'll see you later." He slid a dry, calloused hand down her back to her buttocks and gave it a pinch. Right there in the open, in front of the other patients. A redheaded nurse saw but did nothing.

Catherine's body stiffened.

I clenched my left hand into a tight fist, nails digging into flesh. I reached for the scar on my forehead with my other hand. As I scratched to stop the crawling sensation moving down to my cheeks, I fought an overwhelming urge to kick him.

When he walked off, Catherine relaxed her shoulders.

Leaning close to her ear, I mumbled. "You okay?"

Without answering, Catherine looked at the nearby cracked window that invited the harsh winter weather inside. She reached a hand to the bars. As Catherine gave the metal a squeeze, the pink color drained from her knuckles. I put my hand atop hers. The chill on the rusty iron took the warmth from her hand. She stood there grasping that bar for dear life. I wanted to cry. For her. For me. For the rest of the unfortunates who didn't belong there and would never have a chance to prove their sanity. I wanted to sob enough tears to float us all away from this hell.

Catherine remained quiet for a while before removing her hand and looking at me. Pockets of tears threatening to overflow stood still on her bottom eyelids. I reached a hand to wipe them before they streamed down her cheeks.

On that day, there would be no assistance from Barbara Lincoln or Harriet Brownstone. The redheaded nurse I saw earlier was assigned to our group. Like in the hallway with Roy, she would continue to be no help at all to us.

Midmorning was when the ordeal began. The inside temperature had risen a bit from the combination of body heat and steam escaping from soup cooking in the kitchen. Roy stormed down the hall with Albert at his side. Like men on a life-or-death mission, they quickly pointed out women who were to have their baths. I knew they would choose Catherine. He made a sleazy evocative motion with his index finger on Catherine's arm. Locking my knees together in an emotionally protective gesture, Roy then pointed to me. Cringing, I flexed my thighs together.

Roy gave Albert a strange nod then grabbed Catherine's dress and pulled her off the bench. I rose and followed the procession to the bathroom. It smelled musty and stank from urine and feces; it probably hadn't been cleaned in days. The filth, worse than the last time I had had a bath, made me want to turn around and leave. If only I could.

Another shorter nurse accompanied the redheaded nurse. The short nurse, giving smiles and winks with hands on her hips, cozied up to Roy. What she saw in him was beyond me. I found him physically repulsive with those long, frizzy sideburns that needed trimming and the opening between his two front teeth that he spat through when he talked or belched. Even when his breath didn't have that offensive alcohol odor, it smelled rotten. Keeping the short nurse at arm's distance when she neared him, Roy's attention remained focused on Catherine.

The redheaded nurse pointed to an unkempt patient chattering to herself and laughing in a way that seemed fiendish. The nurse ordered the demented patient to pick up a gray, soiled rag and, "Go over to the bath." When she ignored the nurse's order, Albert was instructed to drag the woman over to the washtub. She went peacefully enough, cackling the entire time.

The redhead then looked at me and told me to undress. Right there in front of Roy and Albert. Feeling trapped, a panic flushed through my body. Furious about being so humiliated, I stood unwavering with my chin held high. I'd had enough.

Catherine tried to intercede. "I'll go first."

Roy became livid. He turned his attention away from Catherine and onto me. "You want to disobey?" His jaw contracted, and his teeth locked together as his eyes bore hatred through me.

He moved in on me with such ferocity that I thought I would faint. In one swift arc, his massive, steel-like fist slammed my left cheek.

I dropped to the floor.

Still conscious, I saw Catherine's shoulders lean in my direction. I held out a hand to her to stop. I shook my head no to tell her to stay put. I didn't want her to suffer any further on my behalf.

Roy drew his right leg back. Catherine and I both saw that his heavy boot was aimed at my face.

Catherine jumped between Roy and me.

As Roy went to push Catherine away, she grabbed his arm.

He stopped.

She then rapidly removed all her clothing. Standing naked before him, Catherine repeated, "I'll go first."

Her tactic had worked. Roy had forgotten about me. Catherine went to the tub and got in. The shorter nurse motioned to the crazy woman holding the tattered gray rag in her hand to wash Catherine. Roy's blatant, obsessed gaze followed the hand strokes of the woman scrubbing my sweet, brave friend. The wide-eyed look on Roy's leering face, with his hand grabbing hold of his crotch, turned my stomach. When Catherine got out of the bathtub and wiped herself with an old, filthy towel, Roy left the room with a hand covering his genital area.

My left cheek ached with a prickly burn radiating from the place where Roy punched me. Embarrassed and dreading being naked and washed with Albert looking on, I now feared what would happen if I continued to protest. I turned away from Albert and removed my clothes. I had my bath and hair washed, dried off, and got back into my dress just like the rest of the patients who were herded through like a flock of sheep.

When the day was over, we were all funneled back to our rooms. I was ready to get in bed and let sleep take me. But when I arrived in the dorm and saw Catherine's bed, I got sick. The measly evening meal I had consumed came right up.

If Catherine felt anything, she kept it hidden.

None of the others seemed to notice either the mess around Catherine's bed or the one I had just made.

The blanket that was on her bed was now on the floor next to the book, which was torn to shreds. Bundled sheets revealed a small bunched up area that looked like it had thick yellow-tinged discharge on it that smelled like bleach and urine. At first, I thought Roy had urinated on her bed. But then I recalled the moaning sound from that night when he sought Catherine out. The next morning her sheets had had a new stain that looked just like this one. I knew what he'd done both then and now. And to destroy the book, our only source of enjoyment, was unthinkably cruel. He was a sick, corrupt, perverted human being.

A Different Kind of Angel

Catherine bent down to pick up a few of the ragged pages that still had readable words and sentences. Tears dripped from her eyes onto them. I found something to clean up my vomit then helped her. The torn pages screamed abuse. Even the hard cover was ripped into pieces. It was evidence of Roy's cruel, vulgar, explosive nature. Catherine took the pillowcase off her pillow and gathered the fragments of pages. I helped her pick up the pieces. The remnants of his evilness burned in my hand.

There was no comfort in our mutual tears. Catherine quietly got into her bed, and I went to mine.

I was drained. I was exhausted coping with all that had been savagely taken from me. My family, my religion, my freedom, my future, and now the book. It was one of the only things I had left to look forward to, and it was also violently torn from me. There was no mercy. How much longer could I endure such hatred?

Sleep did not come to me that night. I was too consumed with anger. I wanted to kill Roy and all the Roys of the world that tromp on innocent lives and wreak havoc without a thought about the consequences to anyone but themselves. I wanted to join Annette in her screams to kill. But unlike Annette, I had no God to pray to for help. Had I finally been driven to madness?

The next morning, Catherine looked like I felt. She had dark circles under her eyes, and her skin looked ghost-white. Even her hair, which was usually pulled back neatly, looked distressed. Loose strands drooped all around her head. But it was her forced attempt at a smile that made me want to cry. She was feigning cheerfulness on my behalf.

I went to hug her while still dressed in my nightclothes. I then took the tie hanging loosely from her head and pulled the strands into a neat bun. As I was retying it, Barbara Lincoln entered.

I was not about to remain quiet, like Catherine. "Look," I pointed to the bed and the polluted mark Roy had left. "And," I opened the pillowcase to show her the ripped pages.

She looked around the room at the other women, prancing about and babbling, oblivious to what was going on with Catherine and me. With narrowed eyes and downturned lips, she sighed out a sad low tone when she asked, "Roy?"

Not really surprised by her query, I nodded. Of course, she knew. Everyone knew about Roy. So, why does he continue to get away with it?

She must have sensed what I was thinking. "Roy has an uncle on the board."

I didn't understand the word board or her emphasis on it but gathered that he had a powerful uncle that protected him. Perhaps the best we could expect was temporary reprieves when he was transferred to other units. But then the monster always managed to return to the women's ward. To him, we were the part of his job that he enjoyed most. A bonus. We were objects for his use—outlets for his urges, sexual or sadistic.

As she was gathering us all into a line, Barbara mentioned to Catherine within my earshot, "I'll see what I can do."

Catherine's slumped shoulders raised a notch higher. "Thank you."

"And," Barbara added, "I'll let Harriet know so she can see about bringing you another book."

When I heard her mention Harriet, I knew they had been talking. The two nurses were most likely working together to help us as much they could. Although it wasn't exactly strength in numbers, might or resources, it was certainly a comfort to know we had friends among the staff. I felt less alone.

That night as Annette rampaged on, my urge to retaliate against Roy lessened. I wondered if that was the line that separated Annette and me; whereas my edge smoothed, her apparent deep desire to kill some unnamed evil man never mellowed. But what or who was she bent on avenging? And why?

Chapter Twenty

It was bitterly cold. A blizzard had moved onto the island sending an icy chill through cracks in the windows. Moods were plunging like the temperature, and a fight broke out among patients. It started when poor Rosie stood in the hallway and grabbed her stomach. "It's time!" she yelled. Her faced flushed as she reached high up under her dress. "I feel the head!"

"You crazy loon!" Albert came rushing at her waving his baton.

Holding her hands over her head, Rosie ducked to avoid the hard, wooden weapon crashing down on her head. Fear flashed in her eyes. "Don't hit me. You'll kill the baby!"

"You stupid simpleton." He brought the baton down on Rosie's belly.

Another patient jumped on Albert's back to get him away from Rosie, who was screaming, "Help me! Help me!"

Albert lost his balance trying to free himself from the woman who was flailing her legs as she clamped her arms around his neck. They both tumbled to the ground with the patient on top of him. The redheaded nurse from the other day blew her whistle. If she thought the shrill sound would put an end to the chaos, she was sorely mistaken. That piercing sound set the place off into pandemonium. Patients began screeching, ganging up on Albert and hitting him, frantically running about and wildly talking to themselves. One woman with long, wild hair started pulling out handfuls of knotted clumps from her scalp.

Boot heels resounded like a stampede of horses as five male guards descended on the bedlam. When one fired a gun toward the ceiling, the bullet ricocheted into a patient's leg; her blood gushed out in pulses. The guards quickly locked leather belts around the waists of all the women piled on the floor. Long cables were then hooked to the belts and pulled to separate the women. Some were dragged away to the bathroom. Some were brought to their beds to be restrained. And Rosie, at the bottom of the pile, was dragged away in an unconscious state. The woman with the gunshot wound was lugged like a sack of dirty laundry to the infirmary, leaving a trail of splattered blood.

Frozen in terror, my legs were trembling as I sat huddled on the bench next to Catherine. I didn't dare make eye contact with any of the guards or nurses.

Screams came from the bathroom.

Moans came from dormitory doors left open.

Bang!

Slap!

Barbarian, sadistic laughter came from guards.

Cheering each other on, I heard a male voice say, "Hit harder," and another said, "Kick her. It's easier on you."

I was able to breathe a bit when someone said, "Stop, you're going to kill her."

"So what? They're all garbage. Get rid of them all."

I held my breath again.

Get rid of them all! Soldiers are coming. Fast and furious. They're storming into my home. Killing my mama and siblings. "Get rid of them all!" Stop saying that! I was back in Kiev.

Catherine was still sitting next to me. "Oh, my God," she whispered to no one specific.

Caught between the past and the present, I shook my head to orient myself. But it was difficult. There was no significant difference between then and now. Rage flew through me. I abruptly stood and shouted, "Stop this madness!"

Catherine pulled me down by the back of my dress. "Klara, no," she whispered. "Get a hold of yourself."

They're killing them all! "They killed them," I cried.

From nearby in the hall, Annette ran to me. "Kill them! Kill them!" became "Kill him! Kill him!" Pulled away by one of the guards, she continued to rant, "Kill him." I heard the words, but they weren't spoken with Annette's voice. I heard soldiers. Russian soldiers.

"Shh, Klara." Catherine held my arm and every time she felt my muscles tense in an attempt to stand, she gripped harder to restrain me.

Feeling her hand on my arm, I looked around. Kiev fell away and reality gripped me harder than Catherine's hand ever could. I was in this new hell. Without my papa to help me escape.

A nurse ran by carrying a tray of medications.

The shouting quieted.

The screeching stopped.

The brawl was over.

The masculine laughter grew louder.

I couldn't stop trembling.

Catherine let go of my arm.

Other than some incoherent babbling, no one spoke for the rest of the day. It was as quiet as a graveyard. I feared for the woman who was shot. I feared for Rosie. And all the others injured as the guards laughed.

Minutes moved slower than usual. Boots shuffled. Patients coughed and fidgeted. The sun lowered toward the edge of the earth.

I sat in a dazed fog. The sheer magnitude of the suffering around me was crushing. I was numb. Numb yet shivering.

The rest of that day, I felt as if I was in a slow-moving dream but one I couldn't awaken from because I was not dreaming. My feet mechanically moved my trembling legs until Catherine took my hand and walked me to our beds. Rosie's bed was empty.

* * *

The next few days felt long and shapeless. Day and night, I struggled to locate myself in time and place. Am I in Kiev before the massacre? The Blackwell's Island Women's Lunatic Asylum? Am I dreaming? Am I finally crazy or merely on the brink? What is happening to me?

The asylum faded, and my scattered attention drifted back to my beautiful Kiev. Back to books. Back to singing. Back to hugs and warmth and love. I was reliving the time before my life was turned upside down. Away from persecution. Away from guns. Away from soldiers.

As a baby, my cries never went unnoticed. Mama was there to hold me. My tummy was never empty for long. There was baby talk and adult talk. Life was filled with promise and possibilities. You are so beautiful, my baby girl. Then, I was beautiful. You are so smart and anything you make your mind up to do, you can. Then, I was intelligent. Your body is sacred. Always take good care of it. Then, I did. Never lose faith or become weak. Then, I was strong, surrounded by strength—the power of love. I was an integral part of a family, and I belonged to something meaningful and beautiful. Then…

Now, in this frigid asylum, I didn't exist. I didn't matter. I was a nobody. No. Body.

Vacillating from Kiev to the asylum and back to Kiev, I was in a confused in-between state. Unable to locate happier memories, ugly ones resurfaced. Soldiers! Nooooo! Traveling. An ocean. You are smart. You are smart. Never lose faith. Stay strong. Papa's fading face. Nooooo!

"No!" A nauseating rolling motion hit me. Papa. "No!" The motion continued. Someone whispered something I couldn't make out. I opened my sleepy eyes. Catherine's hand was on my shoulder. It was dark. I was in my bed.

"Klara, you're having a nightmare."

"Huh?" I was disoriented. I wanted to go back to my dream, or nightmare, for whichever it was, it was a relief from the existence I was now living.

"Klara, you're okay." Catherine rubbed my back like she had done so many other nights. But it wasn't her hand I felt.

"Thank you, Mama." I rolled over to go back to sleep.

The next morning, Nurse Barbara walked in carrying a large stuffed pillowcase. It's the first we'd seen of her since that horrible incident with Rosie's outburst about giving birth, the other patients, and the staff. She looked at Rosie's still-vacant bed and then to Catherine. Without lowering her voice, she said, "Rosie will be okay."

"The patient with the gunshot wound?" asked Catherine.

"Lost a lot of blood, but she will be okay also."

She looked at me, huddled in my flimsy blanket, and walked over to me. "Klara, you look a fright." She then reached into the pillowcase she held, pulled out a thick woolen blanket and handed it to me.

Barbara distributed warm blankets to all the women. That was the beginning of some changes for the better. And the timing couldn't have been more appropriate to help pull me out of my melancholy. I endured the rest of that day with my attention on when I would get back to my bed and cuddle in the soft, comforting, pale-blue blanket.

Several nights after that, Nurse Harriet was on duty and brought us a fresh, clean copy of Jane Eyre. Having been too preoccupied, I paid no attention to the fact that Roy hadn't been around since he had violated Catherine's bed and destroyed the book. Unbeknownst to us, Roy had once again been transferred back to the men's ward.

Catherine had returned to her composed self. The bone-tired, bleary-eyed look was gone from her countenance.

And, once again, I had reading to look forward to as 1886 defrosted into another spring and summer. Reality became a bearable place for me, so I let my sweet Kiev fade into the past, but not so far that I couldn't find it when I needed another respite from the horrors of asylum life. And, of course, there would be more horrors.

Chapter Twenty-One

My pale-blue blanket was like a friend. It brought back soothing memories of my "comfy" from when I was young. Mama knitted me an infant-sized covering when I was born. After that, she stopped knitting. She said it was too time-consuming, but Papa told me that it frustrated her to miss stitches. People used to tell her, "If you can purl, you can knit."

"Nonsense," she'd reply to Papa as she made a big swatch for me. That was my comfy. I was the very proud owner of the only fruit of Mama's knitting. She dreamed of knitting us sweaters and frowned at all the money it cost not being able to work efficiently with yarn. She was, however, accomplished at sewing. And so she'd compensate, saying you can't be good at everything, and my sewing is good enough. Although Mama downplayed her talent, she was an excellent seamstress for our family and a few close friends. Her sewing skills were well known in our neighborhood. Before I was born, she made a few extra rubles altering and mending things. After I was born, Papa wanted her to concentrate on mothering me.

My pale-blue blanket reminded me of my comfy, of a time when I was deeply loved. If only I could conjure up that love in my heart to help fill the emptiness…But even if my grief over the losses I had endured could not be pacified, cuddling my new blanket comforted me. It had become a piece of my former self: the carefree girl who only saw goodness and a bright future.

A Different Kind of Angel

* * *

As the last days of a muggy summer settled into fall, autumn colors appeared on trees. The foliage I saw on our precious jaunts out to the garden was glorious. Perhaps living in a shades-of-gray world had numbed my eyes and mind to the brilliant colors outside the walls of the asylum. In winter, I saw white snow; in summer, I saw green leaves and grass. But autumn always took my breath away. It was a relief whenever I got to go outside. Lush, green leaves had turned to various shades of red, orange, and yellow. Their reflections shimmering on the East River reminded me of Kiev, where abundant waterways were mirrors for multicolored trees. Watching leaves drift from limbs was like watching butterflies float out of cocoons. When the trees lost their growth, stunning views opened. Kiev, the land of hills, offered picturesque sceneries that made my heart sing. Here on the island of insanity, there was so little that was beautiful that, by contrast, to see the green shades shift to vibrant, assorted hues was mesmerizing. For me, nature was hypnotizing. Calming. Healing.

I wandered to the edge of the walkway overlooking the river, scanning the city's buildings and traffic across the water. Trains and horse-drawn carriages carried people to destinations they anticipated. Boats heading to the asylum island brought people who were sent against their will or who were unaware of where they were going. While most of those people in the city would return home from their travels within hours or days, those of us sent across the East River might never get sent back. A chill ran up and down my spine. Best not to think about that, Klara, I told myself.

I shifted my focus back to women walking arm in arm with men in suits. I imagined them sashaying in long, flowing, colorful gowns.

I wondered what they were saying, where they were going, what their days and nights were like. Above me, birds landed on limbs now exposed because their leaves had already fallen. Chirping their goodbye songs, I wondered where their next destination would be. The longer that colors, creatures, and movements filled my vision, the more my mind emptied. A gentle calmness came over me. It was a welcome respite from my persistent gloomy contemplation.

That night I read with Catherine. After a very short while, my eyelids grew heavy. It was a welcome ending to the day. I made my way to my bed and my comfy, my pale-blue blanket. As my head rested on my pillow, my attention went to my breathing. Each breath in its own new moment brought relaxation and, finally, an uninterrupted, peaceful, dreamless sleep. Those moments when gratitude found its way back into my heart kept me stable.

Becoming aware of the impact that appreciation had on my mood, I began to seek out the simplest of things to feel grateful for. It surprised me that in this den of lunacy there were so many opportunities to focus on thankfulness. Catherine and the two kind nurses (Barbara and Harriet) topped my list. So did sweet Rosie, who I had grown very fond of despite the fantasy world she lived it. I often wondered if she had been driven to insanity by the loss of a child. She was so convincing during her imagined childbirth or when caring for her phantom baby. I had witnessed many real aspects of Rosie's faux pregnancy, delivery, and motherhood. I was there with Mama during her pregnancies with my siblings, especially with Anna. Mama never went mad. But she knew of a woman who had, and we all heard about it.

Mrs. Mikalev was young when she had her baby back in 1872. I remember because I was around ten-years-old and had a keen memory. I liked Sarah Mikalev, who couldn't have been more than seven years my senior. I recalled that, before being pregnant by her husband from an arranged marriage, she had trouble with sour moods on cloudy, rainy days. She'd complain about it. But no one made the connection with her mood issues from lack of sunshine and her after-delivery episodes. The first week after the birth of her beautiful little girl, Sarah was acting normal. But by the second week, things completely changed. Dramatically. She became easily excitable. Elated with hectic bursts of energy, she said she didn't need to sleep. A serious bout of sadness followed her restlessness. Day after day, she cried. When she began to hear voices telling her to do scary things to her baby, Sarah's mother stepped in to tend to and raise the child. Sarah was never the same after that. The whole thing must have been dreadful for everyone.

Feeling compassion, I looked at Rosie and thought of Sarah Mikalev. Sarah's child lived and was well taken care of. Perhaps if Rosie did have a baby, that child was not as fortunate. Maybe now, in her fantasy world, she was making up for it.

Yes, there were things to be thankful for if I looked for them. Focusing on the few precious positive elements of life in the asylum didn't stop the hurt inside or my emotional ups and downs, but it did help to smooth them over; it sanded down the jagged edges so that they didn't cut so hard and deep. I thought of Roy and how having a hostile attitude toward him caused me to feel worse. I didn't want to hate him but, struggle as I might, I couldn't get over my anger at him. I didn't want to end up in a hostile rage like Annette over some mysterious man. In her maddening prayer rituals, her wrath appeared to be escalating. How did she get to that state? And if my animosity continued to build up, what would be my ultimate response? My challenge was to find a way to channel my feelings so I didn't do something reckless and end up hurting myself. Or as Annette said in her prayers, kill him!

A few days later, I awoke thinking of Roy. Will he be returning to our area? I would soon have my answer. Later that week while out in the garden listening to the sweet chirping of birds, a chill moved in on the island. When the on-duty nurse moved us inside to a warmer place, I heard rowdy bursts of laughter. It was Roy cavorting with Albert. He had returned and, with flask in hand, they were celebrating. I was afraid of what they were so overjoyed about.

That night I hugged my blanket to my chest. Despite the soft comfort it had given me so many nights, that night I had trouble falling asleep. As clouds moved past the moon casting a soft ray of light onto the room, I looked around. All the women were asleep. My attention went to Amelia who barely moved while sleeping. I wondered if she stayed in the same scrunched up position on her side all night. I wondered if she ever snored. She was the quiet one in our dorm group. Her excessively loose and wrinkled skin extended beyond her skeletal frame onto the sheet like an extra blanket. What did she look like before the asylum? And why, like all the others, did she land here? The only clues I had to her "personality" were her usually squinting eyes and furrowed brow. I thought of the night she screamed out because she saw a rat and Nurse Sally beat her black-and-blue. Because she reacted to a rat! More thoughts came about Amelia. About Rosie. About Tillie. About Annette. About Catherine. About the unpredictability of life. I tossed and turned until daybreak. The sky was a cloudless pale-blue. Like the color of my blanket. Perhaps it was a good omen.

Having one last cuddle with my blanket before I got up, I hoped that maybe the day would bring unexpected good. It wasn't easy to slide into pleasant daydreams. But when I was able to, with some newly-formed crack, hole, or stain on the wall, I'd drift off into a new version of an old, amusing memory. Like a while back when a brown stain on a plate reminded me of the day I stepped in dog excrement.

It must have been a large dog because the minute I stepped in the brown, smelly substance it covered the bottom of my new left shoe and sent a clump splattering onto the right one. From the odor and texture, I knew it was fresh. I had nothing to use to clean the smelly waste. I rushed home fearing Mama's disappointment that I might have ruined my shoe by not paying attention. Aside from my winter boots, they were the only ones I'd own until they wore down. Arriving at our front door, I banged and screamed to be let in. I didn't dare enter. When the door opened the scent of bread wafted from the kitchen. One whiff and I started to cry. Not only had I ruined my shoes, but I also spoiled the aroma the family loved when Mama was baking.

Mama took one look at me, from head to toe, and squeezed her lips together. I couldn't make out what her reaction was, but silence was never good. There we were when Abram's voice rang out. "What smells?"

When he appeared, Mama broke into laughter. So did Abram. Bless Mama's heart, after she made me take off my shoes at the door, she went outside to clean them in a bucket. They lost their new look, but I could still wear them. For the rest of that day, I was teased (in good nature) about ruining the heady aroma of Mama's freshly-baked bread. To me, it wasn't funny. Not yet. The teasing went on for days, with my siblings looking at my feet and holding their noses. Before long when I looked at my shoes, I also laughed.

Remembering that, envisioning Mama and the rest of the family, helped lessen the stinging anguish I felt when recalling them.

I wanted to believe that my cozy blanket played a part in my newfound change in attitude. I finally had something I could hold onto that would comfort me when I needed to transform pain into something more tolerable. Caressing it, I came to discover that what was important in life was not what I had lost but rather what I had been given. Love. Kind words. Hugs. Smiles. In that chaotic, inhumane asylum, there was value in someone giving me her time. It warmed the chill of the environment. Seeing that ignited a flicker of light in my soul. I wanted my life to count for something. I wanted to help others. Like Catherine was doing.

My light grew as I reached out to assist others, like with Tillie when I went to help soothe her before sleep. I had a tender connection with her. She didn't have to acknowledge that anything happened between us for me to know that on some level she appreciated our bond. That's when I began to understand where strength really came from. I finally knew I could endure anything this crazy place might have in store for my friends and me. I was alive. I was aware. I was sane. And when others around me could not claim the same, I gained energy by helping them. I immediately found more reasons to smile.

The next several days were okay. Roy was not working with us, and I hoped that Roy stopping by to see Albert the other day was just a social call. Maybe he had been permanently reassigned to the men's ward.

My new hopeful disposition was to be sorely tested. Roy had two more weeks to work elsewhere before he came back to terrorize us.

A Different Kind of Angel

Chapter Twenty-Two

It was the last week of fall. Gray, gloomy cumulus clouds covered the horizon. Melding together, they oozed like a bleeding watercolor painting as flashes of lightning cut through the heavy sky. The clouds took on the appearance of leaden bunches of cauliflower. Thunder drum-rolled in the distance, and I paced on shaking legs to try to stay warm.

The approaching storm front was agitating some of the patients. As crashing sounds intensified, a black-haired, dark-skinned woman a few feet away from me belted out a moan that sounded like a constipated mule I once knew. Another woman with white hair huddled in a corner. Rosie was wildly swinging her cradled arms back and forth, muttering, "Shh, my baby. Your Mama's gonna keep you safe. Good. Shh, my baby."

Annette, who was next to a woman who was tugging on knots in her hair, repetitively banged her foot on the floor in an irritating manner. Biting the inside of my cheek was the only way to stop myself from yelling at Annette to stop. I wanted to shake all those stirred up patients by their shoulders and tell them to calm down.

In recent weeks, I had been getting headaches. This pain was new for me, and I didn't like it. Whether it was the impending thunderstorm or the storm brewing inside the asylum, I developed another headache. Attempting to relieve my aching head, I rubbed my temples. I knew the constant anxiety I felt contributed to my new malady. The weather did, too. Cold and damp air settled into my neck and back, making the muscles hard and taut. Feeling as stiff and cold as a block of stone, I picked up my walking pace to get some blood flowing to my limbs.

Nurse Barbara approached Catherine, who was sitting slouched over on a bench. Her eyes were closed, and her head was nodding. Barbara gently touched Catherine's shoulder, startling her erect.

I moved into earshot of them and overheard Barbara tell Catherine, "I'll be off for a few weeks."

Why did she say that? I thought. She has been away before without a forewarning, so why now? On top of a headache, my gut began to feel queasy. The uneasy sensation in my belly exploded when she said, "Roy is coming back here."

Catherine's shoulders slumped.

No! I grabbed hold of my abdomen and went to the nearest chamber pot.

When I returned, Barbara was no longer with Catherine. I sat down next to her, not knowing what to say. I felt the temperature drop. I couldn't tell if the coldness inside the building was real or if the news of Roy's return sent my insides into a dark, frigid pit.

Catherine, sensing my distress, moved closer to me. "Did you hear what Barbara told me?"

I barely nodded.

"It was nice of Barbara to mention it to me."

Nice? How could anything involving Roy be nice? I sat there scratching my forehead, not comprehending Catherine's comment.

Catherine lowered her voice to a whisper. "I asked Barbara if there was any way to keep him from returning."

I remained quiet.

"She told me that he has pull."

170

I tipped my head slightly and furrowed my eyebrows. "Pull?"

Catherine spoke softly. "Power. He has people in charge protecting him. They let him do anything he wants. The most that can be done is to change rotations. Like with all staff."

"Rotation? What mean rotation?"

"Where he works. The building area. Staff has to shift locations. Apparently, it's asylum policy. Barbara may have had a hand in influencing getting him scheduled somewhere else after the last flare-up."

Not fully understanding all she had just said to me, I got the gist of it. I felt annoyed that Nurse Barbara had mentioned it when there was nothing we could do about it but worry. That didn't seem nice to me. "Why Barbara tell you? Just bad news."

"She wanted to let me know she may not be here when he returns. But not to worry as she will be back to take care of us."

The jittery climate escalated with each lower degree of temperature. I wished we could go outside for a walk to ease our nerves. Feeling the frigid air claw through the window, I stood to look out at the approaching storm. Gooseflesh had formed on my arms as clouds covering more sky moved closer. Drizzle hitting the window seeped in through the cracks while the mist of my breath fogged into blurry condensation.

Catherine stood up, hugging her chest to ward off the biting cold.

Watching the droplets of water stream down the window, I flinched as a blaze of lightning lit up the sky. Roaring thunder mixed with the sound of the river's white-capped waves crashing ashore. It scared me that I could hear the river beyond the walls. It had never been so fierce before. Nature's violence had not bothered me previously, but with my headache and my nerves on razor-sharp edges after hearing about Roy, it didn't take much to tip the balance on my already-heightened agitation.

Wild, angry sheets of rain pummeled the ground. A damp, musty smell permeated the air. I recognized it immediately. The old granite walls and neglected windows that defined the perimeter of our world couldn't keep out the smell of the earth or the torrential rain forming rivers around the grounds. Pools of water formed on the floor as rain continued to seep in through the windows. The next flash of lightning and roaring boom of rolling thunder rattled the windows.

The temperature continued to drop with blustery gusts slapping the outside walls. Buckets of water pouring from the sky turned into crystals of snow. Flurries formed hail. The wind blew with wild abandon, sending frozen balls the size of robin eggs crashing against the ground, the roof, the exterior walls, and into the windows. A sudden burst of those frozen balls of snow and ice hit and broke one of the windows in the sitting hall. Another window crashed open. Glass went flying. Large and small shards skated across the hallway sending patients screaming, running, ducking or staring wide-eyed in apparent paralysis. Rosie went into her world of wild imaginings. "Baby hurt! Baby hurt!" she repeated over and over.

I grabbed Rosie. Not knowing where else to go, I led her back to the dorm. Catherine took command of our other dorm mates— Annette, Tillie, and Amelia—and followed my lead. In the shadowy room, intermittent flashes of lightning cast eerie patterns on the walls. I moved Rosie to her bed and attempted to calm her and her make-believe baby. "You are okay now, Rosie."

"My baby scared."

"Keep rocking, Rosie."

Rosie made a swaying motion back and forth.

"Good, Rosie. Now, look. Baby sleeping. Rosie good mama." I no longer feared speaking English in the dorm. When I felt it would calm situations, I spoke it. I think it helped Rosie; I know it helped me.

The night was long as streaks of lightning lit up the sky and thunder boomed. Everyone was medicated except Catherine and me. I didn't want to be drugged. A doctor ordered medication for other women who had night fits or made any kind of trouble for the nurses and guards. A doctor who never saw them. Determined not to lose any more control than I had already lost, I gladly sacrificed medicine-induced sleep. So, I remained awake listening to the blizzard's high winds pound the building.

Bang! Bang! Bang! It reminded me of the 1812 Overture. The frightening intensity of Tchaikovsky's cannon part, which I had once heard on a loud percussion instrument, came to mind. It jolted me when I had first heard it. That same sense of startle hit my body with each crash and boom filling the air. The high winds and low visibility continued into the morning when we dressed and marched to breakfast.

Open conversations between the guards and kitchen staff were rare, but they were talking clearly enough that those of us who were capable could understand them. And worry.

"New York is shut down."

"No coal deliveries."

"Hope we don't run out. Imagine this place with no heat!"

No heat? We never had heat. They must have been referring to the staff's living quarters. Everything in this place was contrary to common sense. Patients were not helped; they were hurt. The staff's lives were comfortable; patients' lives were miserable and uncomfortable. None of the staff looked undernourished; all of us did. The staff offices and quarters had heat; our areas had none. It was upside down.

"It's so cold!" a staff member complained.

Looking around at the chattering blue-tinged lips and pale complexions on the patients, I sipped a spoonful of lukewarm porridge. The protesting from staff continued until a patient stood up screaming. A beetle had crawled up on the table next to her. That was the end of breakfast for all of us.

By the time the storm stopped, it had looked like five feet of snow had fallen, with drifts significantly higher. Traffic to the island had stopped for two days with impassable roads to the river in need of shoveling. Food stopped being heated as staff continued to bicker about having to sit for their breaks in a cold room.

Four days passed before the snow was shoveled and boats reappeared crossing the East River.

Four days closer to when Roy would be returning. From a freezing tempest to burning hell.

Chapter Twenty-Three

Nellie

1887

What happened after that winter's blizzard is hard to talk about. And so I digress again to Nellie's arrival. Yes, there were plenty of dreadful things that occurred when Nellie was there but none as explosive as what happened when Roy returned. And none with a more significant emotional impact on my time in the asylum. I need a breather before returning to the horrors of that part of my story.

It was late summer or early fall when Nellie arrived. The day was hot and humid. The patients weren't given any means to cool themselves. I was perspiring vats of water. My dress clung to me like a second skin. I pulled my top away from my chest and fanned it in and out to get some air.

Catherine made room for Nellie beside us on the bench. She looked to be around my age (twenty-five, plus or minus a year or two). She sat for a while and was rather open with her conversation. Right away, she claimed that she was not insane. To my surprise, Catherine shared some of her story with this newcomer. Nellie was chatty and friendly. After a short while, Nellie got up.

"Very hot this day," I whispered as I leaned into Catherine.

"It sure is." The additional heat of her breath on my cheek drew more beads of sweat. Wiping myself with my hand, I watched the attractive new patient walking around the hallway.

Greta Smidt was on duty. She was also new to the asylum. My first impression of her was mistakenly favorable. Misinterpreting her pleasant looks for a pleasing personality, my assessment of her changed when she opened her mouth. She was heartless. Obnoxious. With no provocation, she seemed to enjoy tormenting patients. I watched her laugh and blow cigarette smoke in a woman's face until the woman coughed and wheezed, but that didn't stop Greta. A patient's suffering seemed to motivate her to continue the abuse. To get another patient's attention, Nurse Greta pinched her arm with fingernails longer than any of the other staff, drawing blood. To a patient who was innocently looking out of the window, Greta grabbed hold of her hair and held onto it until she sat the patient back on the bench. The poor woman wasn't disturbing anyone. Greta was just plain mean-spirited.

If someone told me while I was growing up that I would meet a woman who gained pleasure by being cruel to others, I would have said, "Nonsense!" Seeing Greta in action certainly changed that naïve opinion.

Greta was at the door to the garden, just opening and closing it. I think she was attempting to cool off. But when a patient wandered up to her (probably to get a bit of relief from the slight breeze), she slammed the door shut and kicked the woman. The patient hobbled back. Her shin was already discolored.

Nurse Greta took nastiness to a whole new level. She was on duty when the new, pretty, blue-eyed Nellie arrived.

Nellie ambled about, flush-faced, looking as hot as the rest of us. Her short brown bangs, wet from sweat, stuck to her forehead.

Pushing her hair off her face, she continued to watch the patients closely. When she looked back and made eye contact with me, I smiled. My smile quickly disappeared as I watched Greta approach Nellie.

"And what do you think you're glaring at?" Greta asked Nellie.

"Being as I'm new here, I'm just having a look around."

With a puffed out, busty chest, she scolded, "Well best keep your eyes to yourself if you know what's good for you." She dug a pointed finger into Nellie's side. "Keep being nosy, and you'll see what it gets you."

Standing erect, Nellie did not appear to be put off. She simply continued to walk around casually, looking where she pleased. Greta's face turned red as her narrowed eyes followed Nellie.

Nellie moved back toward the bench and made a comment about Greta. "Bad mood?"

Catherine responded in a whisper, "Looks like it. It's her first day here."

Nellie spoke a little too loudly when she responded. "She's not behaving like a nurse should."

When Nurse Greta overhead this, she stormed over to Nellie and grabbed her by the hair. "You crazy piece of garbage. I warned you about being nosy!"

Nellie politely replied. "Being nosy? What in the world is wrong with walking around and talking with others? I'm new—"

Before Nellie could finish, Greta palm-punched her right in the middle of her face, giving Nellie a bloody nose.

Nellie licked the sticky substance off her upper lip and swiped her face with the back of her hand. "What did you do that for?" Seeing the red, sticky blood on her hand, she protested. "Why are you treating me like this? I am not insane. And even if I were, this is no way for a nurse to—"

"Oh, this one thinks she's smart! Don't know your place yet, do you?" Greta blew a loud whistle and called out, "Guard!"

Harry Phelps, a big, burly, balding man, appeared. He looked at Greta then at Nellie. "A troublemaker?"

Greta didn't bother to answer Harry's question. She just ordered him, "Get a hold of her and follow me."

When Nellie returned, her dress was wet and her hair was dripping. Despite the hot day, her teeth were chattering, and her skin was gooseflesh. Later she told Catherine and me that she had been put in the bathtub and several buckets of ice-cold water were thrown over her head. "I tried to defend my sanity. To protest the harsh treatment. Belligerent treatment. All to no avail. I experienced a sensation of drowning as they dragged me, gasping from the tub. It was then I thought I probably did look insane."

The rest of that afternoon on the bench, Nellie exercised more restraint than earlier in the day. After several hours, she asked, "How long do you sit here?"

"It depends on who is on staff," Catherine muttered under her breath. "With the awful ones, anywhere from eight to ten hours."

Between her teeth, Nellie softly responded. "That's insanity in itself."

Catherine and I remained silent. So did Nellie until Greta took a break and the nurse watching us was way down the hall out of hearing range.

In a quiet, nearly garbled way, Nellie said, "Between a false diagnosis, confinement, and the disregard and objections to my claims of injustice…the abuse is maddening," she sighed. "I attempted to defend myself. But the more I protested my lucidity, the more the professionals shook their heads and arrogantly said it confirmed that I was rightly diagnosed. I don't see how—"

Catherine, seeming annoyed, crossed her arms over her chest. Looking down at the floor, she huffed when she interrupted in a whisper. "I experienced the same!"

Nellie's eyes grew wide. Her pupils dilated. Keenly interested, she leaned closer to Catherine. "Huh?" Restraining any further communication, she waited for Catherine to continue.

"Oh, there's no use in further discussion about my situation. It's a sorrowful and hopeless one. Like you who wasn't believed when declaring your sanity."

The conversation was interrupted when Greta returned with a brown-haired nurse. She was the tallest and sturdiest woman I'd ever seen. I overheard them loudly gossiping. "The supervisor put me down to work a night shift next week. That old biddy." Greta's voice was as bitter as her disposition.

"I don't like working when she's on," responded the other nurse. "You're new here?"

Greta looked up to the brown-haired woman. "Yes, why?"

"Don't be smoking around her or taking long breaks. She'll be all over you. You won't believe this, but I was called in for pulling a patient's hair. The nerve! How about what the looney did to me?"

Greta nodded her head in agreement.

"She don't let you get away with things like the other supervisors," said the tall nurse.

Nellie whispered in Catherine's ear. "That's very unprofessional for them to be gossiping like that. And right in front of the patients."

I watched Greta talking to the other nurse, hands on her hips, bellowing how she hated this or that. Then her manner and voice softened when she said, "Do you know anything about Dr. Robinson?" I had no idea who that doctor was, but by the look on Greta's face, he was someone of great interest to her.

The brown-haired nurse slanted her head and narrowed her eyes. "Why? What about him." There was an odd tone of hostility in her voice.

Greta appeared to understand something in the unspoken words, the bearing of the women. She backed off from her a few inches. "Oh, never mind."

"Greta. He's hands off."

From their posturing, I thought that a catfight was about to break out. I wondered if there was something territorial going on with the mention of the doctor.

I had that same sick feeling I had when around Roy. I didn't like or trust her, and this was only her first day. It bothered me that she was a woman. I was raised to believe that women were the trustworthy ones who took care of others. Women were the ones with compassion, and it was men that I had to watch out for. But since being admitted to this institution, I'd come to realize that cruelty isn't limited to any one category of people.

The next time Nellie got up to stretch her legs, Greta marched over to her and commanded, "Sit down on that bench and stay there until I tell you to get up." She looked at the other women on the bench. "And that goes for the rest of you pathetic animals."

We spent the remainder of the day, close to four hours, without moving. When we were told to do so, we stood up and marched to dinner. After we ate, we went back to that hard, wooden surface. We remained quiet until nightfall when Catherine mentioned to Nellie, "We have a spare bed in our dormitory. You can room with us."

Nellie nodded approval.

I thought of Annette's now empty bed. Still feeling the loss, I held back my tears. But that's getting ahead of myself with how things unfolded in 1887 before Nellie arrived. And how Annette's bed became unoccupied. And what happened with Roy.

A Different Kind of Angel

Chapter Twenty-Four

Klara

End 1886 –1887 before Nellie arrived

The blizzard ended, but the despair of being cooped up behind dull walls had gotten me down. Smothering boredom had undoubtedly contributed to my doldrums. Thinking of Roy's return made it harder for me to daydream, to escape into the relief of my fantasy world. Thankfully, with enough effort, I was able to drift away. Far away from the asylum. Back to better times. Into fantasies. Perhaps it was the Roys of the institution that drove the women deeper into those fantasies, never to return to reality. Maybe that was better than my choice: hanging on to my sanity and the pain that went with it.

Looking out the window at the snow, to the piles of icy, white, sparkling drifts that had formed into mountains, I thought of Kiev. I used to love watching the snowfall. It was exhilarating to see the white, glistening flakes defy uniformity. I'd see so many different shapes when I looked very carefully. Some looked fat with spikes while others appeared like threads. I once saw a snowflake that looked like a spider. Papa used to compare snowflakes—frozen then melted—to people. On the surface, we all appear different. His deep eyes held mine, making me feel warm on those cold days when he'd continue. But inside, my Klara, in here, his hand went to my heart, here we are the same. I used to ask him if our hearts and lungs were all the same. He'd laugh and shake his head. No, sweet child, but our feelings, our emotions, they are the same. We grieve when a loved one dies. We get angry at abuse and cruelty to the innocents. He'd have to repeat that to me many times as I was growing up. It took me a long time before I understood it.

Papa's snow comparison started to take root one day in temple. I saw one of the girls attending the service who looked very sad. Dorothy Finklestein was smart, beautiful, popular and from a well-to-do family. I envied her. She was the girl with the fine garments and the handsome boyfriend. Dorothy had what I wanted. On that day, she looked as if she was about to cry. I went to her after the service to ask if she'd like to talk. This popular girl, who seemed to have everything going for her, was inwardly insecure and lonely.

"I have no siblings," she sobbed. I don't know why she was sad about that and didn't ask. She continued, "I envy you with your happy family."

She envied me! And I envied her!

When I told her, she laughed. I laughed, too. I then invited her to my—meager compared to hers—home. We were friends for several years before she became ill with a cold that she never recovered from. I went to her funeral. My papa and mama came with me. It snowed that day. There in the falling snow were her parents and very few other people. It was then that I gained a deeper understanding of her loneliness. I thought of our shared envy when we first became friends. We grew close, Dorothy and me, discovering how similar we felt about so many things; yet outwardly, we were so different. Papa's lesson about common human emotions when he talked about melted snow all being the same became clearer.

I felt sad thinking about Dorothy. I couldn't help wondering if the snowstorm had unleashed that memory. Just making the connection that something in the present might have stirred up a past painful experience lightened a heaviness that sat on my chest. The crisp air became more comfortable for me to inhale.

Four days had passed since the storm, four days closer to Roy's return. The fierce, overpowering blizzard and its peaceful, gentle aftermath taught me something about myself. I realized how much my emotions were like the weather. Like the blustery front that had moved on. All on their own, my feelings came and went. I held onto the tiny hope that my spirits would lift.

Gazing out at the melting snow, I saw something move onto a tree limb. It looked like a little snowball. I scrunched my eyes to gain a better focus. There, in that white ball, was a pair of yellow eyes and a black beak. It fluffed out its feathers, and I saw that it was an owl. A beautiful, white, snowy owl. The minute I swiped a hand to the window to clear my breathy mist, it extended its broad wings and flew off. As it disappeared into the sky, I felt Catherine's presence behind me.

"Did you see?" I asked.

"Yes, wonderful."

Wonderful. The sound of that word after seeing something wonderful to behold put a smile on my face. I was lost in that moment. That magical creature came into my life exactly when I needed it. For the time being, I felt back in the external world. I went about the rest of that day, Catherine by my side, without worry about what was to come.

A few more days passed. The weather still held a chill, and the staff didn't want to take us outside. I didn't care how cold it was, I simply longed to be out of those gray walls and escape into nature.

I remembered sulking when Papa wouldn't let me play in overly cold weather. But then he knew what to do to lift my spirits. Come, Klara, dance with Papa. He'd hum a tune, and off we'd go dancing around the living room.

It started when I was younger, still the only child, and Papa would put me atop his shoes and dance about. With me on his feet, he'd sing and laugh, my very own princess. That was his nickname for me, Princess. Oh, those were happy times that extended to when Abram, Shakna, Josel, and Anna were born with song and dance erupting in our home. One at a time, the girls took turns on Papa's shoes with the boys following his moves from behind. Mama didn't want to join in, preferring to sit on the couch laughing and cheering us on.

A patient let out a high-pitched sneeze. In an instant, I was pulled from my comforting memories to stark, forlorn reality. Another sneeze. It sounded like a kitten I once had. Ah, Mr. Skvik, my kitty. My forehead itched, and I rubbed it as, once again, I flitted off to a happier time. Mr. Skvik earned that name because he made a tiny little squeaking sound when we got him. (Skvik is the Yiddish word for "squeak.") Holding him sent me into fits of sneezing. My sneezes turned into wheezing and trouble with breathing. Mama and Papa were worried.

"Klara, I am sorry, but that kitty is not good for you. We must remove him from our home." Papa spoke softly but firmly.

Tears filled my eyes. "But Papa, I love him! Maybe he just needs a bath. Or there's something else in the house making me sick."

Papa shook his head. "The only thing that has changed in this house is the kitten."

I cried all night when Papa gave him away.

My sneezing and breathing problems stopped after three days. For a while. I made friends with a girl who had a cat. After a visit to her house, I came home red-eyed and sniffling. Mama gave me a knowing wink when I went to visit that friend. She never let on to Papa.

But Papa had his secrets, too. A couple of weeks after he gave Mr. Skvik away, he was late to supper. He said he had to put in extra time for carpentry work on a special job. It turns out that the special job was for me. He spent those secretive hours in his shed whittling a wooden cat. After eight days, he came to supper at the regular hour holding a bag tied with rope.

"For you, miss animal lover," he smiled.

I untied the bag. There was my hand-carved Mr. Skvik replica, painted to perfection with a label on its chest. I hugged Papa, kissed him on the cheek and said a heartfelt, "Thank you, Papa! I have the best Papa in the whole wide world!" From then on, I slept with my toy cat.

More memories came and went as noise or some commotion would bring me back to the present. I walked around the hall, noticing different patients. Some looked distracted; others appeared quite normal. Perhaps they were. I'd seen people in distressful situations look worse than some of the women surrounding me. I turned to look back out the window and wondered if that owl would return, just as one might eagerly anticipate a treasured guest coming over for an evening of delicious food and interesting conversation.

Just then, I felt arms around my waist and a gentle, lilting voice in my ear, "Mama."

It was Tillie. She'd really taken to me. And truth be told, I thought our connection was sweet. Sweet with bitter undertones. I was curious about her story. She was unable to tell me, and I never pushed. Same with Rosie. Aside from Tillie's insistence on calling me Mama and Rosie's baby fantasy, they didn't act much different than various people I'd encountered at different stages in my life. There is a fine line between ordinary and unusual, I thought to myself. Where does sane end and insane begin? I've no idea. Perhaps we're all just one traumatic experience away from crossing that line? I certainly had pondered where my limit was, and many times I probably had crossed it only to be pulled back by something in the present moment, like the owl. Or Tillie's arms around my waist.

I turned around to face Tillie, her smile warming my insides. "Look, Tillie." I motioned to the last of the melting snow. "Almost gone. Soon we go outside. Walk."

"Walk in cold. No!" She hugged herself and shuddered as if she was cold with all the apparent soundness of judgment as I possessed.

"Yes, cold."

"Walk when warm," she smiled.

Smiling back at her, I nodded.

With that, she returned her arms to my waist.

Her affectionate cuddle warmed me.

That night as I was changing into my nightgown, I looked at Tillie. She seemed unaffected by being in the asylum. The loose smile on her lips and her distant eyes reminded me of grandma Gelfman, Papa's mother. Bubbe Adel sat in her rocking chair for hours. With a grin on her face, she gazed empty-eyed into space, not recognizing her family when we tried to make conversation. That was the first time I saw my papa cry, and it made me feel sad for him. But I didn't feel sorry for my bubbe. Although she seemed far away, she looked peaceful. Contented. At eighty-two-years old, how could simple contentment be a bad thing? But Papa missed her. He missed his mama looking into his eyes and lighting up with recognition. That was something he didn't get philosophical or objective about, like with so many other things he found tragic. A terrible shame to see this, were the words that brought his tears. My zayde, Papa's father, handled it better than Papa. I assumed that it was his stage in life, being Bubbe's age as well, that gave him the strength and grace to accept the ravages time takes on a person's body and mind.

When I shared my thoughts with Mama, she shook her head. Then she smiled. "Klara, you are young. These things are not easy to understand. A boy losing his mother… it's different."

A boy? My papa, a boy? The thought of him as a young boy had never occurred to me! I smiled back at her, my beautiful mother.

I realized I was smiling when I returned to reality. Before going to Catherine to read a few pages, I went to Tillie to hug her goodnight.

A Different Kind of Angel

Chapter Twenty-Five

In the middle of the night, someone's coughing awakened me. It was Catherine. I waited to see if she would fall back to sleep before getting up to see if I could help her. She stopped coughing, and her soft, regular breaths told me she had fallen back to sleep. But in the morning, her voice sounded raspy. Her face was flushed, too. The thought of Catherine getting sick gave me a stomachache.

I quickly dressed and went to her. "You look sick."

As she tried to clear her throat, a gurgling noise came from inside her chest.

My eyes widened. "Oh! You not sound good. I get—"

"I'm okay." She looked away from me.

Clearly avoiding telling me how she was feeling, I reached for her forehead. It was the warmest my hand had felt since summer. "Catherine, you have fever."

She took hold of my hand and gave it an affectionate squeeze. Then her watery, bloodshot eyes focused on mine when she said, "Please, Klara, don't worry."

Annette had been listening to our conversation. I was completely surprised when she approached Catherine and me. In a manner I can only describe as natural and normal, she agreed with me when she said, "If you're ill, you need to go to the infirmary."

I remembered that the infirmary was where Annette went on the night she was brutally beaten by Nurse Candace. During that earlier incident, she incoherently babbled to the nurse. I wondered, is Annette—the woman who wanders about the dormitory giving herself make-believe baths, squeaking odd sounds and making death wishes—more coherent than any of us imagine? Her concern about Catherine and her advice was clearheaded and appropriate. I was gradually learning that determining whether a person is sane or insane is more complicated than all those "experts" might think; it certainly was in Annette's case.

Catherine put a hand on Annette's scab-laden arm. "Thank you, Annette."

Nothing further was mentioned about Catherine's condition as we all readied ourselves for another long day. At breakfast, Catherine didn't have an appetite. She moved her spoon around in a bowl of porridge.

I had to say something. "Please, drink tea. Have something."

She stared at the cold cup of light-brown liquid. Rubbing a finger over its rim first, she then lifted the cup to her lips. She drank a tiny sip but struggled to swallow it. A protrusion in her neck bulged out as she exerted effort to wash down the fluid. Spittle ran from the corners of her mouth. She shook her head. "I can't." Catherine sounded like she had a mouth full of rocks.

I felt so helpless seeing my dearest friend suffer. A sudden, overwhelming wave of fright overtook me. I felt as if I was drowning in the very air I was breathing. I sat up as straight as I could to try to gain control of myself. I took a few rapid breaths, slowing them down one after the other. Clarity returned.

The rest of the day, my attention was pinned on Catherine, who was on the bench beside me. My nervousness intensified as her condition worsened. By mid-afternoon, she looked pasty and exhausted with sagging shoulders and drooping eyelids. She coughed up thick, dark mucus and gasped. Spasms of high-pitched wheezing came from her before her eyes rolled in her head, and she fell over onto me. Passed out.

That scary sight sent me into a panic. I screamed, "Help!"

Chaos followed with other patients crying for help, laughing, or wildly prancing about. Harry, the guard on duty, rushed up to us with a scowl on his face. He slapped Catherine's cheek.

Any composure I might have had was instantly gone. I grabbed his arm without thinking about the consequences and pleaded, "No! Please, do not hit her! She sick and—"

Pulling his arm back, Harry then landed a solid, rounded fist onto my mouth. I sucked on my lower, cracked lip, tasting blood.

Nurse Edith took her time getting to us. "Sit her up," she ordered.

"No." Blood dripped down my chin. "Please. She need doctor."

Taking no notice of my having spoken in English, Edith squawked, "Shut up!"

Harry gritted his teeth and looked like he was about to punch me again. I stood up, out of his arms' distance and pleaded with my eyes for help. Just as I was about to say something else, Edith gave me a menacing look that shut me up. Then she put a hand on Catherine's forehead. "This one is sick," Edith sighed. She whistled for another guard to help Harry.

They carried her off to the infirmary. I prayed that she would be okay. I couldn't bear to lose her. But I knew that a simple cough could be fatal, as it was with my friend Dorothy Finklestein. The day was long and frustrating. No word came about how Catherine was doing. I was worried to death about her. Drowning in worry. Feeling utterly useless and consumed with anguish, I wanted to smash a fist on the bench.

When I rubbed my forehead raw, I started in on my lower lip. As soon as a clot formed, I licked it off. And when fidgeting didn't help, I got up to move around. Worrying will get you nowhere. Mama's voice came to me. Worry is the thief of daylight, she would tell me. When I looked at my mama with what must have been bleary eyes, she knew I didn't understand. You spend time on worry, and you miss out on spending your time on what's important, she had explained.

As I frantically paced, I let the thief of daylight get its way. Earlier, Catherine had told me not to worry, but I could no more change my concern than I could change the color of my eyes. There was no lever to pry me out of my apprehension. I continued to aimlessly move about the hall until Nurse Edith barked an order at me. "Sit down! And stay still!"

Unable to jiggle and squirm to release my tension, my mind became extremely active. Please don't die. Please don't die. Please, I moaned inside my head. If Catherine died, I didn't know if I'd want to continue living in that pit. It was then I saw Tillie across the way tapping a foot on the floor. And Amelia sitting quietly with her head down. And Rosie baby-talking to her intertwined arms. And Annette watching me with eyes as bright and clear as polished silver. She seemed to be keeping watch over me with the same clear-headedness that she demonstrated when Catherine became ill. Despite all her ranting about killing, I had grown to feel safe around Annette. Continuing to look at my dorm mates all going about their antics undisturbed helped calm my frazzled nerves. Because of them and the other patients I interacted with from time to time, I would continue to find meaning in this miserable place. As long as I had someone to tend to, someone to smile at, someone to touch, I would occupy my time with heart and purpose.

Thankfully, two days later Catherine returned to join us for breakfast. Appearing weak and pale, she slowly ate her food and drank her tea. My body relaxed. My smile returned. The heavy weight of my worries melted away. Across from us at the table sat a smiling Annette.

I thought I would sleep better having Catherine back. I thought I was more settled since my realization that I had found a way to exist in the asylum with meaning. I was wrong. Fires raged in my dreams; homes were burned to the ground. Women and girls were raped. Men were dragged away, and if they resisted, their heads were chopped off. Blood gushed everywhere, and families were torn apart. In the middle of it all, a menorah burned to the ground. A flaming Bible opened to the page that described the menorah—the seven-pronged, ancient Hebrew lampstand—used by Moses in the wilderness as a portable sanctuary. The symbol of Judaism burned into a blob of unrecognizable putty in my nightmare. Just before the Bible was completely ash, I startled and sat up erect. Disoriented, I tried to get my bearing, to stop the room from spinning. Sweat poured from my face, my chest, and my underarms.

The rest of the women remained asleep. The moon shined a sliver of light through the window onto dull, stained, cracked, beige walls. I was imprisoned in the worst kind of jail. Unjustly robbed of my freedom, my captors forced me into filth and starvation while subjecting me to continuous physical and emotional abuse. How could I accept that fate?

Before that, I had floated upon a vast ocean enduring sickness and the loss of my papa. I had been driven from my homeland. But before any of that, my village had been pillaged and plundered. Homes and businesses were looted and burned by mobs and rifle-wielding soldiers. Many people were injured and killed. For what?

Why did this hell on earth befall me? What crime was I guilty of? What sin did I commit? What sin did any of my people commit? Why us? Because we were Jewish?

From the depths of my soul, the torment awoke. It happened the night Catherine returned. I had no idea what had opened the floodgates. My body shook from disbelief and the sheer enormity of everything I had gone through since 1881. Tears of anger, hatred, revenge and overwhelming grief surged through me. At the bottom of the well was a pain so deep and wide that I could hardly breathe. I don't know how my heart continued to pump, or my lungs continued to take in air.

Enough! I've had enough. In that concave bed, in the middle of the night, I wanted to die.

To stop feeling.

To stop remembering.

To stop sensing.

To stop existing.

I had good cause to feel that way. Good reason. The candle of brutality that blazed in Kiev also burned in America. Was there anything left to hope for?

Chapter Twenty-Six

A soft feathery sensation moved across my forehead and down my face, tickling my left cheek. I opened my eyes to see Tillie's hand. "Breakfast," she said smiling. "I made you pancakes."

There standing over me was a bundle of sweetness that took the sting out of the horrific night I had just had.

My sleep-deprived, grainy voice squeaked out, "Pancakes," as I took hold of her cold hand. Latkes, my favorite pancakes, were different than the flour-made ones I'd had once in America. We also had flour pancakes, but potato latkes were my favorite. Topped with Mama's homemade applesauce, it was a special treat. And just like I had received Mama's gift, I smiled to welcome Tillie's. It didn't matter that she was in a world I would never know. She had reached out to me, in her trusting way, to offer comfort. I needed that. Real or imagined, it didn't matter, her kindness helped me feel less lonely. What I had felt earlier when I awoke into the black room in the middle of that dark, sweat-soaked night was emptiness. A devastating, crushing sense of loss. And now, here before me was a different kind of angel filling me up.

In that freezing room, I sat up to receive the embrace of Tillie's warm good-morning hug. The affection of her arms around me spread through my body. The outside snow had all but melted into the new day. But the chill in the room directed my attention back to the snowstorm. Once again, I thought of Papa comparing snowflakes to people. It was more than just emotions we had in common. We had needs. I was pretty confident that, just like when the sun comes out and melts ice to water, our needs are very much alike when we soften from love.

I tightened my arms around Tillie. I had a need, and she helped to fill it. There with our bodies touching, I felt a sense of belonging. In this lonely, desolate place, it was Tillie who was satisfying this most fundamental need. I had also been helped by Rosie who let me into her dream world, and yes, Annette who had just started to open up. At times, in a strange way, Amelia's mostly quiet demeanor helped to calm me, too. Along with Catherine, those women met some of my most basic longings: to belong, to feel safe, to trust, and to be understood. It seemed so contradictory that I had moments of feeling safe when surrounded by so much brutality. But I did. These simple connections ignited the resilience my soul had all but lost. And I was better for it.

As I got up and dressed, I watched Tillie. Did she know how much she helped me? Was her mental illness a flimsy façade? Was she stuck in it like a fly entangled in a spider's web? Was she blind? Or could she see through the unreal translucent fibers of the fantasy she had created? There was something that appeared alive in her that morning. Like a child having a make-believe tea party, she was sparkling.

I remembered when Bubbe Raisa was on her deathbed. When Mama's mother's ankles swelled, and she had difficulty breathing, the doctor told us it was her heart. "Like everything else in life," Dr. Feldman said, "our bodies break down." With a sad look, he told Mama, "It is Raisa's time." Not long after that, Grandma took to her bed. When she slipped into a coma, we all took turns at her bedside. In a silent moment, Mama spoke to Bubbe.

I asked her, "Why are you talking to her when she can't hear or understand?"

Mama said, "What appears to be might not be what is."

I tilted my head, "I don't understand, Mama."

She went on to explain, "Perhaps our dear Bubbe is still aware but inside a body that is breaking down and can no longer respond. Perhaps she can still hear us."

I nodded. Perhaps Bubbe could hear us. Who could know? I thought of that when I wondered about Tillie. I looked at the women in the room and wondered if they were aware like me.

I held Tillie's hand as we marched to breakfast with a slow-moving, smiling Catherine right behind us. For the rest of the day, Tillie followed me around like a puppy. It was every bit as endearing as her offer of pancakes. Catherine took great pleasure in watching us. She commented to me (once Tillie was out of earshot), "Our little Tillie has taken a liking to you."

Our little Tillie. I liked the sound of that. I liked a lot about how the day had unfolded. Something had changed inside of me. It felt like a reprieve from the tight-chested, heavy-hearted feeling I had had since leaving Kiev.

Three days passed without incident, probably because Nurse Greta, Harry, and the other especially mean ones weren't on shifts during that time. And we had a little over a week before Roy was due back. That break from the horrific days filled with unprovoked abuse was a relief. But was it only a brief lull that would not serve to feed the seed of faith that Papa had planted in my soul? Never lose faith. How many times had I heard those meaningless words repeated inside my head? When I looked to the sky, all I saw were moving clouds. There was no God to trust in and to be loyal to. There were only the slightest acts of kindness that had begun to seep into my shattered heart. Never lose faith. Papa's voice was firm. Certain. Even as he was dying. As for me, I was a disaffected, confused Jew. It would take a miracle to restore my belief in God.

The few good days came to an end when Greta returned to work. Her mean streak flared to holy hell. It was during our lunch meal. At the other end of the table I sat at, an unusually pale woman must have swallowed something the wrong way and started to choke. Greta was on her like an angry honeybee, screaming obscenities. As the patient continued to struggle, Greta did nothing but yell. "Shut the hell up!"

"She's choking," A patient near them dared to say.

"So what?" hissed Greta.

The patient who had spoken got up and shook the coughing woman until she spat out a piece of dry hard bread.

Greta, now really riled up, smacked the woman who helped and shouted, "Get back to your seat! Now!"

The woman who had choked cleared her throat. Greta roughly lifted her chin. "Open your mouth." With her other hand, Greta proceeded to lift the woman's cup of tea.

The unfortunate patient raised her hands as she submissively pleaded for mercy. Greta proceeded to pour warm tea into the patient's mouth, nose, and down her front side. The woman's eyes were bulging and darting back and forth. I thought for sure Greta was going to suffocate her. The disturbing scene came to an end when someone dropped a bowl to the floor. The sounds of the shattering bowl seemed like a cannon blast. All of the patients and staff suddenly froze in silence watching Greta. Greta stopped, looked around at all the eyes on her, shoved the patient back to her seat, adjusted her uniform and said, "Go on. Finish your food, or you'll spend the afternoon hungry."

As much as I wanted to hold onto the pleasant feeling from my encounter with Tillie, I could no more make it last than I could reverse time. I was frustrated that awful things always seemed to crush and replace the favorable ones.

For the rest of the day, I couldn't stop thinking of that choking woman. I hated that Greta had been so cruel to her. In bed that night, as the moon cast light onto cracked walls, my forehead burned. My itchy skin crawled with nervous energy. Feeling the lines of tiny muscles contract on my upper arms, I tensed my hands into fists. I wanted to strangle Greta. I squeezed my pillow so tightly, I ripped the material. Feathers escaped. I didn't care.

Where is the help? Where is it? After over four years in the asylum, I asked that less and less. I had almost stopped caring. At times (like that night), I felt drained and empty. There was no help when I was unjustly committed. There was no help when the same happened to Catherine. There was no help when we were all starving from malnutrition and appetites failed us because of the gut-wrenching, mercilessness treatment from the staff. There was no help when women were thrown from a cold night into a yet colder bathtub of water and strung up like wet clothes. There was no help when women were hit, kicked, had their hair pulled, or were belted and chained. A stabbing pain settled into my chest.

With one slow, painful inhalation I wondered if the little things that Barbara and Harriet tried to do would change anything? Would the pleasant moments with Catherine and Tillie and Rosie ultimately do any good? Would they give me back an appetite for food? For life? And who could possess such yearnings when malicious hands were always near?

When will it end? And how?

Before long, I'd have an answer.

A Different Kind of Angel

Chapter Twenty-Seven

The days moved along with the same rhythm and routine. But something was agitating me. I couldn't say why, but I was as skittish as a wild horse. I was too preoccupied with all that happened in the last week to think clearly.

My attention went to what looked like a new stain on the floor in the hall. It looked like a long-armed monkey. That sent me off into mental pictures of animals and, very oddly, something I had read a while ago by a Russian writer, Ivan Krylov. It was a fable titled, The Inquisitive Man. Why, in the middle of this stark, cold, terrible environment, would I think of a fable that was about a man who goes to a museum? I tried to remember the story and figure out why it would come to mind now.

Then it came to me. The man in the story noticed all sorts of things, tiny things, but didn't see the elephant in plain sight. A sudden moment of illumination struck me when I also recalled that Dostoevsky later referred to that scene in his writing. He stated that the supposed inquisitive man didn't notice the elephant in the museum. Why? Perhaps he didn't want to see it? Maybe this was my answer, too. I didn't want to see what was building up inside of me. I didn't want to see it or mention the big, dark cloud looming over me. The one threatening Catherine, too. Roy. He was due back very soon. I used the constant daily distractions to help me block mental images of him. If only the diversions had absorbed my agitation…

I was brooding when Rosie approached me after lunch. Her arms were huddled tightly to her chest. She was breathing rapidly. Her eyes were darting this way and that. She had pressed her lips together so hard that her mouth was just a straight line. Looking both frantic and dismayed, she said, "I have to go to the doctor."

A hot flush of alarm ran through my chest. "Why, Rosie?"

"Come with me. Come with me."

"Rosie, you sick?"

"Not me. The baby! Come, baby turning blue. Blue!" Rosie screamed.

A guard named Jackson came running over. Nurse Edith followed quickly behind him.

My body recoiled back against the damp wall. My shoulder muscles knotted, and time moved slowly until Edith smiled. "I'll take it from here," she said to Jackson.

I couldn't read the look on Edith's face. She had an odd smirk and faraway expression.

"My baby!" Rosie pleaded for Edith to help the imagined infant that she was now rocking back and forth on her lap. "Blue. Help!"

"Yes, I heard you. I heard you halfway down the hall, Rosie." Edith's elsewhere-look disappeared into a sharp focus. "Just calm yourself down, or you'll rile up the rest of the lunatics."

Rosie stuck her lips out in a pout, like a stubborn little child wanting to get her way.

I flinched when Edith raised a hand toward Rosie.

Edith then patted Rosie's shoulder. "You calm down, and the baby will calm down." She smacked her lips, and, with that, she turned around and walked away mumbling something that sounded like, "Pathetic."

That was strange compassion. I wondered if Nurse Edith knew something about Rosie's past. I saw a reaction in Edith when Rosie said the word blue. I didn't know what that meant, but it seemed to suggest that perhaps Rosie was committed because something happened to a baby she had given birth to.

Rosie broke out in tears.

I felt at a loss, but I wanted to help her. Without thinking, I leaned into her. "Rosie," I whispered. "Give me baby. I can help."

"Thank you! Thank you! Thank you!" Her tear-stained eyes lit up.

"Shh," I breathed into her ear as I held out my arms. "The baby needs to sleep." I wanted to calm her any way I could. Who knew what another outburst would bring? How many times would she be so lucky as she just had been with Edith? "Shh." I continued to sway the baby as Rosie cuddled next to me.

The day moved on.

* * *

In 1887 changes were happening outside of my small, isolated world. I learned about many of the events that took place while I was in the asylum after the fact. Perhaps I was attempting to recapture the years that were stolen from me. Once I was out, I craved information. I asked questions. I read newspapers. And I discovered that the Interstate Commerce Act authorized federal regulations of railroads. Plans were implemented for American Indians to receive allotments of land, and those who accepted were granted US citizenship. Germany, Italy, and Austria-Hungary renewed their triple alliance. A woman named Anne Sullivan taught the word water to a deaf-blind girl named Helen Keller. And Oscar Straus, a Jew, was appointed the United States Minister to the Ottoman Empire.

While the world outside had changed, 1887 also brought two major changes to my life inside the asylum. The first change concerned Roy's return. The second would happen towards the end of summer with Nellie's arrival.

I awoke with unease three days before Roy was due back. We had heard rumors the day before from a couple of nurses gossiping at breakfast that he was expected to return any day. "He's so handsome," giggled a stout one.

Handsome! There was nothing about that ugly, vindictive pervert with his receding hairline and frizzy sideburns that was attractive. The way he spewed putrid-smelling saliva through the opening in his front teeth was disgusting. My lips tightened as revulsion squeezed my gut. Breathe. I looked to the floor beneath the table to avert my attention off the wildly inappropriate chatter. Feet were wiggling and tapping, creating new smudges. My attention went to the cleaning woman who came to the facility. With her bucket of dirty water, she mopped the floors leaving new stains. The swish marks from her mop gradually took my attention elsewhere.

My mind transformed the blotches on the floor into the cleaning woman's bucket overflowing with grimy, dirt-filled water. Water that some patients stuck their hands into to wash when no one was looking. I, too, wanted water to clean myself. To wipe away the layers of filth and grease that covered my body would've been such a gift. And I needed to do something to clean myself of the images of that evil, deviant man who lurked around the halls preying on innocent women. Roy was possessed with the most wicked of demons; he was Satan incarnate.

Satan! That was the horrible monster I overheard Papa philosophically discussing one afternoon with some of his men friends. He seeks to seduce humans into falsehood and sin. Satan. Not being a great believer in everything I heard about the Bible, I thought that was a ridiculous, made-up story. What person would believe such nonsense? But after the pogrom and being in the asylum, I felt differently. I saw Satan (or his henchmen) in the Russian soldiers who laughed as they massacred innocent men, women and children. In Roy. Were they born evil, or did something (or someone) corrupt their souls as boys or men?

Spoons rattled, and plates shifted as women finished their breakfasts. I drank my porridge and all but a small portion of my tea. I poured the rest over my hands and attempted to wash the sticky, filthy layers of dirt off my face. My hand moved to my matted, greasy hair stuck to my head. I pulled the loose strands into a knot on the back of my neck. It was going to hurt to untangle it with my next bath. But just the thought of a bath and the idea Roy might be there on our cleaning day made me put my knees together. I wanted to protect my virginity that felt threatened by him. I wanted to save the last untouched part of my body. I wanted to keep myself pure and hold onto my dream that someday I would be felt, touched, caressed in loving intimacy. I wanted my virginity to be unbroken when I fell in love and for nothing to travel through my sacred feminine place but my husband and our children at birth.

The whistle blew indicating breakfast was over. I released the tension in my knees and my thighs. But I held onto the tightness in my privates. It was hard to let go of the tension down there. I wanted to continue to hold myself tight like I did when I held in my urine.

"You were far away, Klara." Catherine touched my clammy hand.

It had taken Catherine a couple of days to regain her energy. In that time, she pretty much kept to herself. Looking at her now, the lightness in her amber eyes, the dark under-eye circles all but gone, and her pasty complexion looking less pale, made me feel somewhat less nervous. I caressed her hand.

The next two days passed without incident. But as each minute shifted to the next and the sun met the moon, it was hard to sleep. Hard to get my mind off what would come. I tried to convince myself that maybe things would be different this time, but it was impossible. I'd seen what Roy had done, heard his words, saw him swallow liquor as if it was water, and could never forget his twisted, ugly, diabolical face while he was abusing a patient.

Word came that Roy was returning the next morning. I don't remember breathing for the rest of that day. That night, dinner felt like a funeral. A gloomy heaviness pressed in on my chest as I listened to the sounds of teeth hitting cups and slurping liquid, forks rattling, and chewing sounds. It reminded me of the gathering after Bubbe Raisa's burial. Being that Catherine was quiet and withdrawn, I assumed she felt the same.

I looked at the slab of something dry and hard on my plate. It was surrounded by a couple of tablespoons of watery, slimy white rice that looked like it was about to turn moldy and a few wilted lettuce leaves. My mama would have tossed that plate of food in the waste pile.

My fork broke when I attempted to cut the hard square of meat. I picked it up with my hands. When I bit down on it, I thought I'd chip a tooth. I dipped it into a brown liquid that I wasn't sure was tea or dirty water. That didn't soften it either. A balding woman sitting across from me looked around for extra handouts. When she saw my failed attempt to eat the rock slab on my plate, she opened her mouth. With yellow teeth showing, she sat there drooling like a dog waiting for a handout. After another unsuccessful attempt, I handed her my piece of meat. Without so much as a word of thanks or a nod, she put the whole thing in her mouth. She was still chewing when we left.

The procession from the dining room moved to the hallway. I sat on a chipped, flaking bench next to Catherine and hoped I wouldn't get a splinter. I tried to unglue my attention off rapidly arising thoughts that served me no good. As dusk approached, we were marched to our dorm. Still preoccupied while I was undressing, I heard retching. "Who—"

"Rosie," replied Catherine. "You okay?"

I turned to see Rosie on her knees by the side of her bed, vomiting nothing. "Morning." Rosie gagged.

I had no idea what she was trying to say until the second word came out of her mouth. It made me cry.

"Sickness," gasped Rosie.

"You have morning sickness?" asked Catherine, now by Rosie's side.

"Yes," replied Rosie.

I wiped the tears from my face and went to offer them support. Rosie had stopped walking about swinging her crying baby. She was no longer patting its back nor screaming that it was blue. Now she was back earlier in her pregnancy. Back to the beginning.

Rosie smiled when she pointed to her abdomen and said, "Baby."

"I'm happy for you, Rosie." Catherine smiled in return.

I nodded agreement. Down there on her knees with Catherine beside her, Rosie never brought up any food or liquid. But when the gagging stopped, she said, "All better." Continuing to smile, Rosie held her belly. "A baby." She got in bed and went to sleep.

Tillie, eyeing me, sat up. I went to her. As I hugged her, Annette waved a goodnight gesture with her hand while Amelia snored.

All seemed normal, but, oh, how quickly that changed.

Chapter Twenty-Eight

Annette's voice woke me up in the middle of the night. I had been tossing and turning and only just fallen asleep when I heard her say something that sounded like killing. That woke me right up. I watched as she got up out of her bed and roamed around the room rubbing her scabby arms as if she was bathing. The sound of her dry hands scraping crusty flesh made my forehead itch. But I remained still. I didn't want to move and disturb her.

"God," she whispered loudly enough for me to overhear. "I did it for you. I did what you told me." She mumbled more that was unintelligible as she continued to pace.

Hearing God along with killing piqued my interest.

Annette continued babbling until she stopped pacing and looked to the ceiling as if seeing through it to the heavens above. "I hear you," she raised her voice.

I wanted to tell her to lower her voice. I was fearful that one of the night staff would hear her. She'd been punished enough. But just as I was about to say something, she quieted. I took in a slow deep breath through my dry mouth.

"He was a bad man. I couldn't have done it without your guidance, dear Lord," she muttered. "Candace was also mean. But you told me to leave her alone because she's a nurse."

Nurse. Candace. She must have been referring to the night Candace Millhouse (who dragged her from the dorm), threw her in a cold bath, and hung her up by outstretched arms. Although that incident happened shortly after I arrived, it felt as recent as a week ago. I'll never forget that look of pure hatred coming out of Nurse Candace as she slammed the door open, putting a hole in the wall then taking it out on Annette. My body trembled recalling how she made the rest of us get up and watch Annette's torture.

We hadn't seen much of Candace lately, which made me wonder why Annette was talking to God about it. Just her mention of God brought back the mental image of her strung up like depictions I'd seen of Christ's crucifixion.

Annette stopped pacing. She went to her bed. Got down on her knees. And said, "What do you want me to do about it?"

What do you want me to do about it? Annette's question bounced around inside my head. Do about what? Listening to Annette talk to God in such a direct, personal way made me feel sad. Why? At first, I thought it was because of our collective pitiful and often dangerous life in this asylum. But, it was more than that. Annette had something I lost long ago: an intimate connection with God. I had stopped praying. I had stopped talking to God. I believed that my words to Him went unheard. And I was sick and tired of feeling neglected. Annette, you pray for me. You pray for the rest of us. Maybe God will hear you and have mercy on all of us. I closed my eyes and hoped nothing horrific would happen to any of us anymore. Being here was torture enough.

Pitter-patter. Pitter-patter.

Something moved across the floor. Annette got into her bed. And thankfully stayed quiet. The tiny footsteps quickened toward what looked like a big, long-legged spider with glowing eyes. A cloud moved over the moon, and the light was gone. So was the uninvited guest in our room.

Hugging my pale-blue blanket to my chest, I tucked myself into a bony ball. Thoughts of the rat-infested, den of disease we lived in and the wicked, perverted Roy ran through my head until I must have dozed off.

Dawn finally came. The day had arrived.

I didn't want to get out of bed. I didn't want to get dressed. I didn't want to march in line to breakfast. I didn't want to slurp another bland, liquid morning meal. And I didn't want to go to the next destination, only to sit in the hall and wait for torment to descend upon us. Trudging through those early activities was like walking through sludge.

Sitting next to Catherine, who had been quiet and withdrawn all morning, I looked around. On that cloudy day, a chill ran up my spine as I anticipated seeing Roy. We hadn't seen him yet, and I was curious why. Albert and Harry were on duty. So was Greta. Finally, around mid-afternoon, he bounded down the hallway. Loudly slurring words. Spittle was spewing through the space between his front teeth. The bulge from his liquor flask was visible in his shirt pocket. Laughing at something, he slapped Albert on the back. He looked around and locked eyes with mine before putting his attention on Catherine. To my surprise and relief, he made no effort to come near us. Instead, Roy continued to joke around with Albert.

Still, I remained nervous. I feared it was just a matter of time.

Nerves sent me to the chamber pot two times before I decided I had to try harder to get my attention off of Roy and what might happen. I tried to think of things to occupy my thoughts. Mama came to mind.

Mama's soft lips spread kind words. Her touch was always warm with compassion. I thought of her generosity: sharing her sewing prowess, bringing baked goods to neighbors along with pots of soup when they were going through hard times. When we complained that we weren't getting enough or were hungry, she'd say, "Sharing will fill you better than food."

"My stomach disagrees with you, Mama," Abram once retorted.

"Shh, my boy, your belly has not been invited to this conversation," she laughed.

The rest of us, except for Abram, laughed along. Shakna snorted her food up her nose in fits of amusement. Laughter. Those were the best moments. Even Abram finally gave in. One couldn't hold onto anger or resentment in the midst of so much affection. Thinking back to those precious times was painful.

Catherine changed her position refocusing my attention from my aching heart. "Want to walk," I asked her.

"No," she whispered. "I don't want to move right now."

She was like a motionless squirrel, alert to danger.

The day progressed. It was dinnertime. An image of Mama calling us to dinner, gathering around the table, noisy laughter and good conversation, came to me. I remembered the love that permeated our home just as the aroma of baked goods did. It was always such a lonely, nostalgic feeling when marching off to eat in the asylum. There I was in a large room filled with clanking silverware, offensive odors, and disturbing noises coming from deranged, unhappy, and unjustly committed women. Nothing could have been further from being with my family around the meal table in Kiev.

"Boiled mutton," someone yelled as she slammed a fork into a small, tough piece of meat. "Do you know what this is?" She stood up on her chair as if speaking from a podium, swinging her arms wildly. "Sheep! They killed sheep. Death to those who kill sheep. And death to—"

Albert kicked the chair out from under her. As she fell to the floor, she grabbed hold of her plate and flung it at him. Roy ran in from the hall with a cigarette hanging from his lower lip. He put it out on the woman's forehead then joined Albert in kicking her. When she stopped protesting—stopped making noise, stopped breathing—they lugged her out. All order dissolved in the dining hall; mayhem resulted.

"Murder!" screamed a patient.

"Murder!" repeated several others until a chorus of howling women joined into a riotous rebellion.

Plates flew.

Some women hid under tables.

Food and drinks landed every which way.

Annette, hands-in-fists, stood in a corner panting.

Rosie ran out holding her belly.

A guard fired his gun into the air. Thankfully, no one was wounded.

Catherine grabbed my arm and led me out.

I was stunned from the horror of what I had just witnessed. The rest of the evening, I bowed my head and held back an ocean of angry tears.

That night Annette kneeled at her bed in silent prayer.

Catherine quietly undressed, got in her bed, and closed her eyes.

Amelia snored.

Rosie huddled with her arms around her belly rocking back and forth.

Tillie called out for her mama. I went to her. And we cried together for our mamas.

A Different Kind of Angel

Chapter Twenty-Nine

Annette's pleas to God continued well into the night. She kneeled on the hard floor with palms held together, head reverently bowed, beseeching Him to give her answers. I couldn't help listening intently.

"Ouch," she whispered before standing and moving about shaking her legs to rid herself of what seemed like a cramp. She clasped her hands over her heart. Walking in long strides, stretching her legs, I noticed a twinkle of something between her fingers flash a reflection from the unclouded moon. Then it disappeared from view; it looked like a jewel.

Annette's communing with God had increased since the snowstorm. I had no idea why until she looked upward and said, "Look what I have." I couldn't see it. Yet. She smiled and lifted the object in her left hand above her head. The shimmering object was pointing to the ceiling. Or perhaps, in Annette's mind, it was pointing to heaven above—God's house. The higher she moved her arm upwards, the more dazzling the object became. "Thank you for sending this to me during the storm that broke the window in the hallway. I knew it was You, God. Grabbed the best piece I could find for Your purposes. Been keeping it under my mattress. I'm ready now."

Finally getting a better look, I saw that what she held in her outstretched hand was a shard of glass. It must have come from a window that was damaged in the hailstorm. I knew that a couple of windows had shattered, and glass flew, but I had no idea that she had confiscated a piece. A piece that looked like a dagger.

Annette's throat began to gurgle as she continued to speak, and what came out was hard to understand. What I did hear sounded like he's an evil man. He did a bad thing today. After a long pause, as if she had been listening to someone talk to her, she responded in a perfectly clear voice, "Not now?"

Not now? What on earth was running through her head? I assumed that the mention of an evil man was in relation to what happened at dinner with the poor woman who was killed in the dining hall. Earlier in her prayers, she had mentioned killing.

I knew that word from the reading I had done with Catherine through the years. In our time together, she had helped translate words using the book or by pointing to objects. I remember when the word killing came up. She moved her hands into a very light choking position around my neck. She then pretended to stab a dagger into my chest. She acted out various examples of killing. I understood. Yes, I knew that word and couldn't help asking myself, Does Annette have some deep, dark, secret plan?

Although she didn't feel like a threat to me or appeared as such to any of the other women, the mention of killing and the shard of broken glass foretold trouble. Certainly for Annette but who else might be in danger? I couldn't hear the rest of her mumblings as I tumbled in and out of a very fitful sleep preoccupied with the misery I felt over the indefensible violence that caused the patient's death earlier that day. I was consumed with outrage that Roy and Albert would most likely not be punished for their crime.

For the next few days, Roy kept to himself. He seemed to look for ways to minimize contact with patients. Although he appeared more tempered, my fury toward him intensified. I hated looking at his smug face with a cigarette hanging from his lower lip. I resented that he drank openly from his flask. I detested the beastly sound of his laughter. And I was right about him not being punished for murdering that woman. Neither was Albert. Both were guilty vermin, but I hated Roy more. I clenched my fists at the sight of him. Given a chance to act on my feelings, I don't know what I would have done to him. My attention went back to Annette and that sharp piece of broken glass.

Four days after Roy had returned, he made his way toward where Catherine was sitting quietly on a bench. He stumbled over one of his feet and nearly fell, cussing words that should never be used in front of women or out in public. That ill-mannered pig turned my stomach. Attempting to stand erect, he swayed back and forth before approaching Catherine. When he wiped sweat from his beady forehead, I wanted scream for him to get away. I wanted to kick and stomp on him, just like I had witnessed him do to others.

Standing near where Catherine was sitting, I walked over to them and reached out for her hand. Leaning in toward her ear, I whispered, "We go for walk, yes?"

Roy moved in front of me, slapping my hand back. "Geh ou the way. She goin' wit me. Moof it, Stupit!"

I had never heard him slur his words so badly. I reached for Catherine's hand again, knowing he could knock me senseless. Or worse. I didn't care. Any fear I harbored had transformed into nervous energy motivating me into action. At that moment, there was just that threatening, murderous hulk targeting my friend. I moved between Catherine and him, facing Catherine. I felt his breath on the back of my neck. The heat of his body came closer.

"Roy!" Albert's call interrupted us. "I need you."

There they were. Two guilty villains. Criminals who got away with too much! For much too long! But Roy was the instigator. I saw how different Albert was when Roy wasn't around. However, it was no excuse for Albert going along and not standing up to Roy. Not doing right by the women. They both deserved to be put in prison. And never released.

I was fuming, but that break gave me a minute to think. What would my lack of control, my forthrightness with Roy, have done? What beneficial result could have possibly come from my foolish action? I trembled just imagining what I had most likely just escaped. Hoping that Roy was too inebriated to remember what had just happened, I grabbed Catherine and walked to the opposite end of the hall.

That day I was lucky. He didn't seek out Catherine. Or hunt me down.

The next day, we didn't see Roy before lunch. It was a relief especially since we knew that Nurse Barbara was due back the following morning. But that afternoon, he returned. Again, he stank of alcohol, sweat and foul breath.

Keeping my anger restrained, I didn't interfere with his approach to Catherine. It hurt to stand by and watch him point a finger into her chest, right between her breasts, and command her to have a bath. Greta stood by, smiling like a co-conspirator. Why in heaven did she gain any pleasure seeing patients abused? Why did any of them do what they did?

I watched them cart off Catherine with a group of other women. I was not included. The rest of the afternoon and evening dragged on without Catherine's return. Finally, I saw Catherine when I was marched back to our dormitory that night. She was on her bed. Her sheets were wrinkled and dangled to the floor. Her blanket was bunched up at the foot of her bed. I knew this wasn't her doing; she always kept her bed neat. One look at her swollen red eyes, her hands gripped between her legs, the bleachy pungent smell, and I knew Roy had raped her. In her bed. Right there for anyone to walk in on and witness. Her sheets stank from that familiar, disgusting odor he had deposited on her bedding once before.

When I reached a hand to touch her bare shoulder, she pulled back. "Catherine, how I can help?"

She cried and shook her head back and forth. Catherine's sobs turned to wails. Overwhelmed, feeling too many emotions all at once, I sat there, not knowing what else to say or do. I sat beside her into the night while Annette talked to God, Amelia snored, Tillie moaned in her sleep, and Rosie tossed and turned.

What had earlier been lewd overtures and vulgar conduct had turned into an immoral, degrading, criminal assault. Roy had taken Catherine to the bath, watched her undress, and grabbed hold of her inappropriately while Greta stood by, passively inciting him. Then he dragged her to her bed and had his way with her. At my prodding, Catherine finally told me what had happened. I felt murderous rage. Not just at him and his obscene wickedness but that it was allowed to happen. Once again, no one was held responsible. No one was made to account for the unlawful behavior. Damn them! Damn them!

The next day, Nurse Barbara returned looking refreshed and relaxed from her vacation. I envied her. When she got around to where I was sitting with Catherine, I asked if I could talk to her. I trusted her enough to risk speaking English. To open up. Someone needed to do something!

"Of course, Klara. Come let's walk."

Not wanting to leave Catherine alone, I took hold of her hand when I stood to join Barbara.

In telling her what had happened to the woman in the dining room the other night and to Catherine the day before, she sorrowfully shook her head. She surprised me when she admitted, "I know about it."

Taken aback, I stuttered, "You…you do? Wh…Why…Why isn't any—"

"Shh." She moved me down the long hall near the doors that led to the dorms.

When we were far enough from anyone's earshot, I asked. "Why these men get away with…with…that? Why!" I was so shocked that my questions sounded more like demands for answers.

When the volume on my voice became dangerously high, Catherine squeezed my arm to get me to calm down. She was the one traumatized, yet she was tending to me. "Shh, Klara," whispered Catherine. "Shh." She grabbed me into a hug.

Feeling Catherine's breath on my cheek, tears spilled from my eyes. "Sorry. But not right!"

Nurse Barbara wiped away the tears pooling in her own eyes. With a deep, slow sigh, "This is very difficult," she said as she reached a soft hand to my arm. "I can only tell you what I know. I am violating policy, but I owe you two that much."

When Catherine saw I had calmed down, she released her hold on me. I looked at the pained expression on her face, then back to Barbara and waited while Barbara took a moment to inhale a couple of slow, deep breaths. Halfway through telling us, she had tears running down her face. Barbara repeated what we knew: Roy had family in powerful places, which was the reason he wasn't fired. What we didn't know was that the administrator in the asylum who had him transferred out from time to time was retiring. "Roy's family doesn't care what he does. He will never be dismissed. It would prove to be an embarrassment. I'm so sorry, Catherine."

Slumped shoulders, drooping eyelids, and slow, shallow breaths—Catherine's hopelessness felt like a ton of rocks pressing on my heart. "They do nothing?" I murmured.

"I'm afraid not. I'm so sorry."

So was I.

A Different Kind of Angel

Chapter Thirty

When 1887 moved well into another sweltering, humid summer, things changed dramatically. And not for the better.

Earlier, Catherine had told me she could endure Roy's sexual abuse.

"Why?" I was outraged.

"If I resist him, then what? What happens to me? And everyone I associate with? He can't be trusted. He's a very evil man, Klara."

There was no arguing with that.

It saddened me even further when she said, "I am not a virgin like you are."

In our conversations through the years, I had told Catherine about my life in Kiev, my family, and what happened to us. I had also told her I had never been intimate with a boy or a man. Perhaps, I thought, someday I will be free to find that love. I dreamed that, in time and by some miracle, someone would realize that I had been sent to the asylum by mistake, and an ethical person with power would help me. For nearly five years, I had endured misery and squalor without losing faith that justice would somehow prevail for me. And for Catherine. And God knew how many others. That was the hope that kept the fiber of my dream alive. Catherine knew everything about me with one exception—that I was a Jew.

"Catherine, virgin or no, it wrong what he—"

"It's an evil I can live with, Klara," she interrupted. Then attempting to shift the topic as she had done so many times in the past when it came to Roy's abuse, she softly said, "Perhaps one day we will be free of this place. When that happens, I'll cleanse myself of his filth."

"Yes, when free. We will have proper bath." I forced a smile. What I wanted to say was, Don't let that beast touch you again! But what good would it do?

Her eyes were drowning in lakes of sorrow. She hugged me.

Feeling her arms around my ribs and comforted by the connection we had, I whispered in her ear, "Some things we live past, and we be okay." That loving embrace from Catherine, her warmth, helped me endure. That was the last time I protested to her about Roy's sexual advancements.

Whenever he had the opportunity, Roy seized Catherine and had his way with her. Too many nights she went to bed crying. So did I. By summer, his drinking had gotten worse than ever. I didn't know how he was able to stand upright. When he entered the dorm at night, I feared for all of us.

My dread intensified when Annette made her appeals to God both loud and clear, at least to me. "When should I kill him?" she asked the ceiling in the middle of the night when everyone but me was sleeping.

Kill him! Reflecting on what Annette had just said, my legs trembled with fear. What was bouncing around in that head of hers? I had no one to talk to about Annette, no one to tell. There was no one to help any of us. Catherine was my usual confidant, but I couldn't say anything to her; she had enough worries. And talking about it with Annette was out of the question.

When I scratched my forehead bloody raw, I began to chew the inside of my cheek. I was in a state. Too many breaks to the chamber pot at night. Too many knots in my neck and shoulder muscles. Too many horrible images flashing before my eyes. I couldn't think straight.

As Roy's drunkenness escalated, Annette's praying increased. She began pacing down the halls, extended hands braided together and lifted upward, talking to God. "Tell me when Lord!" Her tone varied between beseeching reverently and demanding forcefully. She wore a wide-eyed, dark, icy, haunted look that gave me shivers. The Annette I had roomed with for so many years seemed inhabited by someone else. No longer was there a light of recognition when she looked at me as I waved goodnight.

Scarier than the way she looked was what she openly said in the hall during the day. It became worse at night when she'd loudly scream to God, "Tell me when!"

When?

I was especially frightened when, on a sticky, smothering, hot day at the end of the summer, Roy picked on a relatively new patient. She was young and shy in manners, huddling into herself on the floor with knees bent to her chest. She rocked back and forth, minding her own business when Roy came back from a break. Wobbling up to her, he slurred, "Ged uph!"

A woman behind them, out of Roy's sight, snarled, "Leave her alone."

Turning around to where the interruption came from (and nearly toppling over), venom shot from his eyes. "Leaf her alone? Who shed that?"

No one responded.

"D'you wan me ta leaf her alone?" He yelled into the air. His arms flew out to correct his balance as he swayed. Gobs of slobber and bits of tobacco spewed from his mouth, landing on the curled-up patient on the floor.

Continuing to hold her knees with one hand, she shielded her head with the other. Moaning inaudible words, she continued to rock back and forth.

"Shee how I leaf her alone," Roy's face twisted into what appeared to be intense concentration as he pounded a thick-soled boot down on the woman's head. Nearly falling on top of his victim, he somehow righted himself. Roy's whole manner changed after that. It appeared as if he was less drunk, more in control. More dangerous. He kicked her until blood came out of her nose and mouth. He didn't stop even when she was lying flat on the floor.

Before he landed another blow, Nurse Greta came out of the break room and yelled at him. "Stop!" She stepped between the woman and Roy.

"Come on, Greta," he grumbled.

It surprised me that Nurse Greta, who had been so neglectful and abusive in the past, ordered him to stop. "That's enough." She pushed him back. "Go on outside and cool off." That may have been the only time I witnessed Greta being helpful.

"Cool off," he mocked her, "in this heat?" He trudged off laughing.

While Greta got two guards from another section to help carry the patient to the infirmary, Annette's agitated pleas became frantic.

"Help me! Help me! Help me! He's going to kill us all! When? Tell me when!" She was making wild hand gestures close to the wall, flailing about as if trying to strangle a demon materializing through the flat, dense surface.

That night things turned unimaginably violent.

In our dorm, we were changing into our nightwear. A nearly full moon cast a bright light into the room. The door creaked partially open, but no one entered. I had my nightgown on and got into bed. Amelia and Rosie were already medicated and drifting off. Tillie tossed and turned. Annette was down on her knees, her brown, oily hair slapping around each time she rotated her head to the right then left. Catherine took off her day clothes and reached for her nightdress when the door flew fully open.

Roy charged in waving his metal alcohol flask in his right hand.

Catherine froze. Naked with erect nipples, she covered her genitalia with a hand while grabbing for her blanket with the other.

Four long, clumsy steps and Roy was upon her.

He ripped the blanket from her. Dropping his flask to the floor, he pushed her onto her bed.

Annette screamed, "When?"

"Shut up," Roy barked as his hands groped Catherine's breasts and he used his knee to separate her legs.

Once again, Annette shrieked, "When?"

Roy was pumping up and down and letting out throaty moans. "Yes, yes, yes!" He was too preoccupied to see Annette slide a hand under her mattress. He was still too distracted to notice her pull out the shard of glass.

"Yes," his panting became more rapid. "Yes," his groaning turned to a loud roar. "Yes!"

He had no idea Annette was standing over him.

He opened his mouth to wail another word. All that came out of him was "Oh my—" before he fell off Catherine and grabbed his neck.

Annette let out a high-pitched, screeching, staccato laugh.

Catherine quickly got up and put on her nightgown. Tears streamed down her tight-lipped, wide-eyed, panic-ridden face.

Stunned, I was trembling even though the room was thick with heat and humidity.

Amelia, Tillie, and Rosie slept. They remained asleep for the rest of the night.

There he was, on the floor, his motionless-hand by the puddle of blood surrounding his neck. Red bodily fluid mixed with spilled alcohol. Shocked and numb, doubt flooded my mind. Was he really dead? Or just unconscious?

Annette turned quiet. She seemed to have come out of a dazed state when she focused her attention on me. Gazing into her calm, knowing eyes, I could see that Annette was back.

How many times had I wished him dead? He was the brutal guard that deserved what he got. He was the tortuous Russian soldier that should be wiped off the surface of the earth. He was the face of hatred that I wanted to destroy. But I knew deep down that I couldn't live with myself if I just stood there and did to him what the brutal soldiers had done to my family. As much as I wanted him out of my life, and out of Catherine's life, I had to be responsible. It was in my bones to do right. I turned to the door.

Annette stopped me. Shaking her head, she said, "Not yet." She stood before me, blocking my path to the door.

Not yet? Not yet what? I tried to reason with her. "Annette," I panted, "I need to get help."

I looked over to Catherine who remained in a silent state of trembling shock.

"Not yet!" Annette repeated.

The forceful tone in her voice carried so much command—a resounding authority—that I froze.

230

She watched Roy. And waited. His blood stopped flowing. He had not taken a breath for many minutes. His wide, vacant eyes did not look at peace. Annette finally moved away from me, unblocking my way to the door. She rubbed her left hand through her hair messing it up, so it stood way out, winked and gave me a small smile.

For a split second, I stopped. The expression on Annette's face puzzled me. But I didn't have time to figure it out. I opened the door and yelled for the night nurse.

Harriet entered.

She looked to Annette who had reverted to incoherently babbling, waving the bloody piece of broken glass. Annette looked wild with her hair spiked out, bouncing her head from side to side as if she had no idea what had happened. But when Harriet turned to me, out of sight from Annette, Annette winked at me once again. A tingle ran up my spine.

Did Annette have a moment of insanity that night when she killed Roy? I will never know. I do know that when she looked at me, we made a familiar connection. And at that moment, she appeared as sane as me.

Harriet went for help. When she returned, she helped transfer Annette to a ward where she would be heavily sedated. And she arranged for the cleanup and removal of Roy's body.

I neatened Catherine's bed and assisted her to sit beside me. I remained next to her, listening to our breathing until the dawn broke. We never spoke about that night. Nothing needed to be said. It was another painful memory to stuff down with the others I hoped not to remember.

A Different Kind of Angel

* * *

While the shock of that night lingered for me, life in the asylum went on as usual. Although the constant state of my nervousness lessened with his death, I hadn't gained any pleasure out of Roy's demise. It was another pathetic stone on a path of suffering. While one source of trauma was gone, others continued. If the news of Roy's death at the hands of a wildly mad patient had any impact on the staff, it didn't show in the immediate days following. Greta was still mean to the core. Heartless. She continued pinching us, pulling our hair and ears, kicking us, randomly taking food away from us and giving us degrading tongue-lashings. If that wasn't bad enough, she encouraged Albert to drink more and insisted he beat women. "Slap her, Al," Greta would command.

Albert would gulp some booze and smack an innocent, unsuspecting patient across the face.

"Have another swallow, Al." Greta would invariably find someone half-crippled or a woman nearly blind from malnutrition and agitate Albert. "Go on, grab that whore."

Continuing to incite Albert with orders, one patient who appeared to be like Catherine and me—aware, sane—watched. When Greta turned in that woman's direction, Greta's face turned red. Tendons twisted on her upstretched neck as she aggressively pointed her chin out and said, "What are you looking at?"

The patient started to shiver and bent her head. She put her trembling hands between her knees to calm them. She tried to make herself as small and invisible as possible on the bench.

Greta took the baton off Alberts's belt and stormed toward the woman with her hand raised high. The patient cowered like a fearful dog, with its tail between its hind legs. I didn't want to look, to see

232

any more of the senseless brutality. Torture us enough and we begin to act like ill-treated dogs. But the punishers were the real beasts. They're disgusting monsters! I had had enough!

Mama advocated kindness. Papa promoted strength. Be Strong. When I saw that woman flinching, I vowed that no matter what they did to me, to my body, I would show strength. Be strong. Papa's words echoed in my head. Looking at Greta and Albert and thinking of all the others who have done so much harm, I pledged to the memory of my parents that no matter how they hurt my body, I would never let them rob me of my soul. My dignity. You won't break my spirit. It was when I realized, I will never become like them, that I knew I had finally become the strong person my papa wanted me to be. I recognized that like cream rises and possesses the rich nutrients to fortify a body, rising above hate is where courage lived. To join their battle would only serve to weaken me. I am strong. Being in that lunatic asylum I learned how strong I really was.

The day before Nellie arrived, I saw Annette down the hallway with the group of women who were belted and chained to each other. She smiled as I passed by her. Each night, the sight of her empty bed saddened me. She had been a part of the group that had been my only family for so long. Regardless of what she had done, I grieved her absence.

A Different Kind of Angel

Chapter Thirty-One

Nellie and Klara

Annette's bed was empty for a few days before Nellie's arrival. It pained me to look at the lonely sheets and pillow awaiting a new occupant. My heart hurt recalling the years with Annette. My feelings toward her had zigzagged more than any of the women in the dorm. At first, I was afraid I might catch some disease from all the red, puss-filled scratches on her arms. Then I worried about her as she became the innocent victim of Nurse Candice's and others' unforgivable cruelty. At times, I was mystified by her prayers, rants and fitful behavior; at other times, I was frightened of her. Sometimes, her strange behavior simply wore on my nerves. For as crazy as Annette could seem, at times she surprised me by acting as sane as I was (and much more sensible than most of the staff). In the end, I felt safe around Annette, but I also felt afraid for her. I feared that she would take an action that would cause her more suffering. In some inexplicable way, I surmised that she wasn't motivated by evil but rather a protective disposition towards some unspoken injustice. When they took her away to be locked up with the criminally insane, another scar formed on my broken heart. Despite the little I did see of her when I walked way down the hallway to that restricted area, I missed her.

It was fortunate that Nellie arrived to an empty bed in our room. The blue blanket that Barbara Lincoln had given to each of us the day after the book-destruction incident was missing. In its place was a warm, beige cover. Harriet had taken the blue blanket to Annette. "It belongs to Annette," said Harriet. That may have been a small act, but it showed a mountain of compassion. In hindsight, I see that it was the simplest acts of generosity that began to sew the pieces of my tattered heart back together. Those acts gave me hope that perhaps someday I would be able to breathe without feeling like I was wearing a tight corset.

Next to Annette's old bed, Nellie's glance met mine at the brownish stain on the floor. The dark-red blood from Roy's neck had left an ugly brown blotch. After his death, no one talked about Roy. But each time I looked at the stain he left, nausea born from revulsion rose in my belly. It was a relief not to have him around torturing Catherine and all the others, but the image of his empty eyes and splayed neck was painfully etched in my memory. Alive or dead, that evil man haunted my thoughts. The memories never left, but their jagged edges hurt less over time.

The vile abuse we were subjected to with Roy's obscene behavior had stopped, but the overall brutality at the asylum continued. Nellie keenly took it all in on her first day as a patient. She was very chatty and surprisingly open about the fact that she was not insane and had been falsely committed.

Catherine said, "Same here. And…" She pointed a finger in my direction, "…Klara, as well."

"What happened to you?" Nellie directed her question to Catherine.

Catherine, in her considerate way, responded. "My story isn't as bad as poor Klara's."

"Why is that?"

"She was sent here because she didn't speak English." Catherine reached out for my hand. "My friend is from Kiev. When she arrived here, she only spoke a few words of English."

Nellie listened. When Catherine was finished telling my story, Nellie shifted her gaze to me. "You were taken without your own consent from a free world to this asylum and given no chance to prove your sanity?"

Not completely sure why I hadn't wanted to reveal that I spoke English, I hesitated to respond to Nellie openly. I suppose that it was because I was still suspicious. My early attempts to communicate with the police, the judge, and the nurses got me into this nightmare where I was viewed as incoherent, drunk, and insane. After all of my failed attempts to convince anyone otherwise (anyone with enough power to remedy their mistake), it was hard for me to open up to strangers. To trust. But Nellie seemed so earnest. Did I have to be so cautious? After all, Nellie was a patient just like me. When she remained quiet, I yielded. Finally, I responded. "Yes."

"And do you now speak and understand English?"

"Yes."

Nellie shook her head. Etched on her face was concern. Her eyebrows narrowed and pointed downward toward the bridge of her nose. I could tell that Nellie was interested in my situation by the look on her face and her posture. Leaning forward, she said, "Compare this with a criminal, who has every chance to prove his innocence. Doubtful he would claim insanity." She smacked her lips. "Who would not take that chance for life and choose to be declared insane and never have any hope of escape?"

Catherine shook her head as I tried to comprehend what Nellie had just said.

"Have you consulted with a doctor about your situation?" Nellie asked me.

"Klara hasn't seen a doctor," Catherine responded for me.

"And you," Nellie asked Catherine.

"Early on when I first arrived, I had. But my circumstance quickly became a waste of that doctor's time." Catherine then fully explained her situation, including the part about the affair with a powerful politician who had her committed.

"Oh, I see," Nellie frowned. "And there's nothing—"

"No," said Catherine.

"I've seen the doctor," said Nellie. "And all he did was ask stupid questions. Where was I from? What color were my eyes? I told him, 'I'm not sick in body or mind, and I do not want to stay here. No one has a right to shut me up in this manner.' But he took no notice of my comments, wrote something down on a piece of paper, and then told the nurse to take me away."

Concentrating on Nellie and Catherine, I remained silent.

Nellie looked around the dormitory. The other women had undressed and gotten into bed. "Are they medicated?"

"Yes," responded Catherine. "They received drugs in the hallway before bedtime. Not everyone has to be medicated."

"I assume you and Klara aren't."

"Correct, but if we were to act up, that would change."

Nellie looked around the stark room with the bare walls and windows covered with bars. It had grown darker, and a draft moved into the room. "Well, I won't need them either."

We ended the conversation, undressed, and went to sleep. Once again, I didn't sleep well that night. It was too soon after the horrible incident with Roy and Annette. When the others slept, my thoughts awoke. I felt as if I was at war with myself. Relief and gratitude that he was out of Catherine's and my life conflicted with the horror of watching his murder and doing nothing to stop it. I had vowed always to do the right thing, but, for the first time in my life, I didn't know what was right. I only knew that there was no reprieve in my tortured soul from the removal of one villain. And just like the blood stain left on the floor that would need more than soap and water to be removed, it would take more than Roy's death for me to heal.

I looked over to the new patient. Nellie hadn't been tainted from years of abuse in the asylum. She was still inquisitive and confident; I knew it from her bright, lively eyes. There was something strangely exciting about her. I found her believable, including the manner in which she professed her sanity. But how long would she remain unscathed?

A Different Kind of Angel

Chapter Thirty-Two

Initially, there was something about Nellie that made the cruel moments seem less brutal. She constantly asked questions. She spoke back to the staff. She laughed about the way she thought she looked after her bath. Everything about her was unusually refreshing. Nothing could lessen the intentional cruelty, the squalid conditions or medical neglect, but somehow—in some unfathomable way—Nellie brought a little lightness into our lives during her first couple of days with us. Like everything else good that happened in the asylum, that would change.

If I had known then that I would remain imprisoned less than two weeks more, I think I would have better endured the following events that unfolded. None were as horrible as what Roy had put us through, but the collective impact of these incidents shredded my already frayed nerves. In the remaining days that Nellie was there, she would see the brutality we had been subjected to for years. She would bear witness to endless, unpredictable torture. I had withstood so much torment—directly and indirectly—and it had left its ugly mark on me. My thick curly hair had thinned to filthy, matted nests. I could see most of my bones draped in my dry, wrinkled skin. My once-soft lips had cracks so deep that they often bled if I opened my mouth too much while eating. And that was just my body. My mind was another matter. Anguished. Struggling. I had to continually remind myself that there was still a reason to live, even in this hellish place.

At breakfast, something on the plate smelled foul. When one of the patients vomited up bile, Nellie lifted a piece of stale bread to her nose. "It's rancid. And look here," she pointed to a green, fuzzy section. "It's moldy! Is this what you get to eat?"

Catherine looked around. Not wanting to draw attention and the wrath that came with it, she nodded.

"No wonder that woman is ill," said Nellie.

No sooner did Nellie make that comment than Nurse Candace approached the woman who heaved her meal. "Clean that up." She yanked a clump of the patient's hair then shoved her face down to the small puddle of slimy, yellowish-brown spit-up.

From where we sat, I could see the patient's neck muscles contort and twist in resistance. Refusing to comply with Candace was not wise. She pulled the woman up and out from where she was sitting then dragged her out of the dining room. A few of the other patients followed behind, including Nellie.

The past couple of days had been cloudy, and the weather had turned cooler. It was still early morning, and the sun hadn't begun to offer its warmth. Nurse Candace took the patient to the freezing bathroom with Harry's help. When it was over and Nellie returned to us (we were sitting in the hallway), Nellie told us the all too familiar story. "They kept her standing in the cold water, thinly clad. I watched the poor crazy captive shiver. I opened my mouth and told the nurse that I thought what was happening was horribly brutal."

Catherine's shoulders jerked back in surprise. "Nellie, you are bold."

"Bold or stupid," smiled Nellie.

"Candace did nothing to you? She hasn't been so generous with others."

Nellie looked back over her shoulder to see who may be listening. "She was too busy beating up on that patient to come after me. But I did hear unladylike verbiage directed at me."

"Be careful." Catherine's whisper had an intensity to it. "She could make it very bad for you. And if you make her mad, you won't be the only one she takes it out on."

Nellie rubbed her chin and replied, "Oh, I see. I hadn't thought of that."

The soaking-wet woman with dripping clothes and hair came into the hall. Her arms were covered in gooseflesh, her lips were blue, and her eyes were sunken in despair. She huddled on the end of a bench with her back turned to the other patients and moaned softly.

Nellie looked over at her. "I wish I had something to offer to warm her up with and—"

Catherine interrupted, "Best just stay put." She looked around and not seeing Candace continued. "You don't want to rile Candace."

"I don't mean to bring punishment onto myself or to exacerbate it for anyone else, but it is not right to stand by and allow these things to happen. Won't the staff help?"

I rubbed my forehead while listening to their conversation.

"Most don't. A few do," Catherine carefully scanned the hall, then continued, "but they're not on duty today."

"Um-hum," urged Nellie, prompting Catherine to continue. She listened intently, seemingly absorbing every word.

"It's rare, but we do get some help."

"I would like to hear about it," said Nellie.

"Nurses Barbara Lincoln and Harriet Brownstone have been very decent to us." Catherine went on to give the very inquisitive Nellie a few examples.

The day moved on to lunch. Nellie took one look at another piece of dry toast and strong-smelling, rancid butter and pushed it aside. A patient across from her asked if she could have it. Nellie passed it over then drank from a bowl of tea. "This tastes like it was made in copper." She disgustedly puffed out her lips. "No sugar and as weak as water. Dirty water." That also was passed along to another patient. "I don't think I'll relish dinner tonight."

"You must force food down," said Catherine, "else you will be sick."

Nellie glanced around the room, at mouths chomping food and slurping liquid. Loud chattering—some of it understandable and much of it not—from conversations between patients and individuals talking to someone or something only they could see, also filled the room. Wild head movements. Flailing arms. Indelicate body noises. Nellie frowned and shoved her bowl away from her. It appeared as if she had seen and heard enough. "Who knows, what with these surroundings, one could easily go crazy."

"Certainly. And to have a good brain, the stomach must be cared for." Catherine again attempted to coax Nellie to eat something.

"It is impossible to eat that stuff." Despite all the coaxing, Nellie ate nothing else the rest of that day.

Back in the dining room for dinner, my nervousness heightened when Candace came into the room and abruptly ended the meal. Nellie quietly questioned, "Why is that nurse ending the meal so soon?"

Catherine whispered, "Because she wants to."

244

"That's mean," replied Nellie. "Half the patients have hardly begun. And," she motioned with her forehead to a couple behind Nurse Candace at the door, "They haven't even eaten."

Candace glanced our way.

Nothing further was said as we stood and proceeded into the hallway to sit on hard benches. As another sun cascaded to earth, we marched back to the dormitory. By that time, I had blood on my fingers from scraping my scar raw.

"You're going to dig a hole in your forehead." Nellie was referring to my habit of scratching.

That night Nellie got to see Rosie in full-blown hysterical labor. This newcomer's level of intelligence was fascinating to me. She came to me while I tended to Rosie. Watching for only a few moments, Nellie had one word to offer, "Hysteria?"

Hysteria? My crinkled forehead and tilted head must have expressed my puzzlement over that word.

Catherine was in earshot and responded, "Yes."

"I wonder what happened to her," said Nellie.

"Klara thinks she may have lost a baby and gone mad. She told me that she knew of a case back in Kiev that was slightly similar. The woman gave birth and within a couple of weeks manifested severe emotional problems. The baby was taken from her. It wasn't a loss from death but, a traumatic loss all the same."

"You're okay, Rosie," I repeated over and over to calm the screeching coming out of her as Catherine and Nellie watched. "Shh, now Rosie. You don't want to wake the other patients."

"Ouch!" Rosie thrashed and twisted, knees bent and legs open. "It's coming." Rosie managed to say that with her teeth clenched.

I wiped Rosie's perspiring face then pretended along with her that the baby was out. "Look, Rosie! It's your baby." I was hesitant to refer to it by a gender since I didn't know if my suspicions were accurate that Rosie may have lost her baby. I repeated, "Look, Rosie," moving my arms in a swinging motion.

She took the invisible baby from my cradled arms and held it to her chest. She lowered her nightgown and put the unseen newborn to a breast to feed as I smoothed a matted bunch of her wet red hair back behind her ear.

I was fearful Rosie might have been heard, and any minute someone would come barging into the room. Along with Rosie, I broke out in a sweat. Perspiration dripped from my brow. I swiped it dry with the back of my hand and waited to be sure Rosie would remain calm. She settled back in her bed. Her arms went limp, and her breathing slowed into a snore. I was exhausted. But I stayed there listening for approaching footfalls until I could no longer keep my eyes open.

When Catherine motioned to the book, I shook my head and mouthed, "No."

Nellie, who observed what just took place, asked Catherine, "You read together?" Catherine responded with, "Yes, for years now. It's how Klara learned English."

"You taught her?" asked Nellie.

"I helped. Klara's a very bright girl. Loves to read. She caught on very quickly."

"I can see that," responded Nellie.

The following days were filled with much of the same except for what Nellie brought to the mix of patients and nurses. Some of the events involving her made me smile. And oh, how we needed that.

Years ago, I used to awaken anticipating the wonders of the day; now, I dreaded the dawning of a new day. I didn't want to know what was in store for me. All that mattered were the moments when there was relative peace and freedom from misery. What I did wonder about was how Nellie was settling in by her fourth day.

Nellie's toughness became apparent as the day progressed. Breakfast was the usual. She sipped the tea and forced herself to eat some porridge. Oh, the face she made as she forced herself to swallow that slop! She nearly retched before she had the good sense to choke it down. Poor Nellie, the only difference between her and most of us was that we had gotten used to the stench and the taste of the ungodly concoctions the kitchen staff called our food.

I wanted to reach a hand to her to offer some tiny gesture of comfort. I could easily recall the shock I was spun into when I was committed. Disbelief and confusion muddled my head for days until a deep fear descended upon me when I witnessed the unprovoked, spiteful cruelty from those entrusted with our care.

Once in the hallway, I quickly scanned the area looking for who else was on duty besides the unfamiliar nurses I had seen in the dining hall. My throat tightened when Greta pounced on Catherine, Nellie, and me midmorning. With a sneer, she pointed to me. "You. Up."

Greta stood before me, her brownish-hazel eyes fixed in a cold stare that made my chest ache. My knees banged together as I waited for what was in store for me. Then she pivoted to Catherine. "You." And Nellie, "You." When she motioned a pointed finger to a few other women, my knees stopped shaking.

Her whistle sounded, catching Albert's attention. Greta motioned her hand indicating she needed him.

He tossed his cigarette on the floor and put it out by squashing it with his boot.

Tapping her right toe rapidly, Greta had her arms folded across her chest. "Come on, Al!"

Albert frowned. He shook his head as he shuffled over, never increasing his pace. "What's the hurry? I was busy."

"Having a cigarette?" She rolled her eyes.

He ignored her mocking tone. "What do you want?"

"Bath for this lot." She waved a finger at the other women she had commanded to stand and me.

Albert led the way with Greta in the rear. Nellie whispered, "Is he going to do the bath?"

"No, but he'll probably remain in the room," responded Catherine.

"That's not right." Nellie watched Albert's actions, right down to him unlocking the bathroom door and marching us in.

Greta propped herself up against a wall, tipped her head back and closed her eyes. Either she ignored Albert or didn't hear him when he called the first patient over for her bath. Usually, that was her signal to take over and for Albert to stand guard.

Albert waited a long minute for Greta to respond. When she didn't, he shrugged his shoulders and motioned to the first patient to undress. We all watched as Albert pointed to another patient. "You, get that washcloth," he motioned to a dirty rag on the floor. Pointing his index finger at the naked patient, "Clean her!"

We all watched the next few shivering, embarrassed, babbling, incoherent, women receive their baths. The water muddied. The floor filled with puddles from dripping patients. And Nellie watched with a disgusted wide-eyed, taut-lipped expression.

"Next." Albert's voice was monotone. Bored.

The next woman reacted to the cold temperature. Shivering and attempting to get out the minute her foot hit the water, she groaned, "No…"

Angered, Greta refocused her attention on the room and the patient who disturbed her. "Stop moaning!"

"Please, that hurts," the patient cried from the harsh rubbing.

"Scrub harder," demanded Greta.

When it was over, the woman trembled as she stood wet and naked dripping from head to toe.

Then it was Nellie's turn to undress. She turned pale. She held her hands tight at her side, palms gripping the material of her garment. "I will not remove it," she vehemently said.

"You won't remove it?" Greta was fully engaged and looking for revenge. She marched up to Nellie, stuck a finger in her chest and grabbed her dress. "Al, hold her arms." He held firm and tight while Greta forcibly removed Nellie's garment.

Nellie stood naked. Trying to cover herself with her hands, she looked at the other women in the room. And to a small group that had formed at the door for all of three seconds before she jumped into the bathtub with more energy than grace. Through her chattering teeth, she complained, "Darn, this is cold!" Then, she softened her tone and requested, "Please leave my hair dry."

Ignoring Nellie's request, Greta gave Albert a mean scowl. "Go on, Al." When he hesitated, she shoved the patient who had helped bathe the others aside and got up close to his face. "Take care of her, Al!"

Nellie was submerged into the water, head and all, by Albert, who held her too roughly and for too long. She erupted like a volcano attempting to catch her breath, coughing up the dirty bath water.

"Think again before not obeying," smirked Greta.

The scene that followed Nellie's bath was even more horrible. A fragile, sallow-skinned woman, probably in her late-teens, had a nasty sounding cough. A gurgle from deep in her chest rattled when she pleaded to forgo her bath. "I'm not feeling well," she begged. "Can I please—"

"Shut up! I'm not running a hotel." Greta's face turned red, and her breathing intensified like she was going to erupt. "Where do you think you are?"

Without an ounce of consideration, the patient was plunged into the bath. And again, she pleaded for leniency. "Please, I ask, do not have that woman," she looked at the patient holding the dirty washrag, "scrub me too hard. My head hurts from fever. My skin is painful." Tears streamed down her cheeks as she begged, "Please, be gentle."

Greta viciously responded to Albert as he stood by grinning, "Scrub her hard!" To the sickly woman she said, "And shut up, or it'll get worse. Much worse."

That night Nellie was still distressed when she said, "As much as I hated the bath, I would have taken it again instead of that ill girl. Plunging that poor, sick girl into a cold bath when it made me, who has never been ill, shake as if I had been infected with the plague, is criminal."

Nellie looked at me, her deep-blue eyes lined with concern. She surprised me when she changed the conversation away from the ill patient. "I suppose there's been plenty of sorrow to witness."

I nodded.

Catherine remained quiet.

After a long pause, "That bath was awful." Nellie smiled. "I imagine that for once I did look insane," she laughed. "I caught a glance of the indescribable looks on the other patients' faces who had witnessed my fate."

How Nellie had that laughter inside of her was a mystery to me. But what a relief it was to hear it and to see the honest gleam of light in her eyes. Of course, she hadn't been there long enough for that spark to be stomped out of her.

A Different Kind of Angel

Chapter Thirty-Three

I'd had many milestones in my life; I remember some, but others happened when I was just a baby, so I have memories of my mama and papa telling me about them. My first steps. My first words. My first book. The first cake I made on my own. I remember when I was five years old and was allowed to play with my neighbor Sadie. "I'm a big girl," I chirped to my parents. I felt mature. Trustworthy. I returned at dinnertime (just as Mama had instructed) and was greeted with smiles and questions from Papa and Mama. "How was your day?" they asked in unison. We all laughed.

The joyful highlights ended when my family died. All I had left were days—endless days—each one evaporating into the next. Without noticeable change. Just events. None of them uplifting. Even the small bits of kindness that I found in other patients or staff didn't replace the sorrow that I carried in my charred heart.

I didn't know Nellie's arrival would, in a little over a week, set off a chain of events in the asylum that marked the beginning of something new for me. They wouldn't be happy milestones like the ones I experienced with my loving family. No, they wouldn't replicate any of the past landmark events in my life that lit my soul. But they would be significant. However, that was yet to come, and the asylum was still ever present with all the accompanying brutality.

Nellie was very forthright with Catherine and me. She didn't hold back with her unending questions or direct comments. I liked talking with her; it awakened my groggy mind. But she wasn't always discreet. When she spoke to the staff so directly, I was afraid she would be punished. Catherine and I might be punished, too, just because we were near her. It didn't take much to provoke Greta or Candace or many others whose names I've forgotten. Sometimes it took nothing at all, at least nothing apparent.

I saw how Nellie intently watched a patient when a staff member approached, like the time Candace went to Amelia. Amelia was sitting on a bench in the hallway kneading the loose skin under her arm like it was a lump of dough. Candace stood before Amelia, tapping her foot on the floor. Amelia continued to press and stretch the skin on her left arm with her right hand. She rolled it and banged on it like she was in the kitchen mixing flour, eggs, yeast and milk into bread batter.

Having not gotten Amelia's attention, Candace slammed the heel of her shoe to the ground so hard that Amelia's body jerked back. "You want to pull on your skin?" Candace grabbed Amelia's long brown hair, "I'll show you pulling!" She yanked so hard that she stretched the skin on Amelia's forehead.

"Ouch! That hurt!" Amelia squinted her eyes and dared to look straight at Candace.

Amelia, I thought, please don't provoke Candace. Fear pulsed through my body as terrifying images of Amelia being abused reeled through my head. No, not Amelia!

Nellie stood. She walked over to them. "Ahem," she loudly cleared her throat.

Candace, let go of her tight hold on Amelia's hair and turned to Nellie with poison shooting from her eyes. "What. Do. You. Think.

You. Are. Doing." Her hands were on her hips, elbows out, and her feet were planted widely. She made herself as big as she possibly could.

Nellie took in a deep slow breath. "The city pays to keep these places up," she calmly stated, "and pays people to be kind to the unfortunates brought here."

My mouth flew open in surprise. Catherine gave my thigh a tight, nervous squeeze. We braced ourselves for the wrath to escalate. But to our amazement, Candace replied with, "Well, you don't need to expect any kindness here for you won't get it." She slapped her hands as if cleaning them. "I've had enough of your filth," she scoffed. Then she just walked out.

Candace's reaction made me wonder if Nellie had some mysterious connection on the outside, like Roy with his relatives. I discounted that idea as she had told us that no one had her committed. Candace's reaction was just as much a mystery to me as Nellie's behavior.

Nellie righteously continued to complain. Especially about the hair combing we received after our humiliating baths. The procedure had changed through the years. By the time Nellie arrived, as many as 45 women had had their hair combed by either one patient or one of two nurses during one bath time, each using one of the six combs they had in the asylum. Matted, wet hair was pulled and jerked as screams of pain echoed through the room. There was no reasoning with those doing the combing.

I felt sorry for the women who complained of sore heads. Were they to utter a word, the combing became harsher. If they couldn't endure the pain in silence, the combing got more aggressive. I saw one woman pass out. I'm sure there were more.

Nellie gritted her teeth. When the combing was done, she asked, "May I have hairpins."

"No, you may not!" Her hair was roughly pulled back and plaited. The end was tied with a red rag. The rest of us with long enough hair received the same treatment.

Another change that took place around the time that Nellie arrived was patients were ordered to make beds, clean the facility, and complete other chores assigned by staff. Nellie commented to us one night, "It is not the attendants who keep the institution clean for the poor patients, as I thought, but the patients do everything for themselves. And, I heard today that they even clean the nurses' quarters and clothing?"

"Yes," Catherine responded. "They used to have night staff that came to clean, but that stopped."

I wondered why that changed, why the night cleaning staff stopped working in the asylum. My thoughts were interrupted when Nellie said something about seeing a doctor. That also had changed. But it was only for brief visits checking for breathing problems or diseases that might infect the staff. The jotting of notes took longer than the exam. Again, I was curious. What had he written that took so long? Did he make up a false report about my mental condition? More frequently, doctors were seen in the hallway or on visits to the rooms when patients refused nightly medication brought by nurses. But I never saw a doctor about my mental state.

It used to be the walks that diverted my attention from the hopelessness. But even the walks were different than before. I don't know how long it had been since we'd gone outside. By the time Nellie arrived, we would move about mostly inside the facility— down the hallway that led to the area where they confined the violent patients. It was there I saw Annette in belt and chains. Seeing her that way made me want to cry.

There was a day when we ran into long lines of women guarded by nurses and guards. Horror crept over me as I watched women with vacant eyes and emotionless faces, their tongues uttering nonsense. I could tell they were filthy just by looking at them. When they got closer, the stench confirmed their neglected hygiene.

Nellie asked, "Who are they?"

"They are the most violent on the island," responded Catherine. "They are from the Lodge, the first building with the high steps." She motioned in the direction of that building. "The staff brings them out for walks."

Nellie's head turned to the sound of someone yelling. She stood silent, listening to more hollering, then singing, praying, preaching, and other incomprehensible utterances. "That's the most miserable collection of humanity I've ever seen," she whispered.

As the clamor of their passing faded, another line of belted and chained patients approached. One screamed, "You want to kill me!"

Another woman with dark-brown, hardened eyes cried with a smile. She caught Nellie's attention. "That's a horrifying look of insanity stamped on her face."

The last of the patients had two gossiping nurses following them. "There are over 1,600 women on Blackwell's Island," one said.

Catherine gasped.

We remained quiet for the rest of our walk until we came to a low pavilion. On the wall was a motto: While I live I hope. Nellie drew us near and into our ears breathed, "It should read, she who enters here has no hope of leaving."

The days and nights came and went, meeting us with the routine cruelty and neglect we had learned was normal for the asylum. On her eighth day there, Nellie commented, "I'm getting weak from want of food." I understood. To make matters much worse, on a walk later that day we passed the kitchen where food was prepared for the nurses and doctors. We could only peek, but we saw melons and grapes and all kinds of fruits. Fresh bread and meats, too. The hungry feeling in my stomach intensified. I thought of that sign on the wall, While I live I hope, and Nellie's interpretation. I felt hopeless. I hated feeling that way. I was mad at Nellie for noticing that sign and making fun of it. Why put that thought in my head? I was mad at her for being so outspoken and increasing my anxiety. I wanted to crawl into my bed, cuddle with my blanket, and shrink into a speck of nothing.

Later that day, a flying bug landed on my lap. It must have gotten in through an open door or window crack. I had never seen one like it before. It had a reddish-orange, rounded shell decorated with black spots. I was fascinated with that little creature that was smaller than the nail on my little finger. The top of its body opened into wings. A conversation nearby got loud. I wanted to quiet the sound. To shelter my new little friend. Too much noise or motion could scare it away. And I didn't want to be robbed of the comforting distraction I got from watching that minuscule bug.

Just then Nellie and Catherine approached. Nellie noticed the little red bug. "Ladybug. I love them."

"Ladybug?"

"Yes, that's what they're called. They have other names. They recently became very famous in California. I read it in a newspaper, a story about a fruit farmer and his use of thousands of ladybugs."

"Really?" said Catherine.

Listening, I remained engrossed with the tiny creature.

Nellie told us about a citrus farmer with large groves of orange and lemon trees that were ruined by a destructive insect. He released thousands of ladybugs in hopes they would eat the insect and save his trees. It took two years, but in that time the ladybugs won. The trees began to thrive. Not only did it save fruit for consumers, but the ladybugs also saved hundreds of his employees from losing their jobs. Nellie smiled down at the ladybug and me.

I looked at it and smiled, feeling honored that it chose me to land on. It crawled from my lap to my arm and just before arriving at my shoulder it spread its wings and flew off. No one noticed it drift away back to where the air was free.

Catherine watched the interaction quietly.

Nellie sat beside me. "I think that ladybug will bring you good luck." She patted my arm, right where the ladybug had just been.

I smiled back at Nellie. I was no longer mad at her. Right then, I wasn't mad at anything.

A Different Kind of Angel

Chapter Thirty-Four

Sitting on a hard bench for hours at a time was its own kind of torture. The patients, including me, were stiff, sore, and exhausted. Many of us would sit sideways or on one foot or half-off to create a change. But, depending on who was on duty, we were scolded or hit and told sit up straight. Most of the time, talking was not allowed, so our thoughts were let loose to dash this way and that. I suppose that some women would get so caught up in their web of thoughts that they forgot where they were and started to talk or make sounds. The staff would put an end to that with screams to "Shut up." If that didn't work, a beating usually silenced them. I longed to see nurses Harriet or Barbara or anyone who would allow us to chat or move about or go for a walk. But recently (and way too often) good luck was not with us.

"Take a healthy woman and sit her down for ten hours on a straight-back or no-back hard wooden seat, don't allow her to move or talk, give her nothing to occupy her time, feed her horrible substandard and scarcely enough food, subject her to baths in freezing temperatures without offering heating, and cruel treatment; and how long would it take her to become a mental invalid?" Nellie's usually calm manner was gone, at least it was on the night she spoke those words to Catherine and me as she paced around our dorm.

Nellie had only been with us a few days. I feared that the asylum was already robbing us of our refreshingly optimistic new friend.

"I don't know how you two endured for so long while maintaining a modicum of sanity. I doubt I will last two months." What she hadn't said was that she wouldn't have to weather the harsh conditions much longer. In a couple of days, her nightmare would be over.

"It's difficult to know how one would bear a hardship until the experience is at hand," sighed Catherine.

"Hmm," Nellie pondered what Catherine had just stated.

Somberly, and somewhat defensively, I added, "True, what Catherine said. Some days, not too bad." Although I meant it, my gloomy tone probably cast doubt on my sincerity.

Nellie shook her head and wrinkled her forehead like she still couldn't contemplate any length of stay surrounded by so much cruelty. "And that you both," she looked to Catherine then me, "were committed wrongly. And you, Klara," her eyes held puddles of tears, "did not even speak English when you first arrived. Frightening. I can't imagine."

To this day I'm not sure I know how I tolerated it. I said nothing further.

Nellie mentioned a woman with a story similar to mine. "I talked to her earlier today." Lost in thought, she paused. "Imagine her horrible situation. She speaks French, and when she protested being unjustly committed, she was choked by a guard and given a black eye. Did you see the discolored skin where she was beaten?"

"The woman down the hall with the long blond hair?" asked Catherine.

"Yes."

"You were too far from us for me to see her face clearly."

"She had various shades of black, blue and yellow surrounding her left eye." Nellie smacked her lips. "And what do the nurses do? They flirt with the guards, gossip among themselves, and don't help the patients. No, they offer no help. Instead, they abuse them. This is indeed an insane asylum."

* * *

Nellie increased her visits with patients in the hallway. She ambled over to a woman who had just hollered, "Murder!" which was followed by loudly bellowing, "Police!" When Nellie sat down to talk to her, my flesh felt creepy. That lasted until another patient started to cry.

Greta picked up a broom and beat the crying patient. She then whistled for Harry to help her tie the patient's arms and legs. "Get Al," blustered Greta. "And bring a sheet with you." Upon returning with Albert, Harry threw the sheet over the woman's head and twisted it tightly around her throat, so she wouldn't be heard. They then dragged her off toward the bathroom. Nellie followed.

I very slowly tagged along behind to see what would happen.

"Excuse me," protested Nellie.

When Greta heard the raised voice behind her, she turned and growled, "I've had enough of you!" She smacked Nellie right on her mouth. "Mind your business! Go back to the bench!"

Nellie's hand went to her mouth, probably to check for damage. I could tell Greta's blow was hard enough to draw blood (most likely from a split lip) because I saw red on her hand.

Albert was standing at the bathroom door waiting for Harry to unlock it. The patient was slumped in Albert's arms. I stood at a distance down the hallway, but I could see what was happening.

Nellie wiped the blood oozing from her lip and remained standing there. Greta stretched her arms out with her palms facing Nellie and slammed into her chest. "Move! Or you'll go in the tub," her head motioned to the patient, "right after her!"

"What you are doing is not right." Nellie sounded so confident that she could have been Greta's supervisor. Only she wasn't.

"What you are doing is not right," Greta mockingly repeated. "You want not right." She threw another punch at Nellie yelling, "Get back now!" She gave Nellie another shove with her right hand. "Now!"

I was sweating and itching all over while watching that scene. Finally, Nellie turned around and went back to the sitting hall. Continuing to wipe and tend to her mouth, she sat quietly observing other patients until the one who was lugged off returned. Nellie waited for Greta to take her break then went to that patient. All I could see was Nellie reaching her hand to the woman. It was later she shared what she had heard. The woman told Nellie that she was thrust into a cold bath while the sheet remained around her. They held her under until she fought for air. Greta then pulled out tufts of her hair by the root. "She showed me the proof. The bald, red, swollen places on her head."

"Horrible," Catherine said while I remained silent.

"But," said Nellie, "that wasn't the worst I'd seen today."

She had wandered off from Catherine and me several times, out of visual distance and earshot. And she wanted to relay more disturbing things. "Do you mind my sharing these with you?"

I wanted to say yes, I minded. I wanted to go to my bed. I'd already had five years of living those kinds of gut-wrenching incidents. I wanted to read. To listen to snoring. To the sounds of the night. To try to drift off into sleep where the images wouldn't hurt me. But I also wanted to be there for Nellie. Catherine had been there for me. Without her kindness and support, I don't think I would have survived. I felt letting Nellie talk was more important than my comfort at that moment.

Catherine nodded for Nellie to go on.

"There was this older woman. Must have been in her seventies. She was blind. Looking into her cloudy, pearl-like eyes made my chest hurt. When she was brought into a cold part of the sitting hall, she began to cry that she was freezing and wanted to go back to her bed."

"Oh, dear me," responded Catherine.

"It gets worse. This is the part that made me sick. The poor woman got up and tried to feel her way back to her bed. The guard jerked her back to the bench. She got up again and was slammed back onto the bench. Finally, on her third attempt, she got up and moved a distance banging into benches and other patients, before she lost her balance and fell. The guard called the nurse over, and they laughed at her. She was their entertainment! The cruelty was beyond words."

I smacked my lips in disgust.

"And when another patient protested the unkind actions the guard replied, 'Let her fall on the floor and learn a lesson.' What cold heart treats another human being like that?"

I wish I had an answer to that question, the very same question I'd been asking myself for way too many years. I knew that everything Nellie had relayed to us was accurate. I knew how I had been treated. I knew how Catherine had been treated. And I'd seen what happened to Amelia, Rosie, Tillie, and Annette, plus all the other patients over the years.

I wanted to flush every mental image of the asylum out of my head. Every yell and cry for help, every brutal submersion in ice-cold water, the laughter and scorn at the patients' expense, the shameless restraints, dragging, choking, hair-pulling, and every kind of extreme bullying one could imagine. I wanted to shut out every prayer to God moaning, "Let me die."

When Nellie continued talking, I wanted to stomp my foot and demand her to stop! No more! I wanted to ignore her. Pretending to listen, I put my attention on Rosie's deep, slow breathing, a peaceful lull to distract me. But when I heard Nellie say, "A pretty young Hebrew woman," I instantly focused my attention back to her.

Nellie went on to say that the woman spoke a little English. Her husband put her in the asylum because she had a fondness for other men. This woman spent most of her days and nights crying not just because of her cruel husband but because the staff ridiculed her. She didn't need to know the words to understand what their laughing and finger-pointing meant. She was afraid that no one would help her or even listen to her. "In her fractured English she was not difficult to understand. If only someone took a minute to hear her." Nellie shook her head and continued. "In the middle of my time with her, one of the cooks came out looking for a doctor. She had a plate of raisins, apples, and crackers for him. Imagine that! The hungry patients have to continuously endure eating garbage. I'm surprised the cook wasn't attacked by the starving patients."

All I could think of was a Hebrew woman. And Nellie defending her—having sympathy for her plight—gave me a strange sense of hope. If I were to ever get out of here, maybe I would be safe. Perhaps, I thought, not everyone hates Jews. Imagine, I might someday be free to say, "I am Jewish." Perhaps I was meant to listen to Nellie go on about all the patients. Had I not been listening to her,

I would have missed this seed of fruit that grows from the tree of life.

A Different Kind of Angel

Chapter Thirty-Five

Nellie's tenth day in the lunatic asylum started out like all the rest. But there was something different in the air. Not the air we breathe but the mood that infuses our hearts and souls. I can only describe it as the way I felt seeing the first blooms in spring after a confining, harsh winter when nature's perfumes flooded the air, and the rivers rushed with melted snow. Back in Kiev when the new vegetation began to appear, I was exhilarated. In the asylum, whatever it was I was sensing felt new and moderately refreshing. It started with a subtle yet real change in Nellie's demeanor. I had become sensitive to the delicate changes that occurred in the monotonous asylum, so it didn't surprise me when I took notice of the change in Nellie's countenance: a shining light was back in her eyes, and the tautness around her lips had eased. I was infused with a new kind of hope. The hope that a life other than what I had known for the last five years was possible. I had no concrete idea why I felt that way, but it was as real as the cracks on the walls.

I didn't want to entertain the idea that I was simply daydreaming. The tightness in my neck muscles and the itch on my forehead were gone. That, to me, was a good omen. It was odd I felt that way because the night before Nellie had a run in with the stout, officious evening nurse, Sandra Bergstrom.

Sandra, who very strict about following rules and regulations, didn't tolerate noise after the sleep whistle blew. Catherine and I didn't read when she was on duty, fearing her severe punishment. We didn't even speak. Sandra was also eager to give sleep medications with the slightest provocation. I found that offensive. I had so little freedom left that anything I could control was important to me; keeping my head clear was one of them.

Nellie had trouble sleeping at night just like I did when I first arrived. For a long time, physical and emotional exhaustion forced me to sleep. But I hadn't been sleeping well since Annette was taken away. I knew how to stay still for hours. Nellie hadn't learned that skill…yet.

After a long time of tossing and turning, Nellie finally fell asleep only to be woken by Sandra abruptly entering the room. She walked to Nellie and cast her light onto Nellie's face. I didn't dare move as I watched what unfolded.

"What are you doing that for?" Nellie covered her eyes with her hand.

Sandra's scolding was instant. "You should be sleeping!"

Nellie sat up, bunched her hands into fists, and met Sandra's reprimand with frustration. "I was until you entered and woke me."

Sandra stormed out, waking Catherine and leaving Nellie sitting up and complaining, "That nurse has no business—"

Interrupting Nellie, Sandra stomped back in with a glass in one hand and her lamp in the other. She shoved it into Nellie's face saying, "Drink this."

Nellie looked at the mixture. "I will do nothing of the sort."

Sandra's hand shook with rage. Wide-eyed and grimacing, she raised her voice. "I will say this one more time. Drink it."

"I will not." Nellie stubbornly continued, "You cannot force me to sleep."

When Sandra stormed out again, Nellie looked over to Catherine who shook her head.

"What was that?" asked Nellie. She then added, "I hope that takes care of her for the night."

Nellie's hope was in vain. Sandra returned with the medicine still in her hand and a doctor that I'd never seen. He was carrying a dark leather bag that I assumed contained drugs and medical equipment. He was older, perhaps in his fifties, with streaks of gray mixed with his black hair and wrinkled age-lines around his eyes. Sternly, he insisted. "Take it."

Nellie stood up for her rights and refused. "There are a few hours left to sleep before the day begins. I don't want to lose my wits and be groggy all day."

"You don't want to what?" He reached into his bag and pulled out a syringe. "You're mad, woman! You have no wits to lose!" The doctor's anger was evident in the way his chin lifted, his right foot began to drum the floor, and he tightly gripped the syringe.

"I am not a mad woman. I am not insane. I am sane and demand to be released. I do not belong here."

Becoming rougher with her, he dropped his bag and grabbed her left arm. "You have wasted enough of my time! If you do not drink this," he motioned to the glass Sandra held out, "I will put a needle in your arm."

Nellie looked at the needle in his hand, looked at the liquid in the glass Sandra was holding and reached for the glass. She drank it down.

They left.

The minute the door shut behind them, Nellie shoved a finger down her throat until she vomited up the liquid.

The next day, when the noise level prevented the staff from hearing Nellie whisper, she said, "I smelled that liquid medicine. It smelled like chloral hydrate. I am familiar with that smell from a doctor's visit one time. It occurred to me that if they injected the medication into my arm, I could not get rid of it. But if I swallowed…" She shrugged. "I don't feel too sleepy today."

Nellie's clever way of dealing with the staff made me smile.

"Lucifer! Lucifer!" came yells from a patient partly dressed running down the hallway. "I have killed the devils," she shouted. Two guards threw her to the ground and splayed her legs, exposing her buttocks, then tied her arms. Trying to free herself, she continued to shout, "Killed the devils!"

"Looks like she missed a few," Nellie said under her breath.

"Killed them! Killed them!" echoed down the hall. Candace approached the frantic patient. She was with a young, blond-haired doctor holding a syringe. Within minutes, the patient went limp.

Nellie got up and walked in the direction of the doctor. When she reached out a hand to tap his shoulder, I became very nervous. He turned around to meet her eyes. Without hesitation, in an audible voice, she asked, "What are the doctors here for?"

Brusquely, he responded, "To care for the patients and test their sanity."

Tension gripped my back when I heard Nellie once again protest, "I am sane. I want to be released."

Averting his eyes, without another word, he turned to leave.

I was surprised he didn't scold her. Perhaps it was his youth or inexperience. It was unusual to see what seemed like a mild-mannered young doctor in the asylum.

Nellie spoke to his back, "Excuse me. Please."

When he didn't respond, again she reached a hand to his shoulder. Frowning, I could tell that his patience was slipping. "Miss," he backed away from her, "kindly keep your hands to yourself."

"Doctor," Nellie rapidly responded. "There are sixteen doctors on the island, and yet I have only seen two pay attention to the patients. How can a doctor possibly judge a woman's sanity without examining her? How can a doctor merely judge a woman insane by simply nodding hello when he encounters her yet refuses her pleas to be released? Even the sick ones know it's no use, for their pleas will only be considered as their imagination."

Candace moved in on them and shoved an arm across Nellie's chest. She said to the doctor, "I'll take care of her."

To my amazement, he responded, "Just a moment, Miss Millhouse. Let her have her say." He looked down to a much shorter Nellie, and firmly said, "Then she can't accuse me of not paying attention."

"Try every test on me," Nellie spoke at a rapid clip. "Test my pulse, my heart, ask me to stretch out my arms, to work my fingers, and fully examine me. Then tell me whether I am sane or insane."

"Is that all?"

"No, I must insist on a thorough exam and be released." Nellie then looked over to Catherine and me. "Several of the women here are also sane. Why can't they be released?"

"They are insane and suffering from delusions," he replied. "Like you, young lady."

"You haven't examined me. How can you judge my mental acuteness? Talk to me. Away from the noise and commotion.

Examine me. And find out I am sane. Also," she pointed back to Catherine and me, "examine them as well."

Candace stomped her foot. "That's enough from her!"

Where other doctors and guards tolerated Candace's insolence, this doctor didn't. "I'll not have you interfere when I am addressing a patient. Go take a break."

Candace stormed off. I felt a weight lift off my chest.

When the doctor thought he would solve Nellie's demands by transferring her to a quieter ward, she stated, "That is not the point. I want to be released. And I want my friends to be examined and released as well. We are here incorrectly."

In what I thought was a disdainful dismissal, he said he would consider her requests. "I will see you later." He walked off.

Nellie stood there watching him leave. I waited to see what would happen to her. As the next couple of hours passed, no one scolded Nellie. The feeling I had when I woke up that day resurfaced. And intensified. Something was definitely different.

Dr. Daniels was his name, and he was true to his word. Later that afternoon, he returned. He was with a group including a man elegantly dressed in a three-piece suit. Nellie's eyes widened as if she recognized the man. When they approached us, the doctor addressed Nellie, "This is Commissioner Nichols." Turning to the suited man, "This is the woman I mentioned to you."

He looked at Catherine and me and then spoke to Nellie. "You have an audience now, young lady. Speak your mind."

I nearly choked when next I heard what Nellie had to say. Catherine's shoulders shot up straight.

"This insane asylum on Blackwell's Island is a rat-trap. Easy to get in but, once in, impossible to get out. I have been shut off from all visitors and had no contact with my outside associates. I demand to see my attorney, Peter A. Hendricks, who will explain the matter of my admittance to this facility."

"Hendricks is your attorney?" The fashionably-dressed man took a sudden, intense interest in Nellie.

"Yes," replied Nellie.

The Commissioner squinted his eyes and wiped his graying hair from his right cheek. He looked as puzzled as I felt. The doctors with him, five in total, looked to him for an answer. Leaving Nellie, Catherine, and me standing in the hallway, he said to them, "Come with me."

"Huh?" was all Catherine said.

I didn't know what to say.

Nellie responded to our confusion. "My attorney is well-known. They will contact him."

"What good will that do?" Catherine skeptically asked.

"Wait," smiled Nellie.

We sat with Nellie while she nervously tapped a foot on the floor. I remembered when Annette had done that, and it got on my nerves. Today, I didn't mind. Before long, the Commissioner came back with Dr. Daniels and another suited man. To Nellie, he said, "You'll come with us," referring to himself and the well-dressed man alongside him.

"What about my two friends here who—"

"You are impatient, young lady," said the Doctor. "Miss Gelfman and Miss Bigsby will come with me."

It all came sooner than expected and when it happened, it took my breath away. Taking a walk down the hallway for the last time, Catherine and I were beside the doctor while Nellie, Commissioner Nichols and the other yet unnamed man were in front. When Nellie came to a Mexican woman speaking Spanish, she kissed her fingers and warmly said, "Adios." Continuing along down the corridor, she sang, "Goodbye, I'm going home."

The best part of hearing those words was that I believed them. I hadn't felt that way in years. Trusting in Nellie was the door to my liberation.

There was a certain pain in leaving. My heart ached when the doctors examined me before I was discharged. All that had happened flashed before me. I've heard that happens to people when they die. Perhaps a part of me did die that day. The tormented part. My soul burned when I thought of running back to the dorm for my pale-blue blanket. But it wasn't mine to keep. No, it was for the next occupant of the bed that had been my only home for much too long. All that I needed to take with me was kindness. And the good memories of Barbara and Harriet. And of my angels Tillie, Rosie, Amelia, and Annette. From them, I learned that when you look below the surface—beneath the differences—you meet another's heart. That's where the light of love never dims. I discovered that it's in the light where the power of healing and forgiveness lives. They were all unique. All different. Different kinds of angels.

The whole five-plus years in that dungeon of extreme misery and squalor evaporated into the shadowy place where nightmares live. The last of the ten "Nellie days" was different. The wretchedness transcended into something else: the substance of dreams and fantasies. Of hope and faith. So much of my life had been spent longing to leave that place. And there I was with Catherine by my side, soon to be crossing the East River, en route to freedom.

Chapter Thirty-Six

We hadn't the time to fully grasp all that had occurred. Before Nellie left with her attorney, he made arrangements for us to be examined and released immediately after determining our sanity. Luckily, someone (probably Nellie) made sure that Catherine and I stayed together before leaving Blackwell's Island. What better witness to any questionable underhanded activities than Catherine for me, and vice versa. After everything I had lived through, it was difficult for me to take in what was happening. The thought crossed my mind that this could be a trick or that I had gone insane and was now imagining things. I whispered my concerns to Catherine.

She hugged me, smiled and said with her full voice, "No, Klara. This is real. As real as the floor we're standing on." She stomped her foot.

I did the same. "Real. True." I smiled, glad to have Catherine by my side to reassure me.

Before leaving the asylum, I saw one last doctor. "Everything will be taken care of," he said before giving me my pass to freedom. I had no idea what he had been referring to, but I felt he was sincere from the concerned look on his face. And I could have sworn there was a tad of respect in his eyes. But it would still take many months for me to thaw from the chill of fear hardened into my very core.

Once through the exams, we signed paperwork drafted by Nellie's attorney. Despite trusting Nellie, I needed Catherine to decipher what it meant before I signed. It was a declaration that I had been there and was now officially released. My identity had been reduced to a piece of paper, which I would use to prove who I was. I had to carry the officially stamped document on my person at all times until I received my certified citizenship paperwork, which Mr. Hendricks would also be arranging for me.

In the changing room, I looked at Catherine as we disrobed from our hospital day dress for the last time. In a somber mood, I wondered whose clothing I was adorning. The clean garments might have been from a poor soul still barricaded behind the dull-beige, cracked walls of the asylum. I had dreamed of this day for a long time; I was being set free. But rather than joy, my heart was filled with heaviness. I smoothed the wrinkles in the cotton dress I changed into before departing.

* * *

The salty air flowed through my nose and down into my worn, tired body. I could feel the fresh air deep inside my chest; it was both cleansing and soothing. There on the dock stood Nellie with Mr. Hendricks. Alongside them were two women: Miss Fordham and Miss Armstrong. They ran the boardinghouse where we would room while settling our affairs.

Thankfully, Catherine and I shared a room. In the first few days, Miss Armstrong took us shopping for clothes. Mr. Hendricks had managed to secure some money for us. We were informed that he had filed a lawsuit to compensate us for the false imprisonment. Additionally, he arranged for what he called a "clean politician" to investigate the man who had Catherine committed and all of the other guilty links on that chain of events.

Nellie was extremely busy. Despite her demanding schedule, she kept in constant contact with us. It was then we learned the story about how Nellie went undercover to write her exposé. She forewarned us that all of us would be summoned to appear before the Grand Jury. Soon. She explained to Catherine and me what to expect because we were witnesses.

Nellie said, "I long to help those of God's most unfortunate children who I had left prisoners behind me. If I couldn't bring them that boon of all boons, liberty, I hope to at least influence others to make life more bearable for them."

When the proceedings started, I was taken aback by the civility of everyone in court. For the first couple of hours, I seriously doubted that anything would change at that asylum and was entirely convinced that a noose would tighten around my neck. But as the proceedings moved along, the court's continued professionalism helped me to relax into my new life.

"I found the jurors to be gentlemen," Nellie told me later. It was a great relief to me that for once I could agree about men in powerful positions.

Nellie was sworn in to tell the truth of her story. She related what she had experienced firsthand from her time beginning at the boardinghouse through to her release from the asylum. I became very nervous when Assistant District Attorney, Vernon M. David, examined Nellie. My heart rattled my ribcage when the jurors requested a visit to the Island. Do they want me to go back there, too? No! No! Please, no!

Although Nellie was glad to consent, I felt downright nauseous at the idea of returning there for any reason. The trust that had sprouted in me since leaving vanished. Is this all too good to be real? My body broke out in welts, and I began to hyperventilate.

"There, there, Klara. Please stop fretting. You do not need to accompany us if Catherine is willing to go as the witness." Nellie gently stroked my back as she tried to calm me down.

"Yes, of course. I'll accompany you to help in any way you need, Nellie." I envied Catherine's seemingly bottomless well of strength, grace, and generosity. Catherine continued, "I'm more comfortable than Klara with the whole Grand Jury process and what would most likely be required of me."

On the day they traveled across the East River to the island of the abused, ailing, misplaced and forgotten, I anxiously paced around my room and boardinghouse. Then I burned off nervous energy by walking on the nearby streets. When Catherine arrived back to the room after dinner, I nearly jumped on her with relief. "What happened?"

She inhaled a deep breath before she said, "No one was supposed to know of our planned trip, yet when we arrived, one of the jurors heard that they were notified of our inspection beforehand."

I waited while Catherine's attention went inward. She shook her head and continued. "You wouldn't believe what it looked like there, Klara. Even the boat was cleaned up."

"Huh?" The boat was cleaned up? I remembered the filthy boat that took me to the island. "Boat to the island?"

"Yes. And every room, hallway—even the bathroom—was immaculate. Clean and tidy. And, oh my goodness, when the jury questioned the nurses, their statements bore no resemblance to Nellie's account or reality."

"Oh dear," I whimpered. What does that mean for me? And for Catherine. Will we be returned to that madhouse?

"The staff's reports also conflicted with each other. One of the doctors did admit that, for lack of funds, the food was not what it should be." Catherine went on to say that they had no means to prove that the bath water was cold, dirty or used by the several patients without refreshing it. They couldn't prove that the nurses and guards were cruel or that the doctors neglected patients. And the worse part was when they couldn't verify Nellie's story, they said you and I could be supporting her to gain our freedom."

My arms shook. My knees felt like pudding. "Catherine, I not go back to that—"

"Wait, I'm not done," she smiled.

The curvature of her soft, pink, upturned lips instantly calmed my quivering legs.

"When they challenged Nellie's story, she asked that they call on other patients whom she knew were falsely admitted but of sound mental state. I feared that the sight of so many unfamiliar men in suits would frighten the patients, sane or not. But it all worked out."

Catherine continued to retell the events of the day, including how a few of the coherent patients were questioned about the factual evidence. It was then that what the staff had so quickly covered up came to light. "I felt like clapping my hands and applauding when one of the women told of not having had enough clothing in cold weather, being thrown in freezing grimy baths and dozens of patients having only two towels for drying themselves."

"Were Barbara or Harriet there?" I asked.

"What do you think? No. Absolutely not. No one who was friendly toward the patients was visible. If they were on duty, they were not present when we arrived." Catherine's eyes grew dim, watery, and tears threatened to spill.

"What?" I asked. "You look sad."

"Do you remember the patient who died?" Catherine sniffed a breath. "The pretty young girl who was ill when she was thrown into a cold bath?"

My mind was overwhelmed with too many memories. Too many sick women had been thrown into a cold bath or held under a freezing shower. Too many dragged off by their hair, beaten, battered, or abused. "No, I am not sure who—"

"The one who was ill when she came in. She screamed and pleaded not to be exposed to such a filthy, foul-smelling place when she was burning up with fever."

"Oh, yes. I do." I sorrowfully smacked my lips.

"When asked about her, the doctor said she came in dead. He said she had a fever and convulsions on the boat, and there was nothing they could do for her."

"Lies! All lies!" I stomped a foot. "I hate them! They do such terrible things. Then lie to save own skins!"

Catherine put a soothing, gentle hand on my arm. "Someone finally mentioned that she arrived alive. Ill but alive. And she wasn't sent to the infirmary. The doctor made some feeble excuse that he must have been thinking of another patient." Catherine wiped an escaped tear from her cheek. After a long pause and more tears, Catherine smiled, patted my arm, and continued. "Nellie didn't expect the Grand Jury to sustain her after they saw the place differently than she had portrayed. But they did! Nellie's evidence was accepted as valid."

Unsure of what this all meant, my mouth went dry. "What now? What will happen for you and me?"

"They will submit a report to the court advising all the changes be made that Nellie proposed." Catherine's voice was whisper-soft even though there were no nurses or guards to beat her for talking.

"We are free, Klara. Really free." She took me into a warm celebratory embrace and held me until my pounding heart calmed.

* * *

Catherine took a job working as a saleswoman in a department store. The politician and doctors responsible for having her wrongly committed were investigated and punished. The doctors lost their licenses to practice medicine. The politician agreed to pay Catherine a large sum of money and donate an annual charitable gift (I don't recall the figure, but it was substantial) to the asylum to improve the care and treatment of the patients. He only agreed if his wrongdoing was kept secret. Catherine didn't want his money under those conditions, but the generous part of her nature put the patients' needs over her pride. She accepted his terms. Within a year, he was divorced. He lost in the following election. But he remained true to his word and made a generous annual gift to the asylum designated for improving the lives of the patients.

I received a considerable financial settlement from the City of New York and became a citizen of the United States.

One memorable day, I met Nellie for lunch while I was still living at the boardinghouse. Leaves on trees had turned colors from lush, bright green to orange, yellow, and brown. It was a beautiful sunny day with a moderately crisp breeze floating about. It was a good day to start a new life. That's how I look upon that day.

What had happened from the Kiev pogrom through my release from the asylum was a plodding, agonizing crawl. I had regained my walking legs when I returned to New York City. That luncheon date with Nellie was when I started to learn to fly.

"You said you were excited to meet?" Nellie had sent a note to the boardinghouse for me to meet her.

"Yes, I wish Catherine were here with us, but you can tell her later. After my story was published," Nellie said in reference to the exposé article she wrote in the press, "a committee that provides funding for the benefit of the insane has given $1,000,000. That can do a lot of good to help the asylum. It's a mitzvah," she smiled.

What? I sat straight up and leaned into the table. My teacup rattled. I looked into her beautiful blue eyes, high-arched eyebrows almost touching her short brown bangs, and creamy complexion with a hint of rose coloring on her cheeks. Squeezing my eyes together into a slit, I gave her a curious smile.

"Yes, Klara, I know."

My heart thumped so hard and loudly in my ears that I was sure she heard it. Nellie, beautiful Nellie, told me that she had once thought she heard me use a word that she had heard from other Russian Jewish people. She couldn't remember what word I had used, or the context, but the flimsy shred of memory remained with her. I had no memory of that fortunate mistake of the tongue.

Other Russian Jewish people!

"And with the timing…You must have arrived in America a year after the 1881 pogrom. Yes?"

"Nellie! How…how did you know?"

"It's my job to do research. To pay attention. To see things that others may overlook. Of course, it was an assumption. An accurate assumption but a guess nonetheless. When I said mitzvah, you lit up. That was proof enough."

That was my last, deeply hidden secret. For so long, I lived in fear that I would be persecuted because I was a Jew. When we were still in the asylum and Nellie had mentioned a Hebrew woman, a tiny seed of faith had been planted in me. After being released, my courage had sprouted. Following that meeting with Nellie, the seedling bloomed into a glorious blossom of confidence, and I became less fearful. "You are very smart, Nellie."

When she saw me wipe sweat from my brow, she compassionately said, "You're safe, Klara. Hatred lives everywhere, as you well know from the experience at Blackwell's. But here in America, our Constitution guarantees freedom of religion." She talked a little about that freedom and how men fought to guarantee it, not wipe it out (like what had happened in Kiev). She looked at the piece of cake on the plate in front of me, the one I hadn't touched. "Do you want to eat that? If not, you can wrap it up. I have somewhere I want to take you."

I had no idea what my tear-stained face looked like. Nellie assured me I looked lovely. She had told me many times since our release that I was very pretty. And that day—for the first time in over five years—I felt it.

"Where we're going is within walking distance. It's nice out today. Are you okay with a twenty-minute walk?"

"Sure. Why not?" I smiled.

The New York City streets were bustling with vendors, men and women arm in arm, women walking with their children and carrying babies, all alive and in constant motion. The noise, the different smells and all the movement! Happy chaos surrounded me. We walked without speaking until we came to a large brick structure. When I looked at the top of the entryway, I nearly fell to the ground. There, before my blurry eyes, was the most beautiful statue I had ever seen: The Lion of Judah. Near speechless, all I could say was, "Nellie," before I grabbed her into a hug.

"It gets better. Let's go inside."

A few people were in the main gathering area. An older man in a black suit was talking to a handsome younger man who stood beside three middle-aged women. They had a very familiar sounding accent. My heart beat so rapidly and irregularly that I thought it would flutter out of my chest. A tidal wave of grief flooded my throat. I didn't want to relive all of the heartache, mourning, agony, misery and pain I had held back in a giant pool of hidden memory. But there it was. What these people were saying cracked the dike in the emotional dam I had so painstakingly constructed, and out it came. When my sobs became loud, the group of people stopped their conversation and turned to me. I thought my heart would stop when I made eye contact with the young man. "Klara? Is that you? Is that really you?" In a large bounding motion, he was at my side. "Do you remember me."

I couldn't see through all my crying. But his voice. His accent. I knew it. And then, he said something in Russian. "I am Solomon. Solomon Kliger. I knew your brother—"

Solomon's voice became a blur of breathtaking words as my head spun. Reeling around me like a whirlwind, images of Papa, Mama, Abram, Shakna, Josel, and Anna came to me. Laughing, loving, words came forth. We are always with you. My tears dried. I looked into Solomon's soft amber eyes. In them, I saw the reflection of a woman, a woman whose dreams were about to come true.

Epilogue

1947

That was a long time ago.

Since the time I was freed from the women's asylum, I lived to see remarkable events and inventions like the Wright brothers flight, Henry Ford's mass-produced automobiles, women getting the right to vote, the first talkie movie, the invention of penicillin, television, and the formation of the United Nations. I also bore witness (again) to the violent and cruel nature of too many fellow human beings, like in World War I and World War II. The last war, with that unthinkable Holocaust, rekindled dark memories about my life all those years ago. I told some close friends just a few horror stories about Kiev and the asylum. They were shocked, but they were also curious and anxious to tell their stories about difficult times they experienced. After thinking about their reactions, I felt compelled to do something more about what I lived through than think or talk about it. I also wanted to keep the memories of the Gelfmans alive. So many say, "We must never forget," when referring to what Hitler did to my people. And to all the other unfortunates he murdered along with the Jews. Perhaps that became another reason for me to write my story. Never forget. But where to begin and how to deal with such an overwhelming task?

My answer rested with Nellie. My dear friend Nellie. Years ago, she had introduced me to a friend of hers. Someone she called an apprentice editor. Elena and I became friends. She often told me if I ever wanted to tell my story, she would help me. Nellie said, "She's one of the best editors I've worked with. If she offered to help you, take her up on it."

Long after Nellie died in 1922, I went to seek Elena's help.

"Of course, I'll read your manuscript." She gave me a warm hug. "Nellie would be so proud of you."

Hour after hour I sat at my secondhand Underwood typewriter and pounded out word after word with my two index fingers. It was a slow process that took many months before I completed the beginning part of the book. Feeling extremely incompetent at the task and nervous about all that I was revealing, I wanted Elena to have a look at the first few chapters. I needed support and advice; that's what I told Elena. But what I really needed was an escape from reliving those dreadful times. Too many painful memories came with the images that I wrote. I was foolish to think I'd feel better to take on this massive and painful job.

A fitful sleep was no help as Kiev and the slaughtering of my family came back to me. So much sweat poured from my skin that I had to get up to change my nightgown.

"What's the matter," Solomon asked in a gravelly, sleep-infused voice.

Yes, my dreams did come true. We courted and married shortly after meeting in the temple that day many years ago. "Nothing." I placed a gentle hand on his dry, wrinkled cheek. "Go back to sleep, my love."

Solomon turned over and was peacefully snoring as I got out of bed and made my way to the kitchen. As I passed my children's bedrooms, tears spilled from my eyes. I cried out of gratitude mixed with pain. Oh Papa, Mama, if only you could see them. I continued past the empty rooms. I was never able to feel the pure, unspoiled love a mother should have for her children. No, there was always a sting of pain that went along with the love. Heartache from the past taunted my mind. You could lose those precious grandchildren, too. I loved my family as well as I could. And as completely as my past ordeals would allow. In the times when I didn't feel the nostalgic pain, I could (and did) feel joy and fulfillment, however temporary. These heartwarming times had to share a place in my heart with the losses that had carved themselves into me. Especially now, as so many Jewish ghosts stir in the air I breathe, never to be given a proper burial. Oh, the pain of that awful beast, Hitler. And so many other monsters I encountered.

I went to the kitchen and opened the refrigerator. It was full. I remembered a time when my stomach was always empty. A time when all that filled me was fear. I searched for something to eat, something to calm my mind and the hot rush of anxiety pulsing through my veins. Leftover chicken casserole. Feeling the cold air pouring over my legs, I took it out and closed the refrigerator door.

I don't remember the first bite. I don't remember chewing or swallowing. I didn't feel the saliva running down the sides of my lips. I couldn't see the table through the pool of tears in my eyes. Out it came. Like it always did. Like that blizzard in the asylum, a torrent of rain poured from me. My heart skipped a few beats, distracting my attention from memories that continued to plague me.

Resisting the deluge of emotions—anger, agitation, sadness—I remembered something my eldest son said to me. Irving (named after Solomon's father) was the wise one. "Mama," he'd smile, "why resist what's inside you? Don't fight yourself. Sooner or later it'll just pass."

"Sooner," I'd laugh. "I want sooner." And we'd laugh together.

Sitting at the kitchen table, I thought back to so many other conversations with my beloved Irving. And Lucy (named after my mother, Lucinda). And Anna, the baby. I wanted to name the youngest after my little sister who never had a life. I wanted to give her a life through my womb, my body, my blood. My children were all so different, like my siblings, but together we were a happy, close, loving family. Thankfully, my past didn't come back to haunt me by taking out my buried resentments on my children or husband. Because Solomon and I had lost so much, we were determined to fill our children with love and a sense of belonging. We vowed to give them the family we lost.

Once again, I was successful at replacing my painful memories with happier ones. I realized that what triggered my insomnia was my writing. Perhaps putting my story down on paper would help. All I knew was I had to continue. I just wasn't sure why. Not until Irving came to visit with the news that he was expecting his first grandchild. My first great-grandchild.

When Irving asked me what I thought they should name the baby if it's a boy, I didn't want to answer.

Responding to my silence, he asked, "What is it, Mama? You look so sad."

Not wanting to spoil his joyous mood, I straightened my shoulders and put a smile on my face. "Oh, no, my sweetheart. You mistook my reaction."

"I know you, Mama. Stop trying to be nice, and just tell me what's on your mind."

"Have you thought of names you want?" I digressed.

"Stop avoiding this. The kids wanted me to talk to you. They want to include you in the naming."

With his soft, smooth hand now upon my wrinkled, arthritis-riddled hand, I answered. "Isak."

When he looked deep into my eyes, he understood my hesitation. I could see it written all over his face. "But you've said so many times before that...that you didn't want to use your papa's...Um. The memories?"

I sniffed back my grief. "It's time, as you say, I let my emotions come. Stop resisting."

"Oh, that's terrific." He hugged me.

Whispering in his ear, "You would have loved him. A wonderful man."

I could feel his smile on my cheek. "Yes, Mama, so you've told us a million times."

That happened months ago. I continued my writing. Elena continued critiquing. And like with the first few chapters, there was more red ink on the pages than black.

Composing the story sent me back in time to lively occasions with conversations and laughter. To ominous times when we heard the news of the assassination of Tsar Alexander II in 1881 and the propaganda spread in a leaflet blaming the Jews. To the resulting persecution and annihilation of Jewish villages and cities, including Kiev. I went back to the journey from one continent to another, to the asylum, to meeting Solomon (and our lengthy conversation in which he told me he had lost his entire family during the Kiev pogrom). I went back to our courtship and to our wedding at the temple among many of our Jewish friends. I thought of his skills as a carpenter, like my papa, and how he made a good living for us. And I smiled as I thought of the births and milestones of my three

---

children. Of all of them going to university, having a profession, marrying, and having their own children. I felt warm inside thinking of my seven grandchildren (with a great-grandchild on the way).

I reflected on my lifelong friendship with Catherine. She also remained in New York City (a few miles from our home) and spent the majority of her time involved in women's rights issues. Around 1910, she met and worked closely with Alice Paul, who guided and ran much of the women's suffrage movement. Catherine lived to see the ratification of the 19th Amendment to the U.S. Constitution, giving women the right to vote. Shortly after that, she died peacefully in her sleep. Sweet, kind Catherine never married. The mezuzah she gave me for a wedding present remains nailed to the frame of my front door. Every time I enter or exit my home, I kiss it, and I remember my papa leaving his precious mezuzah behind in Kiev.

In the end, when my story was written and made readable by Elena, I wrote the dedication page, To Isak. This is for you.

Yes, it was for my papa. But it was also for my mama. My siblings. My husband, children, and grandchildren. And it was for Catherine, Nellie, Tillie, Amelia, Annette, Rosie and all who suffered the indignities of persecution and injustices then and now. May I never forget those kindred souls.

Post Note

Nellie Bly's exposé was published in the New York World newspaper soon after her release from the asylum. The article shed light on many of the disturbing conditions at the asylum, including neglect and physical cruelty, spurring a broad-scale investigation of the institution. Significant changes were made in New York City's Department of Public Charities and Corrections. Included in the changes were a larger allotment of funds for the care of the mentally ill, additional physician appointments for more stringent supervision of the nurses and other healthcare employees, and regulations to end overcrowding.

A month after her series ran, Bly returned to Blackwell's with a grand jury panel. At that time, Nellie saw that many of the abuses she reported had been corrected: the food services and sanitary conditions were improved, the foreign patients had been transferred, and the ruthless nurses were gone.

A Different Kind of Angel

About the Author

Paulette Mahurin lives with her husband Terry and two dogs, Max and Bella, in Ventura County, California. She grew up in West Los Angeles and attended UCLA, where she received a Master's Degree in Science.

While in college, she won awards and was published for her short-story writing. One of these stories, Something Wonderful, was based on the couple presented in His Name Was Ben, which she expanded into a fictionalized novel in 2014. Her first novel, The Persecution of Mildred Dunlap, made it to Amazon bestseller lists and won awards, including best historical fiction of the year 2012 in Turning the Pages Magazine. Her third novel, To Live Out Loud, won international critical acclaim and made it to multiple sites as favorite read book of 2015. Her fourth novel, The Seven Year Dress, made it to the Amazon Kindle store top one-hundred bestseller list in its fourth week out. She has been ranked as an Amazon bestselling author for several of her books.

Semi-retired, she continues to work part-time as a Nurse Practitioner in Ventura County. When she's not writing, she does pro-bono consultation work with women with cancer, works in the Westminster Free Clinic as a volunteer provider, volunteers as a mediator in the Ventura County Courthouse for small claims cases, and involves herself, along with her husband, in dog rescue.

Profits from her books go to help rescue dogs from kill shelters.

www.ingramcontent.com/pod-product-compliance
Lightning Source LLC
Chambersburg PA
CBHW060404260626
47160CB00006B/2434